MW00477664

*W*hat the critics are saying...

&

~ *Liquid Dreams* ~

5 RIBBON REVIEW "*Liquid Dreams* is unlike any book I've read before. Playing off the legend of Atlantis, this book provides a fresh and welcome change in paranormal romance... I, for one, was completely engrossed from the first paragraph and didn't move until I had read The End. When I long for an escape from reality, Cathryn Fox will be one of my first choices. I look forward to seeing many more new and exciting ideas coming our way from this talented author." ~ *Jenni Mae, Romance Junkies*

4 ANGELS! "I had a great time reading *Liquid Dreams*. The characters come to life, and both are very likable... I thought the sex in the book was hot and passionate, with a lot of urgency that makes you feel for their situation. I am definitely going to be on the lookout for more from Cathryn Fox in the future." ~ *Fallen Angel Reviews*

4 BLUE RIBBONS! "*Liquid Dreams* by Cathryn Fox is a great page-turn that will keep you up well past your bed time. This story theme is about a man who had loved, lost, and will stop at nothing to find his missing soulmate. Through the use of dreams, Ranek is able to foretell Katrina the tale of their great love affair. Along the way, Ranek encounters many obstacles that will test him, both mentally and physically. I was totally awed the by the sacrifices both Ranek and Katrina were willing to make throughout the book, and how Ms. Fox's conclusion demonstrated the meaning true love. I was swept away by the emotions of the characters and the love scenes between Ranek and Katrina set my blood on fire." ~ *Romance Junkies*

~ *Dolphin's Playground* ~

"*Dolphin's Playground* is another sultry and unique read by Jaci Burton. This time she takes us under the sea and into a one-of-a-kind world filled with the amazing… *Dolphin's Playground* is a wonderfully descriptive and sizzling erotic read… This story will be a winner with any fan of fantasy and the deep blue sea. Don't miss this steamy and adventurous underwater read by Jaci Burton."~ *Enya Adrian, Romance Reviews Today*

"Burton skillfully shows how two beings from entirely different worlds can come together...Watching these two characters realize their destiny, coupled with their fantastic foray into Oceana's paradise, make for a very satisfying read." ~ *Charlene Alleyne, Romantic Bookclub Magazine*

"Jaz and Trey are a powerful couple in Jaci Burton's first take in the *League of Seven Seas: Dolphin's Playground*. Ms. Burton blends knowledge, intrigue, love and passion splendidly in this story. The world of the dolphins and the knowledge the author penned is extraordinary. Not only did Trey and Jaz blow me away, I was enthralled with the information on these beautiful creatures that Ms. Burton added in this tale. I never knew the sea could be so sexy, but Trey, Ronan and Oceania are a sight to behold and could charm the bathing suit off anyone!" ~ *Tracey West, Road To Romance.*

CATHRYN FOX
JACI BURTON

Making Waves

ELLORA'S CAVE
ROMANTICA PUBLISHING

An Ellora's Cave Romantica Publication

www.ellorascave.com

Making Waves

ISBN # 1419952625
ALL RIGHTS RESERVED.
Liquid Dreams Copyright © 2004 Cathryn Fox
Dolphin's Playground Copyright © 2004 Jaci Burton
Edited by Heather Osborn, Briana St. James
Cover art by Christine Clavel

Trade paperback Publication January 2006

Warning:

The following material contains graphic sexual content meant for mature readers. *Making Waves* has been rated *S-ensuous* by a minimum of three independent reviewers.

Ellora's Cave Publishing offers three levels of Romantica™ reading entertainment: S (S-ensuous), E (E-rotic), and X (X-treme).

S-ensuous love scenes are explicit and leave nothing to the imagination.

E-rotic love scenes are explicit, leave nothing to the imagination, and are high in volume per the overall word count. In addition, some E-rated titles might contain fantasy material that some readers find objectionable, such as bondage, submission, same sex encounters, forced seductions, etc. E-rated titles are the most graphic titles we carry; it is common, for instance, for an author to use words such as "fucking", "cock", "pussy", etc., within their work of literature.

X-treme titles differ from E-rated titles only in plot premise and storyline execution. Unlike E-rated titles, stories designated with the letter X tend to contain controversial subject matter not for the faint of heart.

~ Contents ~

LIQUID DREAMS

Cathryn Fox

 co

Dedication

ຂວ

For my wonderful editor Heather Osborn who has made writing for Ellora's Cave so much fun.

For Shelly Hutchinson, Paula Altenburg and Heather Veinotte for their encouragement, their amazing support, valuable critiques, and willingness to read through every draft, but mostly for their friendship.

For my sister Susie Murphy for her love and support.

For the goals group for keeping me motivated and to all my wonderful friends at Sensual Reads.

And especially for my husband Mark, son Alex, and daughter Allison who have always supported me and have helped me make all my dreams come true.

Without all of you this wouldn't have been possible. Thank you.

Chapter One

ဢ

Like a wild untamed panther, he emerged from the ocean and stalked toward her. Every movement sensual, feral, dangerous. She trembled at the dark ferociousness of his potent gaze. Water droplets beaded on the sleek, hard planes of his muscular chest. Her eyes tracked one liquid bead, following it as it dripped down his glistening copper skin until it pooled on the tip of his engorged cock.

She moistened her lips and tried to keep her breathing steady, tried to ignore the elevated thud of her pulse. Her fingers ached to touch him. Her mouth watered for a taste. She needed him with an intensity so raw and powerful it left her shaking.

Words were not necessary. His eyes caressed her with sultry heat and she knew what he wanted. She stripped her clothes off, agonizingly slow, the way he'd taught her.

A muscle in his jaw flexed. "Yes, my love. It pleases me when you follow the rules." A primal growl rumbled beneath his soft voice.

The deep timbre of his tone stroked her in other places. A languorous warmth spread over her skin and she became acutely aware of the moisture gathering between her legs. His gaze roamed over her, stopping to inspect the rise and fall of her milky cleavage. Her breathing grew shallow and she had to fight to keep her knees from buckling. Every nerve ending was alive, on fire. Drunk with desire, she ached to touch herself, to quell the hot, roiling restlessness burning between her thighs.

After he thoroughly studied her taut, pink nipples, his eyes locked on hers again, indicating his readiness. She backed up until the cool ocean waves lapped at her ankles. Instead of doing what was expected of her, she spread her legs in silent invitation and slipped a finger into her warm, slick crevice.

His face went rigid while the heat in his smoldering eyes scorched her. "Lie down," he growled. A fine tingle of anticipation worked its way through her body. That small act of disobedience wouldn't go unpunished.

The darkening of his coal-black eyes told her it was time to obey. His virility frightened her and excited her all at once. She lowered her naked body onto the sandy floor and dutifully squeezed her legs together. Blood pounded through her veins as she craved the delicious feel of skin against skin.

"Why do you test me so?" His voice thinned to a mere whisper as he covered her nakedness with his own, branding her with his heat. Her body molded against his. A perfect fit, as though she were made for him.

"Kiss me," she murmured hoarsely against his throat.

His head descended, his lips, warm and silky, hovered only inches from hers. Desire seared her insides and she whimpered, pleading for him to take her. Tilting her head, she parted her lips, urging him on. But, his kisses didn't come. This was her punishment.

He surfed his lips over the long column of her neck before burying his face into the deep hollow of her throat. The pleasure was excruciatingly exquisite. A jolt of passion ripped through her when she felt the wet tip of his arousal pressing against her legs.

He breathed a kiss over her cheeks and her eyelids before finally moving in for a taste of her mouth. Moaning, she arched into him and undulated her hips, hoping to ease the restless ache in her loins.

Her entire being responded to his closeness, his male heat and his evocative scent. He spread her knees with his long legs. "Yes," she cried out, as the tip of his cock grazed her pussy.

Raining kisses over her skin, he stopped to pull one hard nipple between his lips. Her pink areola swelled painfully in his ravishing mouth. He tracked lower, gracing every speck of naked flesh with his tongue and lips until he reached the damp core centered at the apex of her thighs.

With his shoulders prying her legs open, she thrust her pelvis forward. A wave of lust spread like wildfire through her body, making her lose all coherent thought. "Please…fu-fuck me," she pleaded, aching to feel his hard, erect shaft inside her.

A rakish smile touched his mouth. His eyes held her captive. "All in good time, my love."

Using his thumbs, he parted her dewy folds. Pleasure rumbled in his throat. His eyes softened. "Katrina, my sweet, do you know what it does to me to see you so wet and ready?" His voice was a tender, intimate whisper.

A thrill rippled through her and tugged on her heart. It always surprised her how much she loved pleasing him. She pitched her voice low. "This is what *you* do to me." She ran her palm over his smooth cheek.

When their eyes locked, something comforting and familiar passed between them. Emotions as strong as the man himself filled the hollow that always resided in her heart and she nearly wept from the sheer power of them.

She felt as though she'd known him for a lifetime. But that wasn't possible. He'd only been coming to her for the last three weeks.

The thought vanished when she felt the velvety stroke of his tongue brush her inner thighs. His warm breath whispered across her pussy. He began a lazy journey higher and higher until he reached his goal. When his hot satiny tongue caressed her clit, her head thrashed from side-to-side and her mouth went dry. He pushed one long finger deep inside her, priming her body for his huge cock. Sometimes she feared his thickness would split her in half.

His tongue joined his finger and pushed further inside her tight, hot sheath. Her muscles immediately contracted as a wave began building deep inside her channel. Experienced fingers artfully manipulated her delicate clit, applying just the right amount of pressure to bring her to the brink. But he wouldn't let her tumble over, not until his mouth had its fill.

She fisted his hair and pushed his face into her slick junction. "Faster!" she cried out shamelessly. She was close, so close. One hard stroke of his tongue, and one more flick of his finger would surely send her over the edge.

He obliged. She exhaled a whimper of relief, knowing her wait was over. His tongue sifted through her silky strands until he laved her clit while his fingers picked up the tempo. Soft mewling sounds rolled from her mouth and echoed through the silent air as he delved into her. Her skin grew tight.

"Yes, that's it," she cried out as an orgasm racked her body. Her muscles contracted with enough force that she almost blacked out. Her liquid heat drenched his mouth.

He pulled back, sitting on his heels, and touched his tongue to his bottom lip. His wet mouth glistened in the glow of the rising sun. "You taste like sin." His nostrils flared. "Tell me there is no one else."

"There is no one else." Her voice was a hesitant whisper. "Only you." It wasn't entirely a lie. She hadn't physically been with anyone else, not even her fiancé, James. "I wait for you to come to me at night."

James was her lamb, and this man, whoever he was, was her lion.

She pulled him to her, pressed her lips to his and drank from his mouth. She tasted her sweetness and inhaled her heady scent. "Mmmmm..." she moaned.

He positioned his cock between her drenched legs and breathed her name into her mouth. Somehow, he knew her by name even though she'd never spoken it. "Katrina, you are mine," he said intimately, possessively, pushing into her.

She nodded her agreement.

"Say it," he demanded.

"I'm yours." She wanted to cry out his name but he'd yet to tell her who he was.

His burning mouth closed over hers. He pumped into her harder and faster, his fingers biting into her hips, pinning her to the sandy ground below. Wrapping her legs around him, she gripped his back. Her fingers clawed a path down the center of his spine. Once again the earth began moving beneath her. Her muscles tensed and tightened in anticipation. Hot pleasure shot through her with the rippling approach of an orgasm.

As soon as he felt her climax, his thighs went taut and his motion stilled. He buried his muffled cries into her neck as he spilled his seed into her.

They lay there for an endless moment, their greed for one another temporarily fed. The soothing sound of the waves lapping against the shore lulled her eyes shut.

The sun began to rise on the horizon warming their slick bodies. Her heart sank. For she knew what daybreak meant. He'd be leaving her. The few stolen moments they spent together in the predawn hours simply weren't enough to satiate her cravings for him.

He stood up, gathered her hand in his, and pulled her to her feet. The vision of him grew faint as he backed toward the ocean. Silhouetted against the rising sun, the water rushing over his knees, his hands still reached out to her. "Come back to me, Katrina." His voice was fading, his body melting. "Come home."

And then he disappeared, swallowed by the ocean. The same way he had every other morning for the past three weeks.

"No! Don't go," she cried, reaching for the apparition that had vanished into the cool Atlantic Ocean. "Stay with me. Stay…"

* * * * *

Body drenched in sweat, she awoke with a start. Writhing on her satiny sheets in the shelter of her bedroom, her hands flailed in the dark, searching for something that was no longer there. "Stay…" she whispered, her voice a mere thread of sound as it lingered in the still morning air. "Who are you?"

Who are you…?

The shrilling phone startled her out of her reverie. She twisted and winced as the sun caught her gaze. Squeezing her lids shut, she tried to regain some semblance of composure before answering. Trembling fingers reached out to grasp the receiver.

"Hello." She cursed her voice for sounding as shaky as she felt.

"Katrina, this is Dr. Murphy's office. You're late for your appointment." The crisp, efficient voice on the other end snapped her thoughts to attention.

Katrina stole a glance at her clock and groaned. Not only were her dreams affecting her personal life and her work at the art gallery, now they were affecting her doctor's appointment as well.

She drew a tight breath and exhaled quickly. "I'll be there in twenty minutes," she assured the receptionist and placed the phone back onto the cradle.

This was one appointment she couldn't skip. She'd been seeing the doctor for a little over six months now. Although the erotic dreams had only begun three weeks ago, she'd been having disturbing, tempting dreams of the ocean for much longer. When those dreams grew stronger, more intense and had begun to affect her life, Katrina had known it was time to seek professional help.

Dr. Kay Murphy was the only one she had dared to confide in about her erotic dreams. Anyone else would surely think she'd lost her mind. And truth be told, she wasn't too far from thinking that herself.

She flopped back onto her bed and stretched out her tired, sore limbs. An ache that would remain with her for the day, reminding her of the vivid dreams that swept her away into a land of fantasy—with a man she felt she'd known for a lifetime. A man who knew things about her that she was only discovering herself.

Who was this man that invaded her nightly dreams?

The cool sheets felt scratchy beneath her warm, naked body. Sitting up, she examined her bed. *Sand.* She scooped up the fine granules and rubbed them between her fingers. As the tiny particles slipped from her fingertips and pooled on the bed, she shook her head in bewilderment.

None of this made sense.

Although the doctor assured her that these dreams would pass, that they were simply a nervous reaction to her upcoming nuptials next week, Katrina suspected otherwise.

She suspected her mind hadn't conjured up some fantasy man. Some small part of her felt that someone, or some*thing*, had found a way into her subconscious.

How else could the sand be explained?

Katrina respected Dr. Murphy's professional opinion. However, since she'd never been with a man physically, she refused to believe that she'd conjured up some fantasy man to help her cope with having only one sex partner for the rest of her life.

Unfortunately, the doctor was at a loss to explain the sand in her bed or the bruises lacing her hips. Katrina couldn't blame it on sleepwalking. Surrounded by pavement and cement she'd have to venture pretty far from her Manhattan condo to find a beach.

Katrina flung her legs over the edge of her bed and pinched the bridge of her nose hoping to ward off an impending headache. The dreams that filled her nights left her tired during the day, and had begun to wear her down.

Confused and emotionally drained, she made her way into the bathroom, hoping a shower would help clear her head.

Unfortunately, the last few weeks had proven that no matter what she did, *he* continued to consume her thoughts.

She pulled open the curtain and turned on the shower nozzle. Who was the man that invaded her mind, her body and her heart? What did he want with her?

Turning, she sagged against the bathroom sink and stared at her reflection in the mirror. She tilted her head back as her body tingled with memories of his gentle caress. A surge of warmth flooded her veins as she recalled the way he filled her soul with unfamiliar emotions. It surprised her how the emptiness that always resided in her heart disappeared when he embraced her in his arms.

"*Come home, Katrina…*" His parting words echoed through her mind.

How was it possible that a man from her dreams made her feel so complete, so whole — a foreign, yet welcome feeling?

She played that thought over and over in her mind as she adjusted the needle-like spray on her showerhead.

What was his name?

Then it came to her. As though his name had been planted in her mind all along and all she had to do was search for it.

Ranek.

His name was Ranek.

Her sea god.

* * * * *

With a wave of his hand, Ranek placed Katrina back into the safety and comfort of her bed before returning to his undersea lair. He needed sleep. These nightly trips to the surface were exhausting.

She would be his again. Katrina was his soulmate. And when a Bandara mated it was for an eternity. Soon she'd return to his world, where she belonged. Ranek knew he had to bring her over slowly. A patient man he was not, but such matters required delicacy. It would take gentle prodding to bring her mind around. For it wasn't easy to discover you're not who you think you are.

Like himself, Katrina was a Bandara. Magical descendants of both Atlantians and humans that lived in an oxygenated pocket deep under the ocean.

He pulled open the door to his lair and lowered himself onto his bed. He drew a tired breath as his body molded against the soft sheets.

He took one last glimpse into the mortal world and watched her sleep. "Rest now, my love, for your journey will be a difficult one. You will need your strength for what you are about to endure."

Every night he filled her mind with small bits of information about her past and who she was. Tonight she'd drank her own sweetness from his mouth. Tomorrow she'd drink from his cock, and his seed would fill her with old memories. And when she was ready, he would take her behind the walls of their kingdom beneath the sea.

Fire pitched through his blood as he recalled the way she had been torn from his grasp and killed by mortals. All of this at the hands of his younger brother, Kohan. A man who'd been banished from their kingdom for his treachery. He fisted one hand and pounded it into his palm. His nostrils flared with uncontrollable rage.

Kohan. After the elders had spared his life, he'd been taken to the underworld. Ranek knew if they ever crossed paths again, he would not be so charitable with him.

He'd spent decades searching for Katrina, knowing that when the hands of a human killed one of his kind, then that slain Bandara would be reborn a human with ties to both worlds.

Anger coiled through him. It had taken him far too long to find her. With her wedding to a mortal man only a week away, he had to work fast—being careful not to rupture the part of her that was human, the part that was resistant to believing. For if he did, she would slowly fade and die—this time permanently- and as her lifelong soulmate, he would die along with her.

Chapter Two

Katrina inhaled the salty sea breeze as cool ocean droplets dusted her hair. Lit only by the glow of the full moon, the waves shimmered as far as the eye could see. Their crashing sound against the sandy shore mingled with the call of the gulls overhead.

Drawing a contented breath, she moved toward the inviting water. After her doctor's appointment earlier that day, she'd gone straight to the gallery hoping to finish her commissioned painting, but once again she'd found herself staring at her easel, reliving her nightly dreams. When Susan, her best friend and business partner, offered Katrina the use of her rustic cottage on the ocean, Katrina had jumped at the opportunity. Perhaps a nice, relaxing night on a *real* beach would help her eradicate Ranek from her thoughts and get her mind back on her wedding preparations, where it belonged.

Icy water rushed up to meet her bare feet, but Katrina didn't mind the cold. In fact, she welcomed it. She squeezed her toes savoring the sensations of the cool wet sand beneath her flesh.

As she stood there overlooking the ocean, a feeling of peacefulness and belonging filtered through her. Having spent her childhood searching for something to fill the void that inhabited her heart, Katrina embraced the foreign, happy emotions and clung to them as if her very life depended on it.

Folding her arms across her chest, she tightened her shawl around her shoulders as she thought about her younger years.

Her life had been filled with an intense unfulfilled longing that she'd always attributed to losing her parents at such a young age. Recently, however, since Ranek's nightly visits and the emotions he aroused in her, she'd begun to question her logic. Was the longing a result of losing her parents or was it something else?

Katrina's mind filled with memories of her grandmother. Warmth flowed through her and touched her heart as she recalled how she had tried so hard to fill the emptiness inside Katrina.

Her thoughts drifted to James and his large extended family. Katrina hoped her marriage to him would help quell the longing that has always resided in her heart. James. Sweet, gentle James. A patient man who'd agreed to her wishes to abstain from sex until after they were married. She wasn't sure why she'd always felt such a strong reluctance to sleep with James — or any of her previous boyfriends, for that matter.

She cared for James a great deal. He was a lovely man who treated her with dignity and respect. His family took her in and welcomed her as if she were their own daughter. She loved the idea of belonging to a family and prayed she'd grow to love James the way a wife was supposed to love her husband.

Katrina dug her toes deeper into the sandy ground and willed her mind to clear of the tension surrounding her work, her upcoming wedding, and all the preparations that were still needed. She breathed in the salt-scented air, and gazed at the twinkling stars in the dark night sky. As she drew in a deep contented sigh, her tightly coiled muscles began to relax and she actually found her smile widening. She untied her hair, letting it fall across her shoulders.

Katrina turned and made her way back to the cottage. Although far from a luxury hotel, it contained all the basic necessities anyone required, like a bathroom, bedroom, small kitchen and all the privacy she needed.

After heating the kettle, she poured herself a strong cup of caffeinated tea. She was desperate to suppress her dreams of Ranek, so tonight she would not sleep. Without sleep, Katrina was sure he couldn't come to her. An unsettling mixture of disappointment and need settled around her heart.

What was it that attracted her so to this dream man?

Slipping into a comfortable reclining chair with her favorite historical, Katrina sipped on her tea, becoming lost in the characters.

Hours later, despite her valiant efforts, she was lulled to sleep.

* * * * *

The second her lids closed, Ranek brought her to him. She looked as beautiful and angelic as ever, standing on the shore waiting for him. The moon overhead danced playfully off her golden highlights. He loved the way her eyes darkened with heat and need when she watched him emerge from the ocean.

As he closed the distance between them, Katrina did what was expected of her. She slowly removed her clothes and positioned herself on the sandy ground. Her legs locked together, the way he liked.

She moistened her lips. "I've been waiting." Her voice was a mere thread of sound.

He hovered over her. "You were fighting it." His dark tone held an edge of danger. With such little time to work with, her resistance would complicate matters. Why did she constantly test him? Did she always have to be so strong-willed?

Of course she did, he thought wryly. Some things never change. A slight smile touched his lips as he recalled the way her independence, strength, and determination had got her into trouble on more than one occasion as a young, rebellious girl.

"I can't fight the inevitable." She widened her legs in anticipation.

Ranek could see her damp pussy shimmering with silky, wet excitement. Using her fingers, she parted her swollen sex lips wide allowing her pink clit to come out to play. When she brushed her thumb over it, his blood boiled with intense need and he fought to control the primal, untamed animal in him. His body vibrated and his nostrils flared as a growl rumbled from the depths of his throat.

Katrina's welcoming invitation nearly made him unleash the lustful beast that stirred within.

He shook some clarity back into his mind. Tonight he was on a mission and he needed all the control he could summon.

"Stand up, Katrina." His voice came out harsher than he meant.

Her eyes flickered. "Have I done something wrong?" Nervously, she assumed a sitting position.

Her aroused body glistened in the moonlight spilling over her naked flesh. His whole body trembled at the sight before him.

Aching to find solace in her mouth, in her heat and in her welcoming sheath, Ranek had to fight the powerful urge to drop to the ground and sink into her. That pleasure would have to wait. Tonight he needed her to drink his seed—seed that would slowly penetrate her subconscious with the life and love they'd once shared.

He reached for her hand and pulled her to her feet. "You've done everything right. And for that you will be rewarded." Slipping his hands around her slim hips, he anchored her to him. She felt so good. So right. "In time." He grabbed her fingers and inhaled her delectable female scent. His body ignited and he fought to keep his voice controlled. "Tonight we are going to try something different."

For a brief moment she looked at him in confusion, then slowly nodded her head in agreement. "What is it you wish from me?" she asked. Her tongue skated across her bottom lip and he nearly fell to his knees.

Before he did anything else, he had to taste the sweetness of her succulent mouth. He tangled his hands through her hair and brought her lips to his. His mouth came down on hers. Hard. Forceful. Possessive. She eagerly responded. Sinking into his mouth with the fire, passion and ferociousness only a Bandara could achieve.

He eased back and looked at her. Rubbing his thumb over her satiny lips, he guided her hand to his swollen sex. "I want you to drink from me."

Startled by his suggestion, she opened her eyes wide as though she'd never considered such an idea. Her small hand quivered as it closed around his thickness.

"I've never done that before."

Skittish eyes glanced downward and examined the length of his cock. "It's…it's so big. I'll choke on it." She ran her fingertips lightly over the head of his shaft and he lubricated in response.

He watched her eyes zero in on the liquid pooling on the engorged tip. Small teeth tugged on her bottom lip. She looked mesmerized, entranced.

"Taste it," he whispered. His voice was husky. He watched the pulse on her neck leap. "Taste my juices, Katrina." He brushed his mouth over her warm, pink cheek.

His cock pulsated in her hand and grew another inch. The jerking movement elicited a small moan of approval from her. He watched her look of shock transform slowly into curiosity, intrigue.

Ranek guided her fingers to the dripping slit at the end of his cock. "Go ahead. Tell me if I taste as sweet as you do," he encouraged.

She dipped her finger into the milky substance and drew the liquid to her mouth. "Mmmmm." He watched her lick her finger clean then look down as though searching for seconds.

Ranek dropped to his knees and pulled Katrina down with him. He lay her small body on top of his. Silky blonde hair spilled over his face. Bringing her lips to his, he grazed a kiss over her mouth.

"Put my cock into your mouth," he coaxed.

"Okay," she agreed softly, eyes gleaming in anticipation.

She kissed him lightly, his mouth, his jaw and the damp hollow of his throat. Her tongue skated across the pulse in his neck and his whole body stiffened in response to her slow seduction.

She licked a path down his chest, stopping to lave one nipple with her hot tongue. Her heat seared his skin. The velvety sweep of her lashes against his body sent flames surging through him. He moaned and threaded his fingers through her hair, guiding her head down further.

With a panther-like stretch, her exploring fingers grazed his inner thighs, purposely brushing up against his swollen cock, making it pulse in response.

He reached down and thumbed her nipples, evoking low groans from her that grew louder and louder until her moans of pleasure drowned out his.

She positioned herself between his legs and wrapped her delicate fingers around his thick shaft. Her pink tongue snaked out and caressed the tip of his sex. She ran her lips down his tight skin as though she were testing, tasting and savoring the texture.

His head lolled to the side. "Ah, Katrina, my sweet. You *are* a quick learner."

"You like?" she whispered from somewhere deep between his thighs.

"Yes, my love, I like."

Encouraged by his moans of approval, she drew the head into her succulent mouth. "Mmmmm…" With greed, she laved the soft folds underneath the tip and drank the dripping fluid.

Her moans of pleasure pleased him. He remembered how much she had once liked the taste of cock. Her fingers sifted through his tangle of dark hair and grasped his heavy sac below, gently massaging and cupping his tight balls in her hand.

His breathing grew labored. She teased and seared his cock with her hot mouth, taking time to savor every inch. Ranek's mind began spinning and soon he was panting.

The first delicious flick of her tongue inside the slit of his cock awakened the jealous animal in him. He felt his eyes darken with uncontrollable rage. "Don't you ever kiss another man this way, Katrina. For if you do, I will kill him." His voice was thick with desire, need and danger.

His harsh words didn't startle her. "I will only do this for you, Ranek." Her voice was as warm and smooth as the sand that provided them their nightly bed.

It was the first time she'd spoken his name out loud. He loved the way it rolled off her tongue. His eyes softened.

"Now, I will drink from you." She placed his engorged head on the tip of her tongue and plunged forward, sinking the entire length of him down her throat.

"Dear God, Katrina!" he yelled, his breath coming in a ragged burst. A wave of passion nearly took him over the edge. His muscles clenched and he fought to hang on.

"Come for me," she whispered breathlessly. "Let me taste you."

She buried his cock in her throat, and then slowly began to rock back and forth, his erection sliding in and out of her hot, tight mouth.

A tremor rippled through him and he knew he was close. Her hands caressed his balls then slowly inched downward. She massaged the tender flesh inside the slit of his ass cheeks. He drew a sharp breath and threw his head to the side.

"*Yesssssss*, that's my girl."

The exquisite sensations she evoked drove every sane thought from him and he knew his time had come.

"I'm there, my love," he cried out, fisting her hair as she drew him deeper into her mouth.

His explosion was fast, intense, sending his liquid heat down her throat.

She drank from him, swallowing until every last drop was safely nestled in her mouth.

He grabbed her in his arms and pulled her on top of him. Her dark eyes were lust-filled, her lips wet from his juices.

He smiled at her as he held her tight.

Now the memories would come.

Chapter Three

ဢ

It was dark. Murky. Dangerous…

An eerie, foreboding sensation crept up her spine as she looked around the partially submerged, abandoned ship. Sparks of fear ignited her nerve endings causing her body to involuntarily shudder.

Apprehensively, she bit down on her lip and brushed a wayward curl from her eyes. Darkness had begun to fall, making the walls of the ship feel as though they were closing in on her.

"Kohan, stop fooling around. You're scaring me," she cried.

Except for the muted sounds of creaking metal mingling with her footfalls, silence enveloped her. Reaching into the blackness, she wrapped her fingers around the ship's railing to help guide her forward.

"Kohan, where are you?"

Her senses were assaulted with the pungent aroma of aging rust, rotting algae and palpable fear. Her own fear. A fresh wave of panic prickled her skin.

She took a cautious step forward. Crystals from a fallen chandelier crunched beneath her feet. The abandoned ship shifted and Katrina screamed as she lost her footing and crashed to the floor.

Oh, why had she ever followed Kohan outside the protected walls of their kingdom and into forbidden territory?

Because he'd dared her and she'd wanted to prove her fearlessness.

"Kohan," she cried, grabbing a railing to right herself. "Where are you?" Her fingers gripping the slippery rails, she pulled herself upward.

They needed to get back home before their absence was noticed. Punishment for venturing outside the concealed kingdom walls would be harsh. She shivered to think what the elders would do if they ever found out.

"What's the matter? Are you chicken?" he taunted, sneaking up behind her.

His hands skimmed her full breasts as he reached for her. She spun around to look at him. Her senses went on full alert as she caught his lambent gaze and suggestive smile.

"It's getting late. We should head back before someone notices we're missing." Her voice wavered and her stomach dipped. She didn't care for the way his eyes traced the pattern of her body. She took a guarded step backwards.

He matched her step. "What's your hurry?" He yanked her into his embrace and brushed his lips over hers.

Planting her palms onto his chest, she shoved him away. "Stop fooling around."

His smile was dangerous, wolfish. "Come on, Katrina. You know you want it." He pulled her closer, his breath hot on her neck.

"Kohan," her voice grated in warning. "Stop."

She watched as something deep inside him shifted. Her heart beat wildly as he glared at her for a long moment. When she made a move to go, he gripped her arm harder and slammed her against the wall.

She looked around frantically, wanting to scream for help, but knowing her cries would go unanswered. There was no one around for miles. "You're *hurting* me." She tried to twist away but with each movement he tightened his hold.

He crushed his body against her. "Come on, Katrina, stop fighting it. It's what we both want. Admit it." He closed his mouth over hers, jamming his tongue down her throat. "Let me fuck you. It'll be real good. I promise," he whispered harshly.

She gasped and squirmed, freeing herself from his grip. Anger flashed through her veins. "What is the matter with you?"

His eyes blinded with lust, he pushed his swollen cock hard against her legs. Deftly, he slid a hand between her thighs. "Do I make you wet?"

She clenched her legs together and pushed his hand away. "No!" she yelled.

His nostrils flared. "I bet if I were Ranek you wouldn't hesitate." The dark tension in his voice frightened her.

She knew he envied his older brother. Knew he envied Ranek's authoritative position in the kingdom, but he'd never displayed such blatant jealously before. At least never to her.

She opened her mouth to speak but the rage in his eyes cautioned her to remain silent. Fisting her hands, she prepared for his advances. Not that she would be any match for a man destined to follow in his brother's footsteps and become a warrior.

A deep insidious growl caught in his throat. "That's what I thought." He snarled and stepped back. "I see the way you look at him."

There was no denying his accusations. But, she wasn't the only one who looked at Ranek with adoring eyes. Ranek's virility, power and confidence drew the attention of every unclaimed girl in their kingdom.

Ranek had yet to take a mate, and although it was foolish for Katrina to think he'd ever give her a second glance, she clung to her girlish crush.

A movement beyond Kohan's shoulders caught her eye. She blinked, focusing her gaze, and came face-to-face with Ranek. His dark eyes were hooded, dangerous. His mouth set in a grim line. Katrina wilted under his powerful, angry gaze. A strangled cry caught in her throat.

How long had he been there? What had he heard?

In two easy strides, he closed the distance between them. He stood over Kohan. "If you touch her again, it will cost you your hand." His tone was controlled, deep and dangerous. Ranek grabbed Kohan by the shoulders and pulled him from her, sending him sailing in the opposite direction.

Kohan clambered to his feet and lunged for Ranek, but he neatly sidestepped his advances.

Dark brows quirked over black eyes. "Don't test me, little brother," he warned, wrapping his large fingers around the dagger anchored to his side. Tension lines bracketed his mouth.

As though sensing this a battle he couldn't yet win, Kohan backed down. The look in his piercing eyes spoke volumes. Katrina knew this fight was far from over.

"Go back to the kingdom. I will deal with you when I return," Ranek ordered.

Mumbling curses under his breath, Kohan turned his back to them and disappeared into the darkness.

After Kohan left, Ranek concentrated his attention on Katrina. For a long moment he remained silent as he gazed at her.

Underneath his glaring eyes, her legs trembled, her mouth went dry. She was both relieved and uneasy that he'd showed up when he did. Swallowing past the knot in her throat, she fought to recover her voice. "Are you going to punish me for venturing to the surface?" she whispered.

"Perhaps."

He circled her. Standing behind her, he touched her shoulder and she trembled.

"Do you fear me?"

She could feel the tantalizing sweep of his breath on the back of her neck. It wasn't fear that made her body quiver. "No," she answered honestly, knowing full well that he was a fair man and her punishment would be just.

Ranek was a man as quick to reward an act of honor as he was to punish an act of disobedience.

"I see," he replied, coming back around to face her.

One long finger reached out to stroke her cheek. His movements were sensual, arousing. Katrina knitted her fingers together and fought the pull to touch him back. Such boldness was unacceptable.

She stole a peek at the broad-shouldered, powerful sea god before her. His square jaw was firm, his eyes dark, unreadable. Dressed in armor, his large body hovered over hers. His stance was prepared, as if always ready for battle. She stared at his large hands resting at his sides and wondered how they would feel touching her skin.

He lifted one eyebrow. "Is it true?" His voice covered her like sweet honey.

"Is what true?"

"What Kohan said?" His corded muscles shifted as he took a step closer.

She bit her lip and flushed, knowing full what he was referring to. "I'm not sure I understand."

"Would you have hesitated if it were me?" His words were bold, confident.

"Why is it you ask?" She lowered her gaze.

"Because, unlike my foolish younger brother, if I am going to touch you, I want it to be a welcomed touch." The hypnotic tone of his voice mesmerized her.

Her heart pounded and she was certain he could see the pulse in her neck leap. Surely he wasn't suggesting he *wanted* to touch her?

"Answer me, Katrina," he demanded.

The deep timbre of his voice made her body burn with desire.

He tipped her chin up. The sweet friction of his fingers on her skin made her shudder. Their eyes met and locked, and for a brief moment Katrina became spellbound by the dark intensity of his gaze.

"So it is true. I can see it in your eyes." He pulled her tighter and she molded against him. "Ahhh," he whispered into her hair. "And I can feel it in your body."

To lie to him now would be foolish. "Yes, Lord Ranek." Her voice was a low whisper.

"So if I touch you like this—" he ran his fingers gently along her curves, skimming the outside of her swollen breasts, "—you would not protest?"

Her nipples grew tight alerting Ranek to her mounting desire. He dipped his finger inside her cleavage and stroked her flesh. His rough skin contracting her per nipples.

She drew in a sharp breath. "No, Lord Ranek. I would not."

"Very well then." Using his knee he parted her legs. She felt her pussy dampen and became dizzy with desire. She worked to keep her breath regulated. "How about this?" He pushed her legs further apart. "Would this make you protest?"

She didn't answer. She was too busy trying to control her ragged breathing and her body's evocative response to his invasive touch.

"Katrina, I asked you a question. I expect an answer." He spoke in a clipped tone. He placed his knee deep between her spread legs and she sagged against him. Her breasts surged forward aching to be touched by his strong, warrior hands.

When his touch didn't come, a surge of boldness rushed through her and she straightened. "No, Lord Ranek, I would not protest. In fact, I'd welcome it." Unflinchingly, she met his gaze.

A slight smile flirted with his lips. She suspected her boldness threw him off-kilter. The women in her kingdom were not expected to be assertive.

She watched his reaction. His face was grim, his eyes told her nothing, but the smirk playing on his mouth was all the encouragement she needed. She pressed on. "If I touched you like this, would *you* protest?" she asked, and ran a gentle finger between his hard, muscular thighs, her hand contacting his engorged cock. She was thrilled to discover his arousal, but kept a telltale smile from her lips.

Undoubtedly, there were penalties for such aggression, but Katrina knew she had nothing to fear. She glimpsed a pleased look in his eyes. He seemed rather amused by her assertiveness.

His eyes narrowed. "You have so much to learn my sweet, undisciplined Katrina. And I, and *only* I, shall be the one to teach you."

Chapter Four

ဆ

The beach was noisy, rowdy, filled with playful, rambunctious children making sandcastles or splashing near the waters edge.

Katrina strolled further along the crowded seashore, hoping for a distraction — something, anything to keep her mind off the previous night's dream. Her body still tingled with memories of Ranek's touch.

She stared blankly at the ocean, watching a surfer ride the white-crested waves. Sailboats bobbed in the distance. Inhaling the salty sea breeze she tilted her head back and gazed at the brilliant blue skyline.

Standing there with the midmorning sun heating her skin, her body chilled as a presence passed through her. It was brief, brisk — as though it was searching for something, or someone. If she hadn't been so aware of her surroundings and her emotions, she would surely have missed it.

Her eyes sprang open as an uneasy feeling crept over her skin. There was a hint of danger in the air. Wrapping her arms around herself, she hugged the chill from her body and looked out over the water, searching for signs of Ranek.

He'd never before come to her during the day.

A foreign scent lingered in her nostrils. Although similar to Ranek's, deep in her gut Katrina knew it didn't belong to him.

If it wasn't Ranek, then who could it be?

Katrina wanted answers, and she wanted them now.

Who was Ranek? Where had he come from? And what did he want with her?

She sighed and glanced at her wristwatch, knowing her answers would have to wait. She thought briefly of James and immediately felt guilty. Her thoughts should be consumed with their wedding plans, not some mysterious sea god who invaded her dreams at night and plagued her thoughts in the day.

Katrina made her way back to her cottage, away from the bustling crowd. After gathering up her easel, paint, and brushes she positioned a chair facing the water and mentally prepared herself to begin the seascape she'd been commissioned to do.

Hours later, consumed by her work, she nearly fell from her chair as the powerful presence once again swept through her.

* * * * *

Ranek awoke with a start.

His senses on full alert, he automatically searched for the dagger he kept secured to his side. His knuckles whitened as he gripped it with angry fingers.

Kohan.

He shut his eyes, his mind searching for his brother's presence. Was it possible? Had Katrina's dreams of Kohan roused him from the underworld?

If the rumors about the creatures of the underworld were true — that they could transport themselves to the mortal world during daylight hours — then Katrina's life would be in danger.

Unable to pinpoint his brother's location, Ranek stood and prepared himself physically and mentally for his trip to the surface.

Alone in the mortal world, Katrina would be in danger if Kohan picked up on her signature. White-hot rage raced through him. He snarled and slammed his fists against the wall.

Ranek needed her here with him, in the safety of their home, a place where he could protect her. He wanted to work fast, yet he had to be careful to bring her mind around slowly.

A deep growl of frustration rumbled in his throat. His patience was growing thinner by the day.

He paced as he waited for the last fingers of light to fade from the mortal sky. Finally, after what felt like an eternity, she drifted off to sleep.

With warrior strength, he shot to the surface and was pleased to find, unlike the previous night, that she welcomed his arrival. Standing alone on the sandy shore, fully clothed, she waited for him.

Lust settled deep in his groin and his body automatically hardened at the sight of her. She smiled at him and his heart filled with longing for all the years he'd gone without her.

Soon. Soon she would understand the depth of his love for her and hers for him.

As she parted her legs his fingers tingled, anticipating a touch. He ached to lose himself in her tight, hot sheath. To find solace in her mouth, her embrace.

His heart pounded in his chest as he stared at her for an endless moment. Her eyes were dark, glossy, searching for answers. After a slow perusal of her attire, he caught her gaze and noted the boldness in her eyes.

He cocked one eyebrow. "Is this how you are supposed to greet me?" Shifting her stance, she made a sexy noise as he fingered the silky material of her blouse. Her full breasts tightened before his eyes alerting him to her desire. Saliva pooled on his tongue just thinking about sucking her tight nipples.

"I want to know what's going on. Who are you? What do you want from me?"

In one swift movement that threw her off balance, he pushed his hands up her skirt. An amused smirk danced across his face when his fingers touched her dampness. Without hesitation he tore away the scrap of silk covering her drenched pussy.

She opened her mouth to speak but he silenced her with his fingertips.

"Your answers will come, my love. But first let me taste you. I have thought of nothing else since our last coupling."

* * * * *

The delicate slide of his fingers over her swollen, wet clit overruled any coherent thought Katrina had. She became pliable in his capable hands. Scorched nerve endings screamed in ecstasy with each deliberate stroke.

His lips closed over hers, sending shivers of warm need throughout her body. A wave of passion left her teetering on the edge as his tongue thrust into her wanton mouth.

Although desperate for answers, Katrina quickly discovered her body was even more desperate for his touch.

He released her mouth and licked his damp fingers. "Do you know how arousing your taste is, my love?" he murmured.

Katrina whimpered and nearly dropped to her knees. "What is it you wish for me to do tonight, Ranek?" Need made her voice husky.

A low chuckle rumbled in his throat. "Since when did you ever wish to obey me?"

She smiled. "I want to please you."

"You always please me, Katrina." The soft timbre of his tone warmed her all over.

Lowering herself to the ground, she removed her skirt, unbuttoned her blouse and slipped out of her lace bra. Her fingers circling, she teased her pink nipples until they tightened almost painfully.

Hovering over her, Ranek tensed, chest heaving as his breathing quickened. She watched his throat work and listened to him swallow. Katrina grinned. She liked this bit of control she had over him.

Boldly, seductively, she slipped her hand between her legs and dipped her finger into her wet pussy.

He groaned and dropped to his knees. "You never did know discipline, Katrina."

"And that displeases you?" She quirked a challenging brow.

Taking back control, he mock-glared at her. "You know better than to come to me fully dressed. This act of disobedience will not go unpunished." He pushed her thighs as far apart as physically possible.

Gulping air, he sat back on his heels, a puzzled—if not pleased—look on his face. "Katrina…" His gaze traveled from her neatly shaved pussy to her face and back again.

His eyes caressed her with sultry heat. Under his appreciative gaze, she parted her labia. As her ripe, pink clit sprang out from under its slippery hood, his engorged cock grew another inch. "I'm not sure why or how I remembered, Ranek, but something deep in my soul told me you preferred my pussy this way."

She felt the gentle touch of his fingers over her smooth sex. Her eyes slipped shut and she moaned with the intense pleasure. He stroked the full length of her, his fingers probing, pressing into her opening. She arched forward, offering herself up to him completely. His fingers danced around her puckered asshole, playing with the tight cleft between her cheeks.

Desperate to feel his cock inside her, she wrapped her fingers around his shaft and squeezed. "Please, Ranek. I need you inside me," she begged, her breathing labored, shallow.

He chuckled. "Ah, then you should not have made your pussy so desirable, Katrina. You will have to wait for my cock until my mouth has had its fill of your silky sweetness." He dragged a finger over her smooth, sensitive skin and positioned himself between her legs.

Bending forward, he stretched her wet lips open as his warm tongue licked her sex from the front to the far back. He moaned with pleasure and nuzzled his face in closer. His satiny breath fired her senses. A fine tremor burned through her as her skin tightened under his devouring mouth.

Like a cat licking cream, he lapped at her. She could feel her orgasm building. Blood screamed through her veins at the onslaught of pleasure. He eased two fingers inside her and nipped at her clit, sending ripples of pain and desire onward and upward through her body.

She wiggled, driving his fingers in deeper, hugging him tight inside her. He pushed another finger in. It was a deliciously snug fit. Her pussy grew slick as hot pleasure swept through her. She took deep shuddering gasps. Her feminine aroma mingled with Ranek's scent, drawing her deeper into a haze of euphoria. She dug her fingers into his shoulders and bucked her hips. Her skin grew hot, damp. Her breathing was shallow.

She was close. So close. His thumb climbed higher to stroke her fleshy clit. He rubbed with light, slow circles. It was enough to send her sailing close to the edge. Her muscles twitched. He must have felt her response. He changed the tempo of his touch bringing her to her limit. She pinched her eyes shut as she felt herself tumble over. Her release was swift, intense. She lifted off the ground, her body jerking, trembling. Ranek continued stroking, his fingers and mouth absorbing her tremors.

Katrina relaxed back onto the ground and kneaded Ranek's shoulders. She held him for a long moment, until her breathing regulated. Ranek stroked her damp, folds and looked deep into her eyes.

"I want you on your hands and knees, my love."

Obediently, she rolled over. Bending forward, she spread her labia apart. Her juices trickled down her thighs as they dripped from her sopping pussy.

Straddling her from behind, he reached around and cupped her full, dangling breasts. Groaning in delight, he squeezed and pinched her taut nipples. His shaft pushed insistently between her legs.

He moved his hands, placing them on the small of her back, before whispering into her ear, "Lower your shoulders to the ground." With her ass raised to him, she pressed her full breasts into the cool, scratchy sand.

He ran a finger back and forth over her dripping slit pushing his thumb high into her pussy. Her body convulsed under his touch. Then, in one swift motion, he replaced his fingers with his cock, plunging into her sweetness. She cried out sharply and bucked against him.

His thickness pushed open the walls of her vagina. She felt agonizingly full as she accommodated his massive width. His balls slapped her clit as she raised and lowered herself on his engorged cock.

He impaled her again and again until yet another orgasm swept through her. Her muscles undulated and she sank slowly to the ground. Spreading her legs wider, she drove her hips back to meet his. When her vision went fuzzy around the edges, she struggled to blink her eyes back into focus. She clung to consciousness and concentrated on the last fragments of pleasure, moaning as it slowed. After her orgasm subsided Ranek pulled his still-erect cock out of her slick sheath. She twisted around to look at him.

"Turn over," he demanded. His voice was rusty, intense.

He grabbed her hand and guided it to his cock. It throbbed as she stroked the smooth, velvety head, semen spilling from the slit.

His breathing was ragged. "Put it in your mouth." His voice wavered and she sensed he was on the edge.

Obediently, she drew him to her. Her mouth was engulfed with the tangy taste of sweat, salty drips of semen, and her own feminine juices.

She took him all the way, until the tip poked the back of her throat. She rocked against him, letting him drive his shaft in and out of her wet mouth. She grabbed him with one hand, squeezing the base as she flicked the sensitive tip with her tongue.

She knew he was close. His cock thickened and throbbed as she worked her tongue around his bulbous head.

Ranek moaned and raked his fingers through her hair. "Drink my juices, Katrina. And you will find answers to your questions."

He exploded into her mouth and Katrina lapped up every last drop of his sticky semen.

Chapter Five

ဢ

It was a typical day deep inside the Bandara Kingdom...

Katrina tightened her robe around her waist, opened the door to her lair and greeted one of the council's many servants. The elderly, silver-haired lady nodded her head and averted her violet eyes as she handed Katrina a slip of paper.

"Thank you," Katrina said. Without speaking, the woman bowed her head and left.

Katrina's pulse leapt as she recognized the familiar letterhead. Eagerly, she opened the folded note and read the message.

She skimmed the words twice before the meaning finally settled in. It was a personal invitation from Ranek to join the gala at the king's castle.

Excitement danced in her heart and she had to stop herself from shrieking out loud. She pressed the letter to her chest as a smile stretched across her mouth.

After their brief meeting on the sunken ship, she hadn't been able to further her relationship with Ranek. He'd gone off with a band of warriors soon afterward to battle rebels from the underworld. She had no idea he'd returned so soon.

In his absence, rumors had quickly spread throughout the kingdom that Ranek had chosen a mate. Katrina remained silent in the face of such gossip. It would be presumptuous of her to suggest he'd chosen her.

She swallowed the dryness in her mouth as she considered the idea further. Was it *possible* that he'd chosen her? A nervous, excited flutter made her heart race, and she had to sit before she collapsed. Feeling flushed, she fanned her hand before her heated cheeks.

Gaining control over the situation and her emotions, she immediately quashed her wandering thoughts. The king would insist there be many young women at the castle for Ranek to choose from before he made his final decision. It would simply be foolish for her to set herself up for such disappointment.

Climbing to her feet, she walked to her dressing room. Standing before her mirror, she considered how to style her hair. Should she pin it up into an artful coiffure? Or should she let it fall around her shoulders? She cursed her untamed curls as she ran a comb through them.

How would Ranek prefer it?

After much debate she pinned it on top of her head and set out to find appropriate attire. The note said there would be dancing following a formal dinner. As Katrina reached for a simple but elegant dress from her wardrobe, another knock sounded on her door.

She padded softly across the room. Another servant bowed before her. The girl appeared to be only a few years older than Katrina herself.

"I am Tiera. I was sent to help you prepare for the evening." Dark hair cut shoulder-length framed her porcelain-white face. She lowered her lashes, shadowing her large eyes.

Surprised by such unaccustomed luxury, Katrina stepped back and with a wave of her hand, invited the girl in.

"Ranek asked that you wear this." She handed Katrina a beautifully decorated box. "I will draw your bath and prepare your lotions," she said before disappearing into the other room.

Katrina threw open the lid. She gasped in surprise, certain she'd never seen a more beautiful gown. The palest of greens, it was embossed with emeralds, rubies and shimmering diamonds that could only have been acquired in the dangerous mortal world.

Katrina shivered just thinking about venturing into such forbidden territory.

Had Ranek gone there for her?

"Your bath is ready," Tiera said, indicating for Katrina to follow.

Katrina stepped into the other room and became unsettled at the thought of undressing in front of the council's servant.

"Drink this." The girl pressed a cup into her hands. Katrina examined the dark liquid before inhaling the fragrant mixture of spices and herbs. "It will help relax you," Tiera insisted.

Katrina felt the tension drain from her body when she sipped the syrupy concoction. Her tightly coiled muscles began to relax. The potion was rich in flavor, and the exotic blend of herbs tingled all the way to her stomach.

The girl untied the belt of Katrina's robe. Her breasts jutted forward as her only piece of clothing fell to the floor. Tiera took her by the hand and guided her into the bubbly, aromatic bath.

Breathing in the scented water, she relaxed and allowed her head to loll to one side as the servant began sponging her naked body. She felt almost dizzy, drugged, as though she were floating through time and space.

Katrina's nipples darkened and hardened as the girl dragged the rough sponge over them. If not for the potion relaxing her, surely she would have protested Tiera's invasive touch.

Katrina took another sip of her drink and watched the servant ready her body. A warm glow spread through her veins and settled low in her stomach.

Tiera lifted Katrina's legs one at a time. She ran her soapy sponge down the length of them, careful not to miss a speck of her tender skin.

Eventually Katrina's lids slipped shut and she relaxed against the gentle stroking motion of the girl's small hands. Hands so unlike the masculine, rough-textured skin of the warrior who'd promised to teach her everything. Her body came alive, stimulated just thinking about his long, decadent fingers skimming her curves.

Tiera pushed the sponge between Katrina's thighs. As the fabric scraped her most feminine places, Katrina's clitoris hardened involuntarily. Katrina lifted one lid but the girl was either oblivious to her arousal or chose to ignore it.

Inching her legs apart to provide Tiera with better access to her secret spot, Katrina once again relaxed and enjoyed the massage.

Upon completion of her bath, Tiera poured lotion over Katrina's body and with an erotic circular motion worked it into her skin. Katrina moaned softly as the other girl's warm hands kneaded her tender flesh.

Tiera stepped back and bowed before Katrina. "If that will be all, then I shall return to the council."

Katrina sighed with pleasure and disappointment. Although now relaxed from head to toe, she was disappointed that Tiera had to rush away. She'd *quite* enjoyed the other girl's company.

Katrina ran her hand through her damp hair. The bath had left it a rumpled mess. "Would you mind helping me with my hair? Sometimes I swear it has a mind of its own." Katrina tugged on a wayward curl.

Tiera smiled and followed her into the dressing room.

Katrina sat before her mirror and piled her curls above her head.

"Might I suggest you leave it down?"

"Why is that?" Katrina looked at her inquisitively.

"It is my understanding that Lord Ranek prefers it that way."

Katrina fought a grin. "Then I shall wear it up."

Tiera looked at her in surprise. Her large blue eyes opened wide, her mouth slightly ajar.

"I do not wish to seem too eager to please." She raised one brow mischievously.

Tiera's eyes lit with delight as they shared a private chuckle.

Hours later, Katrina found herself standing in the grand entrance of the king's castle. A servant met her at the door and led her into the large dining hall. As she moved through the elegant room, she felt the glares from the other women. A hush fell over the crowd as she was seated next to Lord Ranek.

She was correct in her assumption that an array of beautiful women from their kingdom would also be joining her in her bid to be chosen as Ranek's mate.

The king sat at the head of the table and nodded his greetings to her. She bowed graciously and accepted a glass of champagne placed before her by one of the king's servants.

When the next lady was brought forth, all attention turned away from Katrina. All attention except for Ranek's. A feminine thrill raced through her.

They gazed at one another.

He looked elegant in his formal attire. It wasn't too often he moved about without armor covering his hard, muscular body. Her gaze roamed over his face. Tiny lines touched his mouth. Laugh lines, Katrina presumed, although she'd yet to see him laugh. Confident as always, he appeared less tense then he had during their previous meeting. With his features softened, he looked more handsome than ever.

His dark sensual eyes studied her with casual aplomb. She shivered with a mixture of excitement and nervousness as she recalled the way he'd touched her and urged her thighs apart only days before.

Would he touch her again that way tonight?

The thought made her tingle with anticipation. She blinked, desperately trying to gain control over her emotions.

Beneath the table, his leg pressed against hers. Ripples of exquisite pleasure swept through her and she nearly leapt from her chair.

As though he could read her every thought, he leaned in and whispered, "The answer is yes, Katrina. I most certainly do plan on touching you again." She caught his smug grin. "However, it will be when *I'm* ready." He lifted his chin as if daring her to question his authority.

So, he wanted to challenge her, did he?

Slipping her hand below the cloth-covered table, she reached between his thighs and found him hard and wanting. She tossed him a slow, sexy grin. "I do believe you *are* ready."

Sexual tension fired between them and crackled in the air.

He flinched and stifled a groan. "I look forward to punishing your bold actions, my love." His jaw flexed.

Katrina moistened her lips. She could hardly wait.

* * * * *

Her touch on his leg made it difficult for him to think about anything else during their meal. He ached to ravage her naked body. To peel away her pale green dress inch by inch to expose her silky flesh. To have his wicked way with her from this night forward until the end of eternity.

Tonight he planned on making Katrina his mate.

Unbeknownst to her, he'd chosen Katrina a very long time ago. He'd been waiting for her to bloom, to develop the healing skills he knew she possessed, and take her rightful position as healer in their kingdom.

Recently however, upon finding his foolish younger brother touching her, he knew it was time to stake his claim. She'd grown into a beautiful, desirable woman and before another man set his fancy upon her, he would make his declaration to the kingdom.

No man would dare touch her once she was his. For if he did, his treachery would cost him his life.

"Shall we dance?"

When Katrina met his gaze, fire and heat splintered through him. Her lips were full and shiny, just begging to be kissed. She looked both innocent and sensual in the gown he'd asked her to wear. A gown he planned to strip from her body the first chance he got.

He held his hand out to her. She eagerly accepted, sliding her delicate fingers into his. He carefully pulled her to her feet as he did a slow perusal of her body. Her full, silky cleavage, barely contained beneath the fine threads of her dress, threatened to spill free.

He licked his lips and she smiled in response. He knew she enjoyed playing with him. He sensed she liked the sexual powers she held over him. Liked to tease him with her voluptuous body. And liked the responses she pulled from his. Tonight he would show her exactly what she did to his body. Especially to the member standing at half-mast between his thighs.

He pulled her onto the dance floor and pressed against her. He eased one knee between her spread legs and glanced around the room. "It pains me to go through these formalities when all I want is to have you alone," he whispered harshly into her ear.

He felt her body go slack against his. It pleased him, the way she responded to his words. He almost chuckled. Now it was his turn to show her just who was in charge of whom.

It was his turn to play.

He inclined his head to look at her. "Would you protest if I touch you again tonight?" he asked, already knowing the answer by the response of her body. He spun her around, skimming her curves with his hand.

"Perhaps," she murmured breathlessly. The soft warmth of her voice flooded him with longing, and he didn't know how he would manage another second on the dance floor.

She clenched her thighs around his leg and pushed her pelvis into his groin. In his semi-erect state her hip connected with his cock. His body tightened and he slowed their dance steps.

He caught her gaze. "It would not be wise of you to resist my touch. Such pleasures are not given out freely." He fought back a rakish grin. "Regret is such a dreadful waste of time."

He became acutely aware of the way she vibrated in his arms. His teasing caused the effect he'd hoped for. What she didn't know was that her sweet response to his seduction made him fairly mad with longing. His body was primed for the night ahead.

He watched her chest heave. That was where he wanted his mouth. There. Right between her creamy mounds. Lust pounded through him and he fought to restrain his arousal in the midst of the noisy crowd.

"Your scent invigorates me, Katrina. What do you call it?"

She smiled demurely. Her gaze drowsy, heated. "Arousal."

He hardened. Right there. In the middle of the dance floor, for all to see.

That was all he could take. He had to get her out of there now. He needed her alone, he needed to bask in her rich female body, her delicate taste and heady scent.

"Come with me now," he growled, grabbing her tiny wrist and putting an end to their game. He practically dragged her to his chambers. He closed his door, shutting out the dull noise of the crowd.

His heart hammered in his chest when he looked at her. "Turn around," he said, his voice husky with emotion.

She obliged. With her back to him, he examined the long column of her neck. Tendrils of hair had slipped from their moorings and flirted with her nape.

"Unleash your hair."

She pulled it free and let it cascade over her shoulders. He gave a lust-filled groan.

"Do not ever wear it that way again." She twisted slightly and he thought he detected a sparkle in her eyes. "Have I said something amusing?"

"No, my Lord."

He came up behind her and gently touched her shoulder. He surfed his hand over her back, down her sides and lower until he touched the sweet tender flesh of her buttocks. His fingers bit into her hips and he pulled her hard against his engorged cock.

When she wiggled her backside, he groaned and began working at the small buttons lining the back of her gown, but quickly tired of the tedious work. In one swift movement, he tore the dress from her body.

She gasped in shock.

"Face me."

She turned, her cheeks flushed from heat and desire.

She stood before him naked and graced him with a becoming smile. Her full breasts prominent, erect, her arousal apparent in the gleam of her silky, wet pussy. He growled out loud at the sheer pleasure of her beautiful body.

Although anxious to take her in his arms, he took his time looking at her. Savoring all that was his. Lowering his head, he captured her mouth in a kiss full of sensual promise.

He deepened the kiss and anchored her to him as he sank further into her warm, welcoming mouth. Using his knee, he urged her thighs apart.

"Are you no longer going to ask for permission?" she whispered between his kisses.

"No," he growled. "You're mine. Tonight we shall mate and belong to each other for eternity."

A whimper escaped her lips. "Yes, Lord Ranek, there is nothing I'd like more."

He dipped a fingertip into her damp, velvety pussy and drew in a shaky breath. His body went up in flames as her sheath tightened around his finger.

As he swirled his finger, he felt her tense. He pulled back and glanced at her. "What is it, Katrina? Have I hurt you?"

* * * * *

She looked into his eyes and saw gentleness there. She glimpsed the tender man hidden beneath a rough exterior and her heart swelled in her chest.

It pleased her that he was concerned with her comfort. She shuffled around and glanced at the dark shadows dancing in the corners of the room. "Someone is watching us."

He twisted around but saw nothing. "Are you sure, my love?"

She gave a quick, tight nod. He picked her up, carried her to the bed and placed her under the safety of his heavy covers.

"Stay here. I'll search the room." He grabbed his dagger from the mantel and drew it from its protective covering. Slowly, he searched the room, drawing back the thick-paneled curtains to inspect every crevice of his chamber. Once satisfied that no one was lurking about, he came back and perched on the edge of the bed.

"Katrina, the room is secure."

She tossed him a hesitant look. "I thought I sensed something."

He drove his dagger back into its casing. "If you're still unsure, I could call the guards and have them search the castle."

"No, I trust you." Perhaps her anticipation of their first coupling was throwing off her senses. "Calling on the guards will take you away from me. And I don't want to spend another second away from you. "

"Very well then, if you are satisfied, as I am, we shall put this matter to rest." He drew back the covers. "Now, let me discover your body as I have been yearning to do for so long." He traced a soft finger over her cheek then lower. He lingered between the satiny mounds of her breasts as his eyes locked with hers.

Overcome by his tender words and gentle hands, she melted under his touch and paid no more attention to her intuition—even though for a brief moment she thought she detected a new scent in the room, one with a hint of danger associated to it.

"You belong to me, Katrina." He stood up and removed his clothes.

She admired his magnificent body. All muscle, strength, and power. She inhaled his rich, seductive scent. Moistening her lips, she stared with fascinated excitement at his jutting shaft. Nodding her agreement, she reached for him.

He took a step back. "Say it," he demanded.

"I belong to you," she whispered, instinctively widening her legs, exposing her swelling clit in silent invitation, her pussy glistening.

He squatted on the edge of the bed and slipped a finger inside her. She felt the room sway. When she gyrated against him, he rewarded her with a gentle kiss that started slowly, but quickly developed into something more powerful.

He stretched out beside her and pulled her down on top of him. Her body reacted quickly to the sensual stimulation of his thick cock resting between her legs. She moaned and thrust her head back.

His male scent intoxicated her. She felt drunk with desire. He once again pulled her mouth to his, her blonde curls spilling over his chest. She opened her lips and accepted his invading tongue.

After a thorough exploration of her mouth, he grabbed her by the waist and rolled her under him. She felt as though she'd suffocate beneath the weight of his large body.

He released her mouth and began a slow, leisurely journey downward. Fire erupted in her veins, her whole body moistened. A growing, aching need settled between her legs.

His satiny tongue seared her flesh as a wild storm began brewing in her virgin body. Growing increasingly impatient for more, she arched her body. "Please…" She bucked her hips against him. "*Please*, Ranek." When she scratched at his back, he took hold of her arms and secured them to her sides.

Tension built inside her as he nipped her tender flesh. She thrust her chest out, begging for him to stop the ache coiling through her body.

He circled a nipple with his tongue, raising her temperature higher and higher. A delicious warmth spread over her skin. His tongue and hands were hot and smooth over her naked flesh.

She writhed beneath him, freed one hand, and reached down to stroke his shaft. She rubbed her fingers up and down his length, increasing the pressure and tempo. He bucked against her hand and moaned into her cleavage.

The torment of his tongue overwhelmed her with desire. Did he have to be so excruciatingly thorough? When he finally took her breast fully into his mouth, she screamed and closed her eyes against the onslaught of pleasure.

As he bit down on her nipple it increased the yearning sensation in her pussy. Desire spiraled onward and upward through her body.

His hand slid between her legs. When he discovered how wet she was, he gave a low moan of approval and rocked against her. She felt his cock pulse in her hand.

"You like me to be wet?" she asked.

He pushed her legs open wider, his eyes darkening with desire. "Oh, yes." His hot breath caressed her nakedness. "I need to taste your sweetness, Katrina." She could hear the urgency in his voice, see the passion in his eyes.

He kissed a path to the seat of her desire. He pulled her sex lips open and let out a deep growl. She shuddered. Her skin came alive as he sank his tongue into her swollen flesh.

The first touch of his mouth on her clit made her blood boil. He spread her labia wider with his tongue and delved in deeper. Her body trembled with white-hot pleasure. She lifted her hips from the bed and shamelessly gyrated against his mouth.

"You taste like sweet honey," he whispered harshly.

Hungrily, he lapped and nibbled and increased the pressure on her clit as he dipped a finger inside her tight cleft. Her breath came in a ragged burst. Fiery heat flowed through her. She fisted his hair and cried out his name as a powerful, earth-shattering orgasm ripped through her.

Sitting back on his heels, he grabbed his cock by the base and began rubbing it along the length of her silky, wet crevice.

"Now I will make you mine forever." The soft timbre of his voice filled her with longing. Her heart and body ached for him.

His eyes softened as he positioned his cock firmly at the entrance of her slit. Carefully, he eased into her, spreading her pussy lips with his substantial thickness. His jaw clenched, his muscles bunching as she sensed his restraint.

"Ranek," she gasped as his fullness stretched her apart. A moment later a stab of pain cut through her. Tears sprang to her eyes.

"Stop," she cried, and tried to push him away.

He held her tight. "The pain will pass, Katrina."

"No, it hurts. You're too big." She tried to squirm away but he pinned her beneath him.

He wiped away her tears. "Trust me, my love, it will get better."

He left his shaft deep within the walls of her pussy, and soon her muscles relaxed and began to accommodate his thickness. He reached between their bodies and gently, soothingly stroked her clit. Her heart began to beat wildly under his tender assault.

When Ranek felt her muscles spasm, he slowly, rhythmically, began to move in and out of her. Each stroke, each push, turned pain into pleasure.

In no time at all raw lust took over and Katrina began meeting and welcoming each agonizingly sweet thrust.

He grabbed her hips and rolled her on top of him. "Ride me, my love."

Straddling him from above, she rocked back and forth, grinding her hips into his. Her clit smashing against his body.

An explosion began building from deep within her. Losing all control, she began bucking, riding him wildly, until tiny sparks of light danced before her eyes and her body exploded into a million fragments.

At the peak of her orgasm, she arched her back, thrust her breasts out, and cried his name as the world shattered around her.

Ranek grabbed her hips and pushed impossibly further into her heat. She felt him pulse as his juices spurted deep inside her pussy. She squeezed her muscles, milking the last drop of semen from his cock.

She collapsed onto his chest and he rolled her beside him. He placed a soft kiss onto her lips and gentle fingers soothed her damp hair from her forehead. "Did I hurt you?"

She glimpsed the gentleness in his eyes. "Only for a minute."

He smiled. "You give me great pleasure, Katrina."

"As do you," she replied.

He smoothed his fingers over her naked flesh, leaving a trail of goose bumps behind.

"Will it always be so pleasurable?" she asked, tipping her head to look into his eyes.

She trailed her fingers over his smooth chest, twirling her fingers around his nipples. She feathered her hand lower and touched his now-flaccid cock. It twitched back to life.

His eyes darkened with passion. "If you keep that up, you will soon discover the answer to that question." His voice was gruff.

She released him quickly and turned her back to him. "Well, we wouldn't want that now, would we?"

He laughed out loud. "Get back here, you seductive vixen."

He smothered her chuckle with a kiss as they once again they became lost in the wonders of each other's body...

Chapter Six

ഌ

Sitting on the sand with the ocean lapping at his feet, Ranek remained by Katrina's side and held her tight against him as her mind filled with memories of their first mating.

When she shuddered, he smoothed her damp hair from her face. When she cried out, he whispered reassuring words into her ear. When she smiled, he smiled along with her.

For he knew these dreams were difficult for the human part of her to acknowledge and accept.

Fingers of golden light broke through the predawn sky and Ranek knew his time in the mortal world was limited. He'd soon have to send her back to her bed and return to his lair.

A moment later, Katrina's body stilled and her long thick lashes flickered open. She looked at him questioningly, but tonight there would be no more answers.

He silenced her unspoken questions with his fingertips. "Shh, my love. That is all you can absorb in one night." As he held her close, her brows furrowed in confusion and he knew the human part of her was resisting. Gently, he rocked her back and forth, soothing her weary mind.

With a wave of his hand he returned her to her warm bed, inside the safety of her cottage. Her eyes slipped shut and she drifted off to a dreamless, restful sleep. Before returning to his lair, he stole a quick glance at the unfinished painting sitting upon her easel.

He smiled and shook his head ruefully. The image on the canvas was of him emerging from the deep swells of the Atlantic Ocean. He stared at it for a long moment.

Soon these visits would end and she would be with him forever. He took one last glance at her and stifled an exhausted yawn.

Not only was he worried about bringing her mind around before her impending nuptials, he was now also worried for her safety. If Kohan were able to locate her signature, she'd be an easy mark for him. A flash of fiery rage raced through him. He snarled as he recalled Kohan's smug look when the elders forbade Ranek from drawing his dagger.

He remembered it like it was yesterday.

Regardless of what the elders deemed justice for Kohan's treachery, Ranek should have finished him off decades ago, when he'd had the chance.

If he was ever given the opportunity again, there would be no stopping him.

Ranek dropped a soft kiss onto Katrina's forehead before returning to his kingdom. She smiled in her sleep and snuggled deeper into her blankets.

These trips to the mortal world were taking a toll on him. As he readied his bed and stretched out his tired limbs, a soft knock sounded on his door.

"Come in," he bellowed, impatient with the intrusion when he was so desperate for sleep.

A young servant entered. "I bring forth news from the elders, Lord Ranek," she said, kneeling before him as she handed him a sealed letter.

"Stand up, my child," Ranek insisted. He turned the note over in his hand and, upon observing the young servant awaiting further instructions, he thanked her and dismissed her from his quarters. She quickly disappeared through the same door from which she'd entered.

Ranek lowered himself onto his bed and tore open the envelope. A wave of rage tore through him as he read the note. Kohan's signature had been located.

Ranek jumped to his feet and began pacing. He stalked back and forth, his mind sifting through many unanswered questions.

Had Katrina's dreams lured Kohan from the underworld? Was he aware of her existence? If so, what were his intentions?

Ranek stopped pacing and closed his eyes. He searched for Kohan's location but came up empty. At least that meant that he wasn't nearby. For now.

Knowing there was nothing more he could do at the moment, he climbed into his bed and forced himself to sleep. Tomorrow, he would send a band of warriors into the underworld to seek and gather information. It was imperative that he discover if there was any truth to the rumors that an underworld creature could travel during daylight hours.

Once Katrina's sun set, he would warn her of the potential danger.

Chapter Seven

஌

Katrina stretched her tired, sore limbs across the bed. Her lethargic body fought against rising. Her lids felt as though they were fastened with weights. She squeezed her eyes tight then slowly peeled them open.

Unlike the previous morning, she was not greeted with rays of sparkling sunshine. She glanced out her small window. A dark, foreboding haze hovered over the Atlantic waters. Icy-cold whitecaps smashed angrily against the sandy shoreline. Gulls cried frantically as the ominous clouds knitted together and loomed overhead, threatening to break open. The scent of the salty air, carried in by the chilly morning breeze, filled the small cottage.

Katrina groaned, pulled the blankets tight around her body, and rolled over. Something sharp pinched her side. She yelped and jolted upright. She flicked on the antique lamp at her bedside and searched out the source of her discomfort.

As her hands patted the mattress, her gaze zeroed in on a small green emerald. Aghast at her find, her mind immediately recalled last night's dream. The beautiful dress Ranek sent her had been beaded with the exact same jewels.

Ribbons of white light danced before her eyes as her blood drained to her toes. As though the emerald was capable of slicing through her palm, she hurled it across the room. She bit her bottom lip and pressed her hands over her face.

No! her mind cried. Overcome with tangled emotions she jumped from her bed. Fresh tears threatened her eyes.

What was happening to her? Her dreams were mingling with reality, and she no longer knew where one began and the other ended.

If not for the small tokens left behind each morning, she'd be convinced she was losing her mind.

She paced the floor with quick hurried steps.

Her gaze caught the painting she'd been working on. With a sharp movement she picked it up and smashed it to the floor. "What do you want with me?" she cried. "Just leave me alone." She turned her back on the mess as a sob caught in her throat.

Her life had been organized and planned before Ranek began to invade her thoughts.

She drew in a short breath and frowned in concentration. Somehow she had to find a way to put an end to these dreams. But how? She didn't know. She just didn't know.

Being at the cottage wasn't helping matters. In fact, her dreams had become more alive, more vivid since she'd come.

Deciding to go back to her condo and back to the gallery, she began throwing her clothes into her suitcase. As she packed her bag, an eerily scented wave washed over her and knocked her off her feet. It was the same feeling she'd had twice yesterday.

The scent prompted her into action. Some deep-seated instinct warned her to be careful. She dressed hastily and arranged her hair on top of her head.

As she quickly readied herself, her thoughts turned to James. Perhaps he would be back from his business trip. Perhaps she'd find security and comfort in his arms.

After determining that was her best course of action, she prepared a plan. The first thing she'd do before going home was head to his place, and spend some quality time with him. Maybe that would help her grow to love him properly, the way he deserved. And maybe, just maybe, once that happened Ranek would stop invading her dreams.

Heavy raindrops beat a steady pattern against her windshield as she maneuvered her car along the busy highway. In her tired state their soothing effect mesmerized her. She blinked to keep her mind in focus. A bolt of lightning zigzagged through the sky, jolting her from her trance.

With renewed concentration she flicked on her signal light, took the next exit, and headed straight for her fiancé's house. He wasn't scheduled to return until later this evening but Katrina hoped, prayed he'd come home early.

It was well past noon when she pulled up alongside his house. Disappointment settled deep inside her as she saw his empty driveway. Obviously he hadn't returned from his business meeting.

Longing for company, for something to help clear her mind, she backed out of his driveway and headed for his parents' home. Every Sunday it was a ritual for his large family to gather for a meal. She was sure to find comfort and security in the crowd.

A smile touched her lips as she pulled up in front of the large Victorian home and spotted cars spilling from the long driveway. They hadn't been expecting her but she knew they would welcome her with open arms. She wanted so much to be a part of this family. She wanted so much to feel loved, to feel as if she belonged somewhere.

The way Ranek makes you feel.

She pushed those thoughts to the back of her mind and opened her compact. She applied blush to her face, attempting to conceal the paleness in her cheeks. Satisfied with the pink hue, she slipped from the driver's seat. The rain had lightened to a mist as she made her way up the flower-lined cobblestone path that led to the front entrance. She tightened her sweater around her waist and opened the front door.

His parents' Victorian home was tastefully decorated in a warm color scheme of walnut and ivory. Persian area rugs covered the chestnut-colored hardwood floors. The walls were adorned with many of Katrina's paintings. They preferred landscapes and scenery as opposed to her less traditional, abstract seascapes for which she was known.

As she removed her overcoat, she breathed in the fragrant aroma of fresh cut flowers resting on an ornate table in the front foyer.

She was immediately greeted with friendly smiles and welcoming hugs. She relaxed a little and felt the tension drain from her body.

Sunday dinners at the Anderson household were always full of lively conversation and scrumptious food. Katrina grinned when the smell of pot roast reached her nose. She hadn't realized just how hungry she was.

Carol, James's mother, rushed around the corner to greet her. James's features were similar to hers. They both had the same gentle eyes, pale skin, and light blonde hair, although Carol's had grayed over the years.

"Come in, child." Carol hugged her and guided her toward the kitchen.

Katrina walked past the den. The men were gathered around a circular card table for a friendly, if somewhat competitive, game of poker. The women congregated in the kitchen where they shared the latest gossip, sipped wine, and prepared the meal.

"Anything I can do?" Katrina asked.

Sherry, James's sister, handed her a glass of wine and a carrot peeler. "If you insist," she said, quickly relinquishing her duties.

Katrina chuckled, grabbed a much-needed sip of wine, and willingly took over. The liquid tingled all the way to her toes. Soft, soothing light from the overhead chandelier beat down on her and took the earlier chill away from her body.

Standing beside Roxanne and Sherry, her soon-to-be sisters-in-law, she joined in the discussion about the weather, work, and as usual, the men in their lives.

Katrina looked at James's family, her future in-laws, and as much as she wanted to belong here, with these welcoming people, emotionally she felt as if she belonged to another.

Her heart was not where it should be.

Ranek.

She thought of his tender smile full of love and her heart filled with yearning. She couldn't understand it. He haunted her. No matter where she was or what she did, he was always with her — in her mind and in her soul.

She shivered as a confusing, unfamiliar mix of emotions and longing raced through her. She bit down on her bottom lip and forced herself to push those thoughts aside. Desperately, she tried to follow the path of conversation going on around her.

Hours later, once they were all seated around the large dining room table, Sherry and her husband Bill, asked for everyone's attention.

"We have an announcement to make," she said somewhat giddily, her bright eyes smiling at her husband as she pulled him to his feet.

As the pair stood, a hush fell over the room and all eager eyes turned to focus on them.

"We're pregnant," Bill blurted out.

Chairs grated across the wooden floors as everyone quickly jumped to congratulate the couple with a hug and kiss.

Katrina was surprised at the rush of emotions she felt at the announcement. As if moving of their own accord, her hands automatically cradled her stomach. Visions of what her child would look like filled her mind.

Tall, male, muscular, with charcoal-black eyes, hair the color of midnight and bronzed skin. She gulped air and drew a tight breath hoping her reaction had gone unnoticed.

"Katrina. Are you okay?" Sherry asked touching her shoulder and pulling her back to the present.

No such luck.

"Of course. I'm just excited for you." Katrina stood and gave her a hug. "I was just thinking about what my child would look like," she admitted honestly.

"Let me guess. You pictured a blond little boy with blue eyes. Just like James," she teased.

Katrina forced a smile. "Yes, yes I did. Blond. Blue eyes. Like James." Oh boy!

Once the dinner dishes were cleared and washed, Katrina became almost overwhelmed with exhaustion. Although she hated to go back to her empty apartment, she knew she had to. With an early morning ahead of her, she made her excuses. Standing in the front foyer, she said her goodbyes.

The hugs she received from her future family were enough to again convince her that this was where she belonged. A smile touched her mouth and she was glad she'd decided to visit with the Andersons. This was where she was meant to be — with James and his family. Not in some foreign land with a sea god from another time and place.

Feeling content with her decision and renewed direction, she returned to her apartment to await James's return.

She knew something was wrong as she inserted her key into the lock. She pushed open her door and her stomach plummeted.

Although everything was orderly and in place, she knew someone, or some*thing* had been in her apartment.

Chapter Eight

ଽଠ

Sitting in his lair, Ranek sharpened his dagger as he waited for word from his warriors. Kohan's signature continued to get stronger, and Ranek wanted to be prepared should they happen to cross paths.

He closed his eyes and took a glimpse into the mortal world. His heart burned with longing as he watched Katrina rest peacefully. Soon he would go to her. Just as soon as word came back on Kohan's whereabouts and his illegal experiments in the underworld.

If such a potion existed that allowed an underworld dweller to travel to the mortal world during daylight, it would have to be confiscated and destroyed. And those in charge of its production would be properly punished. A Bandara's existence was a fragile one. If discovered by mortals, an attack would undoubtedly be forthcoming. Trips to the surface were reserved for emergency purposes only. Those that abused such privileges put the kingdom at risk, leaving Ranek no choice but to destroy them.

A knock on his door drew Ranek's attention. He stood and waved the servant to come forward. "You have news for me?"

"Yes, Lord Ranek." The servant handed him a note and waited for a response.

Ranek read the note and slammed his fist onto the table. The young servant faltered backwards and cast her eyes to the side. Ranek scribbled on the bottom of the paper and handed it back. "See that this gets to my men."

With a wave of his hand, he journeyed into the mortal world. He pulled himself from the water and stalked along the beach. Katrina was nowhere to be found. His heart beat faster with each forward step. He walked on until he came upon a small shadow crouched in the sand.

"Katrina," he said, reaching for her. "What is it?" Worry rushed through him. Had Kohan infiltrated her subconscious?

She wrapped her arms around her bent knees and cradled them to her chest. Her long golden locks fell over her face, shielding her emotions. "Go away."

He closed his eyes with relief. Her words assured him that Kohan had nothing to do with her emotional retreat. He knew this resistance would happen eventually. The human part of her was struggling with her new memories. He bent down on one knee and tipped up her chin.

She flinched away. "I do not wish for you to touch me." Her voice was a whisper of anguish.

She gazed at him. Her beautiful eyes opened wide, buttery locks framing her cheeks and glistening in the moonlight. Warmth spread through his limbs and filled his heart.

With unintentional sensuality, she smoothed her hair from her forehead and touched her tongue to her bottom lip to moisten it. A primitive desire raged inside him.

The sight of her beauty brought out the warrior within and he thought he would go mad if he didn't take her soon.

They stared at each other for a long moment as he stroked the skin on her long, graceful neck. His hand traveled lower, to skim her silky cleavage. Her eyes glazed over and he felt her body shiver with desire, need. Ranek knew her wants, her cravings. And he was about to make her aware of it as well.

"You know not what you want, Katrina. You must drink from me to learn more."

"I no longer wish to learn more."

Her pained voice tugged at his heart. He had to help her find the courage to continue. He circled his arms around her shoulders offering her his strength and comfort.

If only they had more time. Time for her to absorb what she had already learned before pressing on. But with Kohan lurking in the shadows and her wedding to a mortal man approaching, time was a luxury they did not have.

He rose to his feet and hovered over her. "You are a Bandara, Katrina. No matter what you think, you cannot fight it. You must lie with me now to discover the truths of our past."

* * * * *

Katrina tried to scramble away, but he pulled her to her feet and crushed her against him. He pushed his erection against her softness and ran his hands over her curves. Her body betrayed her and began to tingle with anticipation. Moisture gathered between her clenched thighs.

She tried to block her mind to the erotic feel of his long fingers and large hands splayed over her back. But in the end, her efforts were futile.

She took a step backwards and opened her robe. "Just take what you want and leave."

She watched his eyes darken as his gaze roamed the length of her. And much to her chagrin, her traitorous breasts tightened under his smoldering glance.

His eyes zeroed in on her beaded nipples. He arched one brow. "And during our coupling, you shall feel nothing?" She watched him smother a smug smile.

"Nothing," she assured him, working hard to keep her voice from trembling with sheer excitement.

"Very well then." He lowered his gaze. "As you wish." He reached out and stretched open her pink sex lips. "Strange for a woman who wants no pleasure to come to me so wet."

She drew a quick, sharp breath and almost wilted to the ground when he licked his lips.

He forced her legs wider and pressed a finger into her opening. Bending forward, he drew one nipple between his lips and sucked hard enough to form hollows in his cheeks. Her juices began to flow, and she bit back a moan of pleasure.

He chuckled playfully and ran a lazy finger over her clit. Like a blossoming flower, it sprang to life. He plucked at the swollen pearl, making it harder. She swallowed thickly and tilted her head back. Her chest heaved as her breathing became labored.

He dropped to his knees and pushed his tongue into her heated core. "Mmmmm." His finger massaged the tender cleft between her ass cheeks.

His erotic actions forced a moan from her throat, putting an end to any kind of resistance. She arched her pelvis forward, wrapped her hands around his head, and pushed his face deeper into her pussy.

He chuckled. "That's my girl," he murmured from between her open thighs.

Sitting on the ground, he pulled her on top of him. He grabbed his cock by the base and positioned it near her silken slit. In one quick thrust she impaled herself on his long shaft. "Yes," she cried out shamelessly.

She clenched her muscles and shimmied lower, wanting every inch of him deep inside her. She shifted and rotated—anything to drive him deeper into her. Thrashing like a wanton woman, she plunged harder and rammed his cock impossibly deeper.

Frantically, driven by sheer hunger and desperation, she raised and lowered herself, driving his phallus in and out of her tight crevice.

A hot release of pressure washed over her as his fingers found her swollen clit. She grabbed her nipples and squeezed as her creamy release poured down his cock.

"Ahhh!" he cried out, as her heat scorched him.

She listened to his shallow pants and knew he was close. She climbed from his cock and slid down his body. As she guided him toward her mouth, she gazed into his eyes.

A deep-seated longing passed through her when their eyes locked, and her heart filled with a lifetime's worth of love. She drew a shuddery breath as lightheadedness overcame her. "Ranek…" she whispered, her voice tangled with emotions.

He touched her cheek and brushed her hair from her face. "I need you, Katrina." The excruciating gentleness in his voice nearly made her cry out.

"You are my soulmate, and I want you to come home with me. Where you belong. Where you have always belonged." His voice was a tender, intimate whisper. "Drink from me and learn."

Old feelings and emotions that she never knew she possessed ran through her. Her heart swelled in her chest as she took him in her mouth.

She slid her tongue around the textured head and stroked one hand up and down his length while the other cradled his heavy balls. Sucking hard, she plunged forward, drawing out his impending orgasm.

His salty juices exploded into her mouth and she swallowed all of his offering. Gentle hands pulled at her until her lips were poised above his. "You are so beautiful," he whispered.

Smiling, she collapsed onto his chest and accepted the memories that were about to come.

* * * * *

Katrina spent a quiet afternoon resting in their lair awaiting Ranek's return. They'd been mates for many months now and she still continued to find new joy in his strong, giving arms.

He'd been gone for hours searching for one of the children who had rebelliously gone to the surface to explore. Katrina shivered. The surface was a dangerous place. A place where a Bandara was an easy mark for mortals. A place where she'd never again venture without the protection of her lord.

"Katrina, one of the children needs you!"

She spun around to come face-to-face with one of their servants. "What is it, Selin?" she asked, her voice etched with concern.

"Kohan sent me to find you. He didn't say what was wrong, only that one of the children needed you." The elderly lady rubbed her withered hands together, her eyes skittish.

At the mere mention of Kohan, Katrina's senses went on high alert. Katrina knew by Selin's nervous reaction that she wasn't the only one who sensed the dark, angry ferociousness buried beneath Kohan's calm façade.

As the clan's healer, it was her duty to attend to the needs of the children. "Take me to him."

Selin ushered her into Kohan's lair. Sitting perched upon his throne, a dangerous smirk upon his face, he waved an arm for Katrina to take a seat beside him.

She declined and met his gaze unflinchingly. "Where is the child?" She kept her voice tight and serious.

Ignoring her question, he returned his focus to Selin. "You may leave."

Bowing her head nervously, Selin retreated.

Uneasiness began gathering in the pit of Katrina's stomach. Even though this man was Ranek's brother, she did not trust him. She stiffened her back and glared at him. Her gaze settled on the knife scar marring his chin. A scar forged by Ranek's dagger—a recent mark reminding the younger brother not to challenge Ranek's authority.

Since Ranek had stepped into his father's position and became master of their kingdom, Kohan's envy was increasingly evident. On many occasions Kohan voiced his objections to Ranek's rule, and his displeasure had caused numerous battles between the two.

His bitterness had only grown when Ranek had chosen Katrina for his mate.

She narrowed her eyes to mere slits. "Ranek will be joining us in a moment."

A deep insidious laugh burst from his throat. "Do you take me for a fool?"

Her heart drummed but she kept her demeanor calm and unyielding. "He'll be returning from the surface any minute."

Kohan slithered from his seat and closed the distance between them. One long finger reached out and coiled through her curls.

Katrina flinched and drew away. "The penalty for touching me will be high," she assured him. "When Ranek returns—"

Again his laughter seeped into her skin, filling her with dread.

"Your lover will not be returning." He captured her waist and drew her to him. His nostrils flared. "When I am your master, I want you to look at me the same way you look at him." His voice grew dangerous, fierce. "And I want you to moan for me the same way you do for him."

Had it been Kohan watching that first night Ranek made love to her?

She turned her head away from him. Although they were brothers and shared many similar traits, Kohan's dark eyes constantly seethed with anger, while the ruthlessness in Ranek's eyes was reserved for battle.

He gripped her chin hard enough to make her wince and forced her to face him. "You *will* be mine."

She struggled from his grasp. "I'd rather die." She rushed to the door.

"Like Ranek is doing right now."

His words stopped her and she spun around to face him. "What do you mean?"

"He's not coming back from the surface, *my love.*"

My love.

Goose pimples crept over her flesh as he emphasized Ranek's special name for her.

A cocky grin curled his lips. "I've personally seen to it."

* * * * *

71

Ranek held Katrina's quivering body tight and soothed the hair from her face as she dreamed.

Her lids fluttered open and she exhaled a relieved sigh upon finding herself cradled in his arms.

Her eyes opened wider when she caught his concerned look. "Kohan," she whimpered, her voice quivering.

"Yes, Katrina. I know. He's an evil man." He stroked her cheek.

Almost frantically, she grabbed his shoulders. "He's here, Ranek," she cried out.

Ranek stiffened and scanned the semi-dark, desolate beach. "Where?"

She shook her head. "I'm not sure. I sensed his signature at the cottage and then again at my apartment." She looked deep into his eyes and Ranek felt her fear.

"He's dangerous, Ranek." Her nails bit into his skin.

The sun crested the horizon and Ranek felt his naked flesh grow cold. He had to return to his world while he still could. While the sun was still low in the sky. "My time is over here, Katrina." Frustrated at the situation, he slammed his fists into the sand. He was not used to feeling so helpless. How could he protect her and keep her safe from Kohan if he could not return her to the safety of their kingdom?

He cradled her tighter in his arms. "It pains me to leave you. You must believe that." He kissed her forehead, her watery eyes, and then her satiny mouth.

When she nodded, he continued, "You must promise me you will follow my orders." Again she nodded. "In order to stay safe, you must remain with another mortal at all times. Stay with a friend until I return. It is unlikely that Kohan will make his presence known in front of another. I will send my men to find Kohan and I will personally see to it that he is captured and punished for his crimes."

He felt her body shiver. "Tell me what happens next, Ranek." Her eyes searched his for answers. "In my dream, Kohan sent someone to kill you."

He could not tell her it was she who had been killed. The human part of her would surely retreat and her life would be at risk. She needed time to come to terms with what she had learned already.

"Rest now, my love. The answers will come when you are ready."

Chapter Nine

ஐ

Katrina pulled her car into her reserved parking space and nervously glanced around the lot before exiting the driver's seat, her eyes frantically searching for signs of Kohan's existence. Paying no heed to her, people poured from their vehicles and bustled up and down the busy streets.

Katrina was relieved to see it was business as usual on this beautiful Monday morning. She took a deep breath and forced herself to calm down. After last night's dream, calming down had become increasingly difficult.

With the passing of the storm, not a cloud marred the clear blue sky. Warm golden rays of summer sun bounced off the New York sidewalk and glistened in the shop windows. A soft breeze carried the scent of lilac from a nearby florist.

Hurried steps carried her into the gallery. She pushed open the door and relaxed upon finding Susan sitting at her desk. She looked up as Katrina entered.

A bright smile crossed her face. "Hey, how was your weekend?" She pulled her glasses off and dropped them on her desk as she rose. "Did you get some well-deserved rest at the cottage?" Susan took a step closer and stopped mid-stride. "Katrina, are you okay? You look like you've seen a ghost."

She wasn't too far off with that observation.

Nervously, Katrina glanced around to ensure they were the only two occupants in the gallery. She crossed the room and dropped into the soft, cushioned loveseat reserved for clientele.

She blew her bangs from her forehead and drew a weary sigh as she replayed the memories that filled her nightly dreams. Maybe she really was losing her mind.

Susan poured a fresh cup of coffee and sat down beside her. "Want to talk about it?"

Katrina tilted her head back and stared at the ceiling as she thought long and hard before answering. Her mind wandered to Ranek and all the emotions he pulled from her. Like a warm, cozy blanket, silence settled over them as she drifted. She slumped deeper in her seat as she recalled his every touch, his every kiss. She'd never felt so wanted, needed or cherished. Ranek made her feel complete — and for the first time in her life, she felt a sense of belonging. No man had ever drawn such a reaction from her. Not even James.

Susan cleared her throat, cutting off her meandering. She cast her friend a sideways glance. Closing her eyes, Katrina let out a heavy breath. If she were going to ask to spend the night at Susan's place she should at least let her in on what was going on. She swallowed and summoned her courage. "Yes, I'd like to talk about it."

As Katrina relayed the events from the past three weeks, Susan's porcelain-white skin turned ashen. She watched her friend's shoulders stiffen and when she reached out to touch her, she found her hands trembling.

"Do you think I'm crazy?"

Spine straight and eyes wide with disbelief, Susan slowly shook her head from side to side. Her dark hair falling off her shoulders. "Katrina, you must admit this all does sound a little bizarre." Her voice was full of disbelief. She placed her coffee cup on a nearby table and neatly folded her hands over her lap.

"I'll be the first to admit it." Katrina pressed her palms to her forehead and felt like screaming in frustration.

Susan touched her arm gently. "You don't suppose you're just feeling a little stressed about your wedding?" she asked, her voice a hesitant, cautious whisper.

Her reactions were exactly what Katrina expected. And how could Katrina blame her? If anyone were to relay a story like that to her, she'd be calling for a straightjacket.

Katrina stood and shook her head. "I don't blame you for being skeptical, Susan. But I really need for you to believe in me. I need your help and support until I can understand what's happening." She began to pace back and forth across the polished tiled floor.

Susan still had a cautious look on her face when she assured her, "You'll always have my support. Just let me know what I can do to help."

Katrina gave her a grateful smile. "Would you mind if I stayed with you for a few nights?"

"Not at all, Katrina. Stay for as long as you like." She paused and then added, "Have you discussed any of this with James?"

Katrina stilled her footsteps and swallowed past the knot in her throat. How could she share a room, a bed even, with her fiancé when another man consumed her thoughts, her emotions? Until she sorted through her feelings and put the pieces of this puzzle together she didn't know how she was even going to face him. Katrina prided herself on her morals and loyalty, and right now she felt very disloyal to James.

Her heart began racing. He'd always been kind and gentle with her and she didn't want to hurt him. Susan had set them up on a blind date less than six months ago. She cared for him a great deal and it pained her terribly that she didn't feel a burning passion for him, the way she wanted to.

"He doesn't know anything about this, and for the time being I'd rather he didn't."

Susan stood, smoothed her skirt, and gave Katrina a hug. "Okay. I'm here if you need me."

Katrina returned the hug and headed for her office. The sound of Susan's voice stopped her and she twisted around.

"Oh, I almost forgot, you have an appointment at noon. Someone interested in commissioning a painting." She handed Katrina a slip of paper.

Katrina read the note and then slipped into her office. The rest of the morning passed without incident. Katrina sifted though her paperwork and returned phone calls, but in the forefront of her mind, Ranek always remained in her thoughts.

He touched something deep within her and stirred feelings she never knew she possessed. She needed him and hungered for him in ways that almost frightened her.

Just as she was preparing for her lunchtime meeting a rustle outside her doorway drew her attention.

"Morning, sunshine," James called out.

Her stomach plummeted. "You're back." She forced a smile and stood to greet him. "How was the convention?" The words spilled out quicker than she'd have liked.

"Fascinating as usual. I'll tell you all about it over lunch."

Katrina frowned. "I can't go," she apologized. "I have a meeting."

Susan came up behind him and peered over his shoulder. "You two go ahead. I'll cover your appointment for you, Katrina. You haven't seen each other in a while and with the wedding so close I'm sure you have a lot to talk about."

A short while later Katrina found herself sitting across from James at a quaint little restaurant down the street from her shop. A hush fell over the room as the lunch crowd focused on their meals.

Tucked away in an intimate corner overlooking the bustling street, Katrina sat quietly as she listened to the intricate details of the convention. She breathed in the pleasing aroma from a cinnamon-scented candle burning on their table.

James paused his story as the waitress brought their food. Katrina nibbled on her bottom lip and looked at the Cobb salad placed before her. Once the waitress moved on, James continued his animated tale, in much more detail than Katrina would have liked. Feeling her appetite slip away, she sipped her coffee and toyed with her salad.

In technical terms she didn't fully understand, James rifled through papers and excitedly rambled about the latest technology. As he droned on about all the purchases he'd made—purchases he assured her would put his software company on the map—she tuned him out and stifled a yawn.

Had he always been this self-involved?

She tried to listen intently, she really did, but her thoughts were elsewhere. Whenever he looked at her, she smiled and worked hard to blink her mind into focus.

"Don't you agree, Katrina?" he asked.

The sound of her name pulled her back and she nodded.

A pleased smile crossed his smooth face. His light blue eyes sparkled. "Then it's all settled then." He opened his briefcase and began sifting through more files.

She sat there staring at him, wondering what the heck she'd agreed to.

As he brushed his short-cropped blond hair from his forehead, Katrina thought how his light, boyish features differed so drastically from Ranek's. The thick, muscular physique of her warrior, his dangerously dark eyes and intoxicating voice. Moistening her suddenly dry lips, she drew a shaky breath. Unlike James, Ranek was a lethal combination of rugged strength and excruciating tenderness.

The waitress wandered over to refill her coffee, shaking Katrina from her fantasies. Distressed by the direction of her thoughts, she forced her mind back to the present and tried to focus on their wedding preparations.

"James, we need to talk about the flowers. There seems to be some kind of mix-up at the florist." She waited for a response but none came.

"James?" she repeated.

He looked up from the paper he'd been studying and blinked. "Did you say something?"

"The flowers."

He stole a glance at the vase sitting on the windowsill. "Yes, they really are quite lovely, aren't they?" Once again he focused his attention on his paperwork.

Giving it one more attempt, she opened her mouth to speak, then shut it again when his cell phone chimed in the background. He pulled it from his suit jacket and pressed it to his ear, oblivious to the fact that she'd been trying to speak.

Giving up, Katrina sighed and slunk further into her cushioned chair. Crossing her arms over her chest, she studied him as he spoke. Had James always paid more attention to his work than to her?

Their whole lunch had been focused on him and his conference. Never once had he asked about her week or about the wedding preparations. Nor did he offer to help. She cocked her head. Had she always played second fiddle to his work?

And why was she suddenly noticing his inattentiveness now?

Was it because Ranek always put her needs and desires first? Was it the way he looked at her and spoke her name, so intimately, so possessively? Perhaps it was the way his voice seeped into her skin, filling her with warmth and longing.

No other man had ever made her feel so special or cherished, and the depth of emotions in his smoldering eyes when he touched her and kissed her spoke volumes.

Her skin came alive and her body tightened with the memories of him. Craving the feel of his hard body against hers, she could almost taste the sweetness of his skin.

Lost in dreams, she hadn't realized James had hung the phone up and was asking her a question. Damn. She had to find a way to tame her thoughts. In a few days she was to marry the man sitting across from her. She needed to get a grip on reality. Smiling tentatively at James, she battled her conscience.

After lunch, James escorted her back to the office. Standing outside, he leaned in to give her a peck on the mouth. Without fully comprehending what she was doing, she twisted sideways forcing his lips to land on her cheek.

He gave her a quizzical look.

"I'm battling a cold," she lied, as she considered her actions.

Why would she do such a thing?

Because kissing him would be disloyal to Ranek.

She walked into the gallery and nearly fell to the floor as a sense of déjà vu overcame her. A familiar scent perfumed the air. She recognized it immediately. It was the scent from the cottage. From her apartment.

Kohan.

He'd been here.

Her stomach dropped. Had he been her noon appointment?

Susan.

She felt her face drain of color. A jolt of fear cut through her and she bolted to her office. She rounded the corner and found Susan sitting in her chair. "Is everything okay?" she blurted out.

She glanced up from her paperwork. "Fine. Why? Is everything okay with you?"

Katrina nodded and willed her heart to slow down. "How did the appointment go?" She sounded as though she'd just run a marathon.

Susan crinkled her nose. "Not so fine. Mr. Kay seemed rather displeased that you weren't here."

She sucked in a tight breath as her pulse leapt in her throat. Warning bells clanged in the back of her mind and she shuddered with foreboding. She cleared papers from a nearby chair and sank into it.

"Stay away from him, Susan. He's not who you think he is."

When Susan tossed her an incredulous frown, Katrina leaned forward and narrowed her eyes to mere slits. "He's dangerous."

Chapter Ten

ॐ

Silver rays from the crescent moon high overhead sliced through the bedroom window. As Katrina lay in Susan's freshly painted guestroom, she stared at the stark white ceiling and recalled her last dream.

A gentle breeze from her open window fluttered the lace curtains and washed over her skin. Naked atop the linen sheets, her nipples tightened as the wind whispered over them. She stretched out her limbs, allowing her legs to drift apart.

Her body warmed with need and desire as the summer wind stimulated her naked flesh.

Katrina was anxious for answers, but she'd be lying to herself if she believed that was the only reason she awaited Ranek's visit. He'd drawn her in, physically and emotionally, and she needed him with an intensity so strong and powerful that it frightened and excited her all at once.

Restlessly, she shifted on the bed, as she envisioned skin touching skin, hands caressing flesh. Her fingers drifted over her aroused body. She trembled as her belly quivered from her own touch. She cupped her breasts and played with her puckered nipples, imagining they were in the hands of her lover.

Spreading her legs further, her hand slipped between her dewy folds and dipped into her dampness as she pictured Ranek hovering over her, his tongue sliding in and out of her eager mouth.

Heat flamed through her as she tickled her sensitive clit. A feverish longing built with every delicious caress. She bucked against her hand, desperate to take the edge off. A tight groan sounded in the depths of her throat as she gave herself over to the erotic sensations.

She called upon the face of her masculine sea god and soon her skin grew tight as she increased the tempo of her fingers. A tremor racked her body. Her hot creamy release poured down her hand as she continued pleasuring herself.

But, it was not enough. Not nearly enough. She needed the real thing. She needed Ranek.

Her eyes drifted shut, anxiously anticipating the night ahead.

She was losing herself in him, heart and soul, and tonight she wanted to close her mind to the real world and show him just how much he'd come to mean to her.

* * * * *

Ranek spent the day with his warriors in the underworld searching for answers, but in the end he came up empty. And much to his frustration he'd been unable to locate any signs of an illegal potion.

Kohan's men guarded his lair with their lives, and Ranek knew if he were going to find the answers he was seeking then he'd have to plan a surprise attack.

At least during the nighttime hours Katrina would have his protection, and if she followed his rules and stayed with a mortal during daylight, it was unlikely that Kohan would approach her.

He took a glimpse into the mortal world and watched her sleep. Tonight she would learn all she needed to know, and once her memories were complete he could do no more. It would be up to her to make the final transformation.

He gathered his strength and shot to the surface.

Ranek emerged from the ocean and stopped dead in his tracks. His heart gave a hard beat and he drew in a quick excited breath. Standing at the water's edge, his heated blood coursed through his veins. All coherent thought vanished at the erotic image before him.

Lying on the sand, Katrina pleasured herself. Her sultry eyes locked on his as she opened her pink lips and idly stroked her smooth pussy. When he groaned, she delved deeper into her sweetness. Her head thrashed to the side as she cried out in ecstasy.

The sight before him unleashed the primal beast stirring his libido. He stalked forward and dropped to his knees. Grasping her shoulders, he drew her mouth to his, capturing her lips in an explosive, fiery kiss that left them both breathless.

He inhaled her delectable feminine scent and moaned into the hollow of her throat. He pulled back, looked deep into her eyes and saw a tangled mixture of longing, love and desire.

It was beginning.

As memories infiltrated her mind she was becoming more and more Bandara with each passing moment.

Tonight, words were not necessary. They communicated through their eyes and through their touch, the way they had done so many decades ago.

He moved in for a more thorough taste of her mouth. As he kissed her hungrily, she matched the intensity of his passion.

Her silky hands eagerly roamed over his body as though she couldn't get enough of him. Quick, shallow pants burst from her throat. Her dark gaze pleaded for him to make love to her.

He spread her legs further and nestled himself in between. In one quick thrust he drove his cock into her heated core.

She cried out and clung to his shoulders as though she'd never let go, as though she never wanted the moment to end.

He held her to him as he increased the tempo and rhythm. Their bodies were made for each other and she molded into him perfectly. Her breasts crushed against his chest as she writhed beneath him. Her warm, ragged breath wafted across his cheek, filling him with raw, primal lust.

Her burning lips closed over his, drawing his tongue into her mouth. She wrapped her legs around his hips and undulated against him. He felt her pussy muscles clamp down and tighten around his cock.

He held her tight as her explosion overtook them both.

Panting breathlessly, she clung to him. He smoothed her bangs off her forehead and caught her gaze.

The look in her eyes spoke volumes. He could feel the love emanating from her soul. Deep in her heart she knew where she belonged, her mind just needed to accept it.

She shimmied lower and positioned his cock at the opening of her mouth.

He framed her face with his hands. "This will be your last memory, Katrina."

The play of emotions on her face made his heart ache for her. His love for her grew stronger and stronger with each coupling.

She nodded her understanding and drew him into her mouth.

* * * * *

Kohan's insidious laugher seeped into her skin and filled her with dread as she bolted from his lair…

His parting words had left a sick apprehensive knot in her stomach.

"It's too late, Katrina, there's nothing you can do." He shot her a venomous look. "Ranek will die tonight."

He'd summoned his servants to restrain her, but she was much too agile and managed to slip from their grasp.

"Pay her no heed," she heard Kohan shout from behind her. "There is nowhere for her to go now."

Katrina ran to her chamber and secured the door behind her, locking herself in and Kohan and his men out.

She had to warn Ranek of Kohan's deceit. But how? Who was she to trust? An overwhelming feeling of anxiety overcame her and left her legs weak. She sank onto her bed as her mind searched for answers.

Her mind replayed Kohan's words. *"Ranek will die tonight."*

She could not lose him. She *would not* lose him.

Biting back her tears, she reached for the dagger Ranek had crafted for her. She pulled it from its protective casing and turned it over in her hand. The long, sharp blade glistened in the lamplight. After securing it to her inner thigh, she drew in a steadying breath. Now was not the time for tears. If she were going to sneak from the kingdom she had to muster strength and use all her intelligence to outwit Kohan's men.

Fortunately for her, Kohan had underestimated her determination and assigned only one man to stand watch.

She cracked open her door and spotted the guard standing duty. She called on every ounce of bravery and cleared her throat. "Excuse me, sir," she cooed, keeping her voice low, sultry.

He turned in her direction, his eyes immediately dropping to her prominent cleavage. She toyed with the top button on her bodice and pouted her lips. "I'm having a bit of difficulty with my buttons. Do you think you could come in here and help me?" She arched one brow provocatively.

An eager smile curled his lips as he followed her into the dimly lit lair. With the guard distracted by her breasts, she quickly took control of the situation and pulled her dagger.

His dark roar of laughter rattled her confidence. The dagger trembled in her hand. "What is a slip of a thing like you going to do with such a toy?"

He pulled his own dagger. "Now *this* is a weapon."

She swallowed past the fear constricting her throat and held her ground. "And *this* is a locked door," Katrina bellowed, running from the liar and securing the door shut with a heavy metal rod. Listing to his muffled curses from behind her thick-paneled door, she crept down the long corridor.

Expecting opposition, her heart pounded like thunder as she rounded each corner. She found no resistance as she slipped outside the kingdom walls.

With no time to spare, she swallowed her debilitating fear and gathered all her strength as she shot to the surface.

She had to find Ranek and warn him before it was too late. Before Kohan's men killed him.

In her desperate effort to save Ranek, she fought her way to the surface. She battled the enraged sea's powerful current for what seemed like hours until finally her head broke through the wind-tossed surface. Her lungs nearly burst from fear and exhaustion. Her limbs throbbed from the exertion, but she forced herself to go on.

Angry waves crashed over her face as she took a moment to locate Ranek's signature. Nausea took hold and she fought it down. An uncontrollable shiver racked her body as her heart cried out for his safety.

A flash of lightning cut through the dark sky. Wind whipped through her hair as another angry wave pulled her under.

She fought her way back to the surface and raked her heavy, wet hair off her face.

Up ahead she saw a flicker of light and heard the muted sounds of voices.

"Ranek," she hollered out to him, but the loud crash of the swells swallowed her cries. A clap of thunder roared in the distance.

Ignoring the threatening waves ready to swoop over her and drag her under, she pushed on.

She rushed forward when she saw Ranek and his band of warriors treading water a few feet away. She grabbed his shoulders and he spun around, his dagger poised, ready for battle.

His eyes opened wide with shock as comprehension filtered through him. He captured her shoulders in a tight grip and shook her. "Go back, Katrina. It is not safe for you here."

She shook her head and pleaded for him to listen. "You don't understand, Ranek. It is not safe for you," she yelled over the thrashing of the sea. But before she had a chance to explain, a boat came into view.

"Go now," he hollered and turned his attention to the loud cries of the men sailing toward his band of warriors,

Katrina's heart leapt into her throat when one of the sailors shot a spear at Ranek. Her stomach twisted and she shrieked as it missed his head by a fraction of an inch.

She closed her eyes with relief when he safely moved on to battle another. The second she shut her eyes she felt something cold penetrate her skin. She gasped for a breath but it wouldn't come. A sharp stab of pain cut through her. She opened her mouth to cry out to Ranek, but the words were lodged deep in her throat. She touched her hand to her stomach. It was warm, sticky, and in an instant she knew she'd been badly wounded.

Ranek instinctively spun around and caught her gaze. "No!" he bellowed, lunging for her. He gathered her into his arms while his warriors fought off their enemies.

"Katrina?" His face was drained of color.

"I'll be fine," she lied, feeling herself slipping in and out of consciousness.

"You shouldn't have come here." She could hear the anguish in his voice.

"Kohan," she whispered, her lids closing. She felt his warm hand on her face bringing her back.

"What about Kohan?"

She gasped and sputtered for her next breath. "He said he'd sent men to kill you."

Ranek's muscles tightened around her. "I have killed his traitorous men already."

She nodded toward the boat. "Then who are they?" As she drifted, their voices became faint in the background.

"They are drunken mortals, hunting us for sport."

No longer able to move a muscle, she felt her body go limp.

"Katrina, no! Please stay with me." His voice was panicked, anxious. She knew his hands were touching her but could no longer feel their warmth. "I'll take you back to our kingdom and find a way to heal you."

"Is it true, Ranek?"

"Is what true, my love?" He brushed her hair from her forehead, dropped a soft kiss on her cheek, and hugged her against his chest. She heard his breath catch in his throat.

"That when a Bandara is killed by a mortal...they will be reborn on earth?"

He nodded his head.

"Then you shall never stop looking for me?"

"I love you, Katrina, and will never stop my search. I will find you and bring you home. I swear it."

* * * * *

Katrina awoke, gasping for breath. Her eyes were wide with fear, anger and something else, something Ranek couldn't quite put his finger on.

"Ranek," she whispered, reaching out to touch his face. "Please forgive my foolishness. I never should have gone to the surface looking for you." She lowered her head. "I regret not having more faith in your abilities."

The pain in her eyes tormented him. He hooked a finger under her chin and lifted her face to his. "Kohan is capable of great evil, my love. You feared for my life and that is understandable. Trying to save me shows great strength and courage."

She shook her head. "My foolishness has cost us decades." Tears slid silently down her cheeks.

"Shh." He held her tight and wiped her face. "None of that is important now. What *is* important is that I have found you and want to bring you back to where you belong."

She gazed at him, her expression puzzled. "But how? I'm still half-human."

He smoothed her hair from her face. "With every memory, you become more and more Bandara. The final transformation is up to you."

She sniffed. "I don't understand."

"Now that the memories are complete, the only thing left is for your mind to fully accept them. The human part of you must believe in order for the final transformation to happen."

"How will I know when that happens? How will I know what to do?"

"You must will it to happen. Don't worry, Katrina, you will know what to do when you are ready," he assured her.

"But—"

He cut her off by pressing his fingers to her lips. "You have been on a very difficult journey, Katrina. You must rest while your body and mind understand what you have learned."

A comfortable silence fell over them as he held her tight. Her hands trailed over his arms. He loved how she touched him in such a familiar way. The sweet friction began to ignite his skin.

"There is something I don't understand, Ranek. If a Bandara can only travel to the mortal world during the night, how is it possible that Kohan was here today in my office?"

He clenched his jaw and fisted his hands. Anger burned in his eyes. "He's close, Katrina. Too close. He's using a magic potion. My men search for it as we speak." Ranek looked to the sky. Fingers of golden light edged the horizon. "My time is nearly up, Katrina."

"There is one more thing I need from you before you go." Her voice was a low, velvet murmur. She stroked her long fingers over the contours of his body and burrowed her mouth into the crook of his neck. She surfed her lips over his chin and cheek until she connected with his mouth. She broke the kiss and looked deep into his eyes. "Make love to me."

His heart filled with longing. Was she asking for his love, not his memories? "Your memories are complete now, Katrina."

"That isn't why I want to make love to you." The emotion in her gaze held him captive.

His heart swelled with emotion. The gift she was bestowing upon him touched his soul.

She ran an impatient hand over his chest and leaned into him, her mouth poised, her legs widening.

Fierce need took over. He tangled his hands through her hair and urged her closer. She moaned into his mouth and arched her back.

"I want your release inside me," she whispered, and reached down to stroke his swollen cock. "I want to feel your explosion in my body."

His fingers roamed over her scorched nakedness and slid over her quivering belly. He dipped lower and touched her silky, wet pussy. He growled when he felt her moisture.

Her juices dripped over his fingers. She was already so close. He touched her clit and she shuddered.

"You are very excited, my love."

She smiled up at him. The desire in her face matching his own. She squeezed his cock and he drew in a quick breath. "I believe I'm not the only one."

He chuckled. "You are so undisciplined, Katrina."

"You would prefer for me to be docile?" she asked, an amused expression on her face.

He rolled his eyes and grabbed her by the hips. "I prefer for you to be on top."

Without another word, she positioned his cock at the opening of her pussy. She closed her eyes and let the length of him slide deep inside her. "Ahhh," she moaned and thrust her hips forward, rubbing her rigid clit against him. "I believe I may prefer it this way myself."

He reached out and stroked her nipples, pulling on the buds until they were full and erect. Her breasts bounced in his hands as she began riding him, her body lifting and lowering, driving him deeper with each frantic thrust. She seemed almost desperate for an orgasm.

He reached around and pulled her ass cheeks apart, allowing his balls to smack against her tender flesh. She groaned and increased the rhythm.

His blood pulsed at the tip of his cock as he struggled to hang on. Gripping her hips, he drove into her harder. He was panting so loud he barely heard her throaty cries. The sound of her pleasure drove him over the edge. His sharp release was only seconds behind hers.

Minutes later he pulled her closer and smoothed her hair back. "I love you, Katrina," he whispered breathlessly. "You're mine for eternity."

Chapter Eleven

ॐ

Katrina awoke the next morning with her emotions in a tangled mess. There was so much to understand and assimilate she didn't even know where to begin. The human part of her mind wanted desperately to cling to the belief that none of this was real.

In a few days, she was to marry James. How could she possibly go through with the ceremony when her heart belonged to another?

And what if she really *was* losing her mind and Ranek was nothing more than a figment of her imagination?

Would she give up her dream of belonging to a family for something that didn't even exist?

Not so, an inner voice urged. *He* is *your soulmate.*

She flung her legs over the edge of her bed and drew in a weary sigh. Her toes touched the chilled floor and she shivered. The early morning sun filtered through her lacy curtains and shone directly into her eyes. Katrina winced and turned away. Off in the distance, birds chirped as they began their daily search for food.

Katrina's stomach grumbled, reminding her she hadn't been eating properly for the last few days.

As she stretched out her limbs, she stifled a yawn and couldn't remember ever being so tired. The emotional roller coaster she'd been on had drained her of her energy.

The sound of Susan moving around outside the bedroom forced her thoughts to the day ahead. Hopefully her busy schedule would help keep her mind off the jumbled mess that was her personal life.

She didn't want to think about her wedding or the rehearsal dinner with James and his family that was planned for later that evening. All she wanted to do was fall back into bed, curl up into a safe cocoon and forget about the real world, or any other world that existed beyond the realms of the deep.

The knock on her door roused her from her thoughts. She hastily pulled a robe over her naked body.

"Come in," she yelled, climbing to her feet.

"Just checking to make sure everything was okay," Susan said, opening her door. The smell of freshly brewed coffee filled her senses as Susan crossed the room.

Katrina smiled her gratitude and eyed the coffee. "Everything's fine now. Thanks," she replied, accepting the hot cup from Susan's hands. Katrina sipped the warm liquid and felt a little rejuvenated. "I'm sure after a shower I'll feel as right as rain," she said.

Susan took a seat on the bed and patted the empty space beside her. Once Katrina settled next to her, she looked into Susan's questioning eyes.

"Did you dream about him again last night?" Susan asked.

Katrina nodded, took another sip of coffee, and listened to the birds chirp outside.

"Would you like to talk about it?"

She picked an imaginary piece of lint from her robe. "He told me he loved me," she whispered.

"I see. And how do you feel about him, Katrina. Do you love him, too?"

Katrina shrugged. "I don't know. I'm just so unsure about everything."

"I think you better figure it out. Soon. You're getting married in a few days."

Katrina met her gaze. "Susan, do you think I'm losing my mind?"

"You are one of the most sane, reasonable people I know, Katrina," she assured her. "I've done a lot of thinking about this since we talked yesterday. Perhaps there is more to our world then what we can see and touch. And maybe, just maybe, your sea god really does exist."

Paying heed to Ranek's warning, Katrina planned on keeping close to Susan for the entire day. She drove to work with her and then secured herself in the safety of her office, where she planned to spend the day finishing off a few projects that were well past due. Susan assured her she'd allow no one into Katrina's office.

Hours later, Susan peeked around the corner of Katrina's office door. "Are you going to keep yourself cooped up in here all day or do you want to go grab some lunch?"

Katrina stole a glance at the clock. "I'm expecting a phone call."

From across the room Susan's stomach grumbled loud enough for Katrina to hear.

Katrina tossed her an apologetic look. She felt guilty for keeping her best friend chained to the office, but she needed to follow Ranek's orders. "Let's order in Chinese, my treat."

"You sure?"

"Yes, I'm sure." She grabbed her purse. "Would you mind ordering?"

"Okay," Susan agreed. "Since you're paying, I'm ordering one of everything on the menu."

Katrina chuckled before returning to work while she waited for her phone call.

* * * * *

Ranek pulled on his battle armor and summoned his warriors to the front gates. Today he would lead another group of men into the underworld, and this time he wouldn't stop his search until he discovered the forbidden potion.

Standing before his group of warriors, he outlined the details of their attack. Once done, he raised his dagger high above his head. "We stop at nothing. Those that resist our efforts will be killed."

His warriors raised their daggers, mimicked his cries, and prepared themselves for battle.

Ranek opened the great kingdom walls and they all filed out, following their leader into the dangerous underworld.

Deep below ground, Ranek made contact with one of his warriors who had infiltrated Kohan's followers. The watcher led them to the outskirts of Kohan's fortress.

"Be careful, Lord Ranek, you will meet with much resistance from Kohan's vassals." The watcher bowed his head and backed away, allowing Ranek's men to lead the assault.

Moving stealthily, his warriors broke into Kohan's fortress, knocking men to their knees with the surprise attack. While his men battled Kohan's vassals, Ranek's searched for his brother's lair, hoping to find him and put an end to his treachery once and for all.

After kicking in the door to Kohan's quarters, Ranek blinked and forced his eyes to adjust to the dimly lit room. Dagger drawn, he took a cautious step forward, expecting Kohan to attack at any moment.

He inspected every crevice, but in the end came up with nothing. The room was empty.

One of his men came running in, breathless. "Lord Ranek, I think you should follow me!"

He spun around. "Have you found Kohan?"

He shook his head from side to side. "I am not sure what we've found."

As Ranek turned to follow, he felt an icy cold chill move down his spine. The air was forced from his lungs as the room spun before him. He grasped the wall to balance himself.

In that instant, he knew exactly where to find his brother.

Another chill cut through his body, turning his blood to liquid ice.

Katrina.

He could hear her cries, hear the agony in her voice and feel the pain in her heart. His stomach plummeted as a feeling of helplessness roiled within. If anything happened to her, he'd never forgive himself.

She was calling for his help, yet in broad daylight he would die before he could save her.

He needed to work fast, to find what he was searching for so he could save Katrina from the deadly clutches of his brother.

"Lead me to your discovery," he bellowed.

He followed the young warrior into a murky laboratory. Ranek glanced briefly at the slain men lying across the floor. Stepping over them, he studied the display of potions before him.

"Lord Ranek."

He turned in the direction of the voice.

"I think I have found what you are looking for."

* * * * *

The bell strung over the front door tinkled and Katrina assumed it was their Chinese food.

A movement outside her office doorway drew her attention. She looked up expecting to see Susan with their lunch.

"That was fast—" Her words lodged in her throat. She drew in a sharp breath as her pulse leapt in her neck. Frantically, she looked over Kohan's shoulder into the gallery. Susan was slumped over her desk. Katrina jumped up, sending her chair flying backwards. It hit the wall with a loud thud.

He stood before her dressed in an overcoat, his hair slicked back off his forehead, looking exactly as she remembered.

"Kohan," she whispered, taking a step backwards.

"That's not exactly the warm welcome I'd been hoping for," he said, a wolfish smile on his face. "It's been a long time, Katrina. Come closer, let me have a better look at you." He took a step toward her and her mouth went dry with terror.

Her heart pounded so hard in her chest she thought it would burst. She fought to recapture her breath. "What do you want from me?"

He took his time in answering. He shot her a sidelong glance, his eyes gazing at her with lustful hunger. "Ah, my sweet." He cocked his head to the side. "You already know the answer to that question."

She gave a derisive twist of her lips. "I'd rather die than mate with you."

A low chuckle rumbled in his throat as his eyes darkened. "Yes, well, we've already walked that path now, haven't we?" With a swift movement, he closed the distance between them. "And I have no desire to wait another few decades for you to resurface." His body was close enough that she could feel his heat, his arousal.

His eyes slowly tracked her curves. He pushed his cock against her and groaned in delight. "You're still as beautiful and desirable as I remember." He inhaled her skin and scoffed in disgust. "Once I rid you of Ranek's scent, I'll make you mine." He kept his voice soft, but his anger was evident.

She shuddered and turned her head away.

He grabbed her chin hard and tugged her back to face him. "Don't *ever* turn away when I am addressing you. Do you understand?"

"You're hurting me," she cried, clawing at him.

He eased his grip and smirked. "Ranek has been too lenient with you. Under my command, you will learn respect and discipline." The look in his eyes was frightening and Katrina felt her knees begin to collapse.

Kohan pushed his body against hers, anchoring her to the wall. Disgust crept over her skin. There was no way she'd let this man have her.

She summoned her courage and lifted her chin. "I will never live under your command," she bit out tersely.

"I'm afraid, *my love*, you will have no choice in the matter."

"Let go of me." She squirmed and he tightened his hold, letting her know she was no challenge for him.

He ignored her protests. "You will see that the pleasures I have to offer you outweigh death." He smiled and trailed a finger over her breasts. "And soon, I assure you, you will *seek* such pleasures." He buried his face into the crook of her neck and moaned into her throat as he began to unbutton her blouse.

"Undress for me, Katrina. Let me see what I have missed all these years. The last glimpse I had of your beautiful, naked body was the night you mated with my brother." His breath on her neck curdled her stomach and she could feel bile pushing into her throat.

"So you *were* there. How?"

He chuckled. "Magic, my dear Katrina. A magic cloaking potion from the underworld. My foolish brother had no idea I was there, watching you."

She felt his wet tongue leave a slimy trail on her neck. Her stomach twisted and she shook her head. Fresh tears spilled from her eyes as she batted his hands away. "Stop!" He was too strong for her to push away.

He stepped back and laughed. "I must admit, I always did love your spirit."

She closed her eyes in relief when he released her from his clutches. When she opened them again, she spotted movement behind Kohan.

"Ranek," she murmured breathlessly, and felt almost giddy with thankfulness.

"Ranek cannot save you." Kohan's voice was cold, dangerous.

"Don't be so sure, little brother." Ranek's tone was so frigid it turned her blood to ice. His eyes burned with an intense rage and Katrina suspected his fury knew no bounds. He stalked forward and hovered over Kohan like an untamed animal ready to pounce.

She didn't recognize the look on this man's face. Gone was the tenderness he'd shown her. What was before her was the face of a warrior.

Kohan spun around. "How — ?"

"Seems your illegal potion has worked against you." Ranek pulled his dagger from its casing.

"Some would call me a genius. Such brilliance, don't you think?" Kohan said reaching for his own dagger.

Ranek's eyes burned like black coals as they stared into Kohan's. "There is a fine line between genius and insanity." His tone was deceptively mild.

Kohan twirled his dagger in his hand. Light glistened off the razor-sharp edge. "I have not grown soft in the underworld, big brother. You are no match for the strength and agility I have acquired over the years. I shall make short work of you and then return to matters that have more interest to me." He shot Katrina a leer and laughed.

The sound of his poisonous laughter seeped into her skin and filled her body with panic. Katrina stood immobile, frozen with fear. She could taste the tension in the room. Her muscles were unable to move as she watched the battle in horror, brother against brother, warrior against warrior.

The clash of weapons made her ears ring. She gulped air, covered them and cried out for Ranek's safety.

Katrina held her breath when a lethal blow barely missed Ranek's head. Kohan let out a low, triumphant laugh.

As the fight continued, Katrina fought the urge to faint. She felt terror unlike anything she'd ever felt before.

Kohan matched Ranek blow for blow but soon his stamina seemed to dwindle.

"Where is this strength you speak of?" Ranek asked, thrusting his dagger forward. "I believe you *have* grown soft in the underworld."

Ranek's taunting words enraged Kohan. Ranek neatly sidestepped his advances.

There was no place for emotion in a battle of wit and skill. Katrina knew a fight should be fought with intellect, not passion.

She knew this was Kohan's shortcoming and prayed it would be his downfall.

"I wonder just who is making short work of whom?" Ranek mocked. He moved around the floor with grace and agility while Kohan wiped blood from his face and fought to recover his breath.

Rage burned in Kohan's eyes. "I will destroy you once and for all, big brother," he bit out, swinging his dagger with all his might.

Once again Ranek sidestepped his advance, sending the other man sailing to the floor.

In a motion so quick it threw Kohan off-guard, Ranek stood over him. Katrina looked up just in time to see Ranek plunge his dagger through Kohan's chest.

Kohan's cry of agony rang through the air. She tried to block her mind to the sound but it was too loud, too intense.

White lights danced before her eyes as horror twisted her insides. She clutched her stomach as fear and nausea overcame her. The room began to spin and, no longer able to remain conscious, she felt herself slip to the floor.

* * * * *

"Katrina, wake up." Ranek cradled her in his lap, gently rubbing her cheeks, trying to rouse her from her faint.

Her lids slowly flickered open. As her mind began to return to consciousness, he watched the color drain from her face. Her body began to quiver and he held her tighter trying to soothe her.

She glanced at the floor, to the spot where Kohan had fallen. "What happened to him?"

"I sent his body back to our kingdom."

She freed herself from his embrace and pressed herself against the wall. With her knees bent to her chest, she wrapped her arms around her legs and shook her head back and forth.

"I can't do this, Ranek. I can't take any more memories or witness any more battles." He watched her throat work as she swallowed. Fresh tears glistened in her eyes.

Ranek cursed himself for slaying Kohan in front of her. The human part of her could not handle such things and was putting up great resistance. She was retreating, and he needed to bring her back around.

"Katrina —"

She cut him off with a wave of her hand. "No, no more. You have to go." Her voice wavered. Her eyes were dark, haunted, reflecting her every emotion.

Panic cut through him. Blood pounded through his veins. "You know not what you want, my love."

She buried her face into her palms. "I *do* know," she cried. "My life may not have been perfect before you entered it, but at least it made sense. Now I'm confused and emotionally drained. I just want things to go back to normal." She lifted her head and matched the intensity in his gaze. "I want you to leave." Anger sparked in her eyes.

He reached for her and she flinched away. "I've spent decades searching for you, Katrina. I love you and you are my soulmate. I will not let you go so easily."

She sniffed and brushed the dampness from her eyes. "If you cared anything about me, you'd accept my wishes and leave. Let me follow the safe, planned path I was on."

"Is this what you really wish? For me to leave? For you to marry James?"

Her eyes opened wide. "You knew about James?"

"Of course, Katrina. I know everything about you. You are my soulmate."

She turned away from him.

"Katrina?" He needed more time to bring her mind back around. But with her wedding in a couple of days, time was a luxury that wasn't his.

"No more, Ranek. You must go."

"If it is truly your wish, Katrina, then I will not stand in your way." His heart felt as though it had been torn from his chest. "Before you marry, there is something you should know."

"What?" she asked quietly.

"I am your soulmate and if we are denied each other, we will never be able to find true happiness." Ranek deliberately withheld his knowledge of their eventual deaths. He refused to blackmail her into choosing him.

She began to shake her head. A sob caught in her throat. He knew she was scared. So scared.

His heart went out to her. "There is another way, Katrina."

"How?" she whispered, and he sensed she was trying to stay in control of her emotions.

"You gave your life for me once. Now it is my turn to give my life for you."

"I don't understand."

"You died trying to save me, now I will die to save you," he repeated calmly.

"What?" Her whole body stiffened.

"As your soulmate, if I was to willingly die, then you would be freed from me. Free to marry a mortal and live a full mortal life. You would no longer be connected to the Bandara world."

Her eyes opened wide. "You'd sacrifice your life for me?"

"Yes," he whispered.

"Why? Why would you do that?" Her tone softened as her anger melted.

He pressed his lips hungrily against her sweet mouth and smoothed her hair back. "Because I love you, and without you I have no reason to go on." With those tender words ringing in her ears, he disappeared.

Chapter Twelve

જી

He was gone.

Katrina stared at the empty space where Ranek had been standing until he'd faded into mist. With her legs too weak to lift her from the floor, she remained huddled in the corner. Her heart pounded in her chest as she tried to comprehend what had just happened. Oh God, Susan. What had they done to Susan?

"Susan!"

A moment later Susan stumbled into her office, her hand pressed against her head.

"Susan, are you okay?"

When Susan saw Katrina sitting on the floor, she hurried to her.

"Katrina, he overpowered me. Are you okay?"

She took a deep breath and nodded. "It's over. It's all over." An empty feeling settled in her heart and she tried to ignore it.

"You're in shock." Susan helped her to her feet and into her office chair. She glanced around the battered room. "What happened here?"

Katrina sat on her hands to stop them from trembling and explained how Kohan had tried to force her into the underworld. How Ranek had shown up and saved her from Kohan's clutches, and how the incident had ended with bloodshed.

"My God, Katrina. You could have been hurt! You could have—" She stopped mid-sentence, as if what she were about to say was too much for her to bear. "Where's Ranek?"

Katrina stared straight ahead but saw nothing. "He's gone."

"Is he coming back?" Susan asked.

She shook her head. "No. He's gone for good." She struggled for normalcy in her voice when all she wanted to do was curl up and cry.

"But—"

Katrina cut her off. "It's for the best. Now my life can get back to normal."

Susan shot her a disbelieving glance. "Are you sure you want that?"

She knew her too well.

Katrina forced herself to turn away knowing full well her eyes would betray her emotions. "I'm sure."

"Maybe you should go home and rest." Susan leaned in and placed her hand on Katrina's shoulder. "Think on this for awhile."

Katrina gave a defiant shake of her head. She didn't want to go home. At home, in her bed, the memories of Ranek were too strong. Just then the phone rang.

"That's the call I've been waiting for." She looked at Susan, her eyes pleading. She couldn't talk to anyone in the condition she was in. She needed time, time to deal with the events, and time to heal the pain that had ripped through her heart.

"I can't—"

"I'll take it," Susan assured her, putting her hand over the receiver.

"Thanks," Katrina mumbled. She planted her elbows on her desk and buried her face in her hands.

* * * * *

The next few hours passed without incident. Katrina tried to block her mind to all the tumultuous emotions raging inside herself and move on. She forced herself to concentrate on her work and wedding preparations. But, as hard as she tried to forget what had happened in her office earlier that day, she couldn't. Ranek's parting words continued to haunt her.

I will die for you.

The emotions he pulled from her were too painful to think about. The strong resistance from her human side pressured her to block all thoughts of him and concentrate on other things.

By the time she left the office to meet James and his parents for the rehearsal dinner, night had closed around her. She chatted idly in the passenger seat while Susan drove to the restaurant. Katrina was careful to keep the conversation away from Ranek and the events of the day. When Susan tried to bring up the incident, Katrina quickly changed the subject.

Once inside, she was whisked away in a flurry of activity. The maitre d' led her to a private table in back where James's family was gathered. When she caught James's eye, he jumped from his chair and rushed to her.

"Good evening, sweetheart." He kissed her on the mouth. Nothing. She felt nothing.

Her heart sank into the pit of her stomach.

"Is everything okay?" he asked, but before she had a chance to tell him just how *not* okay everything was, he turned his attention to the waiter and ordered a bottle of champagne.

"You were saying?" he asked, turning back to her.

"Nothing," she replied. "Everything is fine. Perfectly fine," she lied.

"Katrina, my dear, just look at you." James's mother reached out and brushed Katrina's mussed hair from her shoulders. "You're as white as a sheet." She shook her head and frowned. "You've been working too hard. I'll be glad when you go on your honeymoon and get some well needed rest."

James winked at her and whispered in her ear. "Don't count on it."

Katrina's stomach churned as she sank into her chair.

* * * * *

The following days passed quickly as Katrina finished her work at the office and prepared for her wedding and honeymoon. Everything was finally in order for the big day.

It was well past midnight the night before her wedding when Katrina, feeling totally exhausted, fell into bed. Kicking her blankets to the bottom of the mattress, she shifted restlessly. She didn't wait for Ranek to invade her thoughts, or her body. He hadn't made an appearance in the previous nights, nor did she expect him to tonight.

A lump caught in her throat and she swallowed past it.

Susan was fast asleep in the other room. She'd insisted on staying at Katrina's apartment to watch over her until the ceremony.

Other than Susan and her husband, she had no other family or friends coming to the ceremony.

This *was* all she'd ever wanted, wasn't it? To marry into a big family? To finally find love, acceptance, and belonging?

As she lay in her bed, she willed her mind to think about James, but no matter how hard she tried, Ranek consumed her thoughts.

Her body quivered as she recalled his touch, his caresses, and his hungry kisses. She twisted sideways, buried her face in her pillow and groaned, praying that she'd made the right decision.

She'd never felt so empty, so alone in her entire life. She'd found solace, comfort and a sense of belonging with Ranek.

Would she ever find that with James?

She was well into the wee hours of the morning when she finally fell into a fitful sleep.

She awoke to the sounds of the birds chirping and instead of feeling alive and elated on this special day, she felt scared and alone.

She'd spent the better part of the night tossing and turning, trying to block Ranek from her mind.

Stretching out her limbs, she reluctantly climbed from her bed. The hairdresser was due to arrive any minute. After that the photographer would be coming, as well as Roxanne and Sherry, her soon-to-be sisters-in-law.

Susan opened the door, filling her room with the aromatic scent of fresh-brewed coffee. She crossed the room. "How are you feeling this morning?" she asked.

Katrina gave her a genuine, loving smile. "What would I do without you?"

"You'd be forced to get your own coffee," she teased.

Katrina laughed and leaned in to hug her best friend.

Susan braced her hands on her hips and narrowed her gaze. "Are you ready for this?" she asked, nodding toward the long white gown draped over her dressing table.

"Yes."

"You're absolutely sure this is what you want?"

Katrina averted her gaze. "Yes."

Susan hooked her arm through Katrina's. "Okay. Then let's go. The hairdresser is here and there is no time to spare," she said, before ushering Katrina down the hall. Before Katrina had time to finish her coffee, her apartment was full of women.

Roxanne and Sherry fluttered about excitedly, as they primped and pampered in preparation for the big moment. The shimmering pale green gowns Katrina had picked looked absolutely stunning on them. She hadn't realized until now that the gowns were similar to the one she wore the night she mated with Ranek.

Katrina sat before her mirror and watched as everyone rushed about. The hairdresser piled her hair on top of her head, allowing a few tendrils to fall over her neckline and jaw.

She immediately remembered Ranek telling her never to wear it that way again.

Sherry's voice pulled her thoughts to the present.

"You're going to need some makeup to cover those dark circles under your eyes," she said, coming up behind her to admire her new hairdo. She twirled a wisp through her fingers and smiled.

Roxanne stood beside Sherry and smiled. "James is going to think he's died and gone to heaven. You look beautiful."

Katrina forced a smile of thanks and squeezed their hands.

The rest of the morning flew by. Numbly, she went through the motions of preparing herself for marriage. She felt as though she was in someone else's body, watching as the activity continued on around her.

Less than an hour later, she found herself standing at the back of the church. Her heart beat faster than the wings of a hummingbird as she watched the guests take their seats.

She closed her eyes and concentrated on her breathing.

She envisioned herself walking down the aisle. Organ music playing softly in the background, all eyes on her, including the eyes of her soon-to-be husband. Except in her mind, it wasn't James standing at the altar waiting for her.

It was Ranek.

Her eyes sprang open and she bit down on her bottom lip hard enough to draw blood.

All of a sudden it felt as if the air was forced from her lungs. She struggled for breath, but none came. Intense pain shot through her stomach leaving her feeling cold, numb. Her chest heaved as her lids fluttered shut. A strangled cry caught in her throat.

Her pulse leapt in her throat and she knew in that instant that Ranek made good on his promise.

I will die for you.

Dear god! What had she done?

A sick apprehensive knot tightened in her stomach and she swallowed the dryness in her mouth.

The connection between them was so strong she could feel his pain, feel the cold blade of the dagger penetrate his skin.

No! This couldn't be happening!

How could she give her heart to James when all along it belonged to another?

Ranek was her soulmate.

Was she too late to follow the path she was meant to travel?

Ranek was everything her heart had been looking for. He was the man of her dreams, the man of her past, and the man of her future.

She had to go to him. To save him.

But how?

The human part of you must believe who you are in order for the transformation to be complete. You must will it to happen.

She looked up to see James watching her. She motioned him to come closer. The wedding guests watched with curious eyes as he hurried to the back of the church. He followed her into a private room where they would not be overheard. Her fingers trembled as she reached out and took his hands in hers. "I can't do this. I'm sorry, James. Please forgive me."

"I don't understand" he said, confusion on his face.

Susan came up behind him and placed a comforting hand on his shoulder. "Go, Katrina. I'll take care of things here for you."

Katrina gave her a grateful smile and hugged her. "Thank you, Susan. I love you."

"I love you, too, now go before it's too late."

Katrina ran from the church and drove the short distance to her apartment. Tears pooled on her lashes and she wiped them away. "I love you Ranek, please don't die," she cried, praying he could hear her. "I never meant to hurt you."

She bolted to her apartment and threw herself onto her bed. How could she contact him? What was she to do?

You must will it to happen.

Katrina closed her eyes and drew a deep calming breath. She folded her hands in front of her and gave a silent prayer. Suddenly it felt as though she was floating through time and space. "I love you, Ranek. You're my soulmate and I'll be yours for eternity," she whispered.

* * * * *

Cold pain sliced through him and he bit his bottom lip to stifle his agony. Blood poured from the gaping wound splitting him open. His hand still clutched the dagger embedded in his stomach.

He jerked and writhed on the floor of his lair waiting for the pain to subside. Waiting for it all to end.

"Ranek."

He heard her sweet, comforting voice, smelled her signature scent and thought he must be dreaming. A warm hand touched his forehead and he struggled to open his eyes.

"Ranek," she whispered. "You're on fire."

He forced his lids open. The silhouette of her body shimmered in the lamplight. Surely he must be hallucinating.

"Katrina?" he mumbled, letting his eyes slip shut again.

"Yes, Ranek. I'm here. I'm going to heal you. But you must rest. You'll need your strength."

"Why? How?" He wanted to reach out and touch her hand to make sure she was real, but he couldn't find the strength.

She frowned in concentration, silenced him with her fingertips, and called forth a servant. Her voice grew faint as he began to slip from consciousness.

A moment later, he felt her long curls brush across his cheek. "Don't even think about leaving me, Ranek," she whispered into his ear.

He forced himself to speak. "It's too late." He tightened his grip on the dagger.

She peeled his hands free and placed them at his sides. "Have you forgotten who I am and what I am capable of? I am this clan's healer and I do not give up so easily." In one quick, painful movement, she pulled the dagger from his stomach and placed her hands over the wound.

The smell of herbs and spices reached his nostrils. He listened to Katrina mumble something to another. Was that Tiera's voice he heard? The muted sound of whispers mingled together and he could no longer distinguish one voice from another. The whispers turned into chanting and he knew Katrina was performing a healing ritual on him.

* * * * *

For days he'd been unconscious as Katrina sat by his side. She'd spent day and night bringing down his fever, cleaning and changing his dressings. When he moaned painfully in his sleep, she soothed him with a touch, calming his agony and nightmares.

She took her rightful spot beside him in the bed and glanced around his lair—their lair. For the first time in her life she felt a sense of belonging. She was home. A smile touched her mouth as her heart swelled with the love she felt for the man beside her.

She checked his wounds. Dark purple bruising spread across his stomach all the way to his back, but thanks to her healing ritual and magic herbs, the wound itself was almost healed.

She sponged his naked body and knew he would soon rouse from his deep slumber. Relief washed through her as his breathing finally returned to normal. He mumbled incoherently in his sleep and Katrina whispered reassuring words, certain that he could hear her.

A familiar knock sounded on the door and Katrina called for Tiera to enter. She placed a basin of water and a sponge on the side table.

"Would you like some help?" she asked.

Katrina shook her head. "We'll be fine, thank you." Tiera nodded in understanding and exited the lair.

She dipped her hand into the basin, wrung out the excess water from the sponge, and began to bathe his naked body. She trailed the sponge over his chest, being careful not to disturb his wound. She trailed lower, until her hand lingered over his midriff. When she dipped even lower and caressed his groin, his cock stirred to life.

Katrina chuckled. "Now is not the time for *that*, my Lord."

* * * * *

Her voice pulled him awake. He lifted his lids to find Katrina sitting on the edge of the bed, her eyes fixed on his body while she cleansed him.

"It is always the time for *that*," he whispered.

"Ranek!" Her eyes opened with surprise and relief. A smile crossed her beautiful face. "Feeling better?" she asked.

He furrowed his brows questioningly. "Why, Katrina? How? How did you get here?"

She took his hand in hers and pressed it to her heart. "It is my will to be here. So I am here." There was so much emotion in her voice, in her eyes. She placed a gentle kiss onto his cheek. "Thank you for bringing me home," she whispered.

His heart nearly exploded with emotion as he pulled her mouth to his for a tender kiss. "Thank you for coming home."

Desire twisted inside him, firing his blood as her throaty purr resonated through his body. He broke the kiss and looked at her. "What is this nonsense that this is not the time for *that*?" he said in his most commanding voice, a suggestive edge to his smile.

He watched her eyes darken with heat as his cock pulsed and brushed against her hand. She moistened her bottom lip. A fever rose in him and it had nothing to do with his wound.

"But you're still recovering. You'll need your strength."

He raised one brow. "You question my strength?" he asked, slipping his hands under her nightgown. His eyes held her captive as he cupped her full breasts and squeezed. A low, primal groan caught in his throat. Katrina's head fell back as she arched into his touch. She practically vibrated as a shiver racked her body.

She bent forward, her hair spilling over his chest, her warm breath on his face. She closed her mouth over his for a slow, simmering kiss. Climbing on top of him, she pressed the heat of her desire against his legs. She was warm, moist, ready. Her arousing scent made him weak with longing.

"Perhaps you are right. Perhaps I do need to conserve my strength," he teased, feigning exhaustion.

"Very well then, my Lord." She began to climb off.

He growled and grabbed her hips, pulling her back on top of him. "You get back here."

Katrina laughed and reached out to stroke his engorged cock. "Perhaps you *are* in need of tending. And I suppose as your wife it is my duty to attend to your every need." She gave a heavy sigh. "And since I am a disciplined, dutiful wife who always follows your rules then I guess—"

His deep laughter cut her off. He gripped her hips and gyrated against her. "Take your clothes off," he ordered.

Slowly, seductively, she began to work the buttons on the bodice of her nightgown. She let it slip over her slim hips and pool over him and onto the bed. Her breasts spilled forward, her nipples swelling under his gaze.

"Bring your pussy to my face," he commanded.

She shimmed over his chest and straddled his mouth. Her skin tightened when he flicked her clit with his warm tongue. She fisted his hair and held him against her as she rode his face. He licked her from front to back as she rocked against his hungry mouth.

She moaned with intense pleasure and cupped her breasts. Throwing her head back, she increased her speed and rode him harder, his tongue delving into her wetness. Ranek felt her pussy muscles contract and a moment later a loud cry sounded from her throat as she tumbled into orgasm. Ranek lapped her juices and felt her body relax.

"Let me make love to you, Katrina, in our own bed, as I've been dreaming of doing for so long." He grabbed her hips and guided her to his cock, her release leaving a path of moisture over his chest and stomach. The pain from his wound was a distant memory as her pussy pressed against his cock.

Straddling him, she leaned forward and kissed his mouth as his cock breached her slick entrance. She moaned, arched her back and sank his length deeper inside her. She bucked, matching the pace and rhythm of each sweet thrust.

Katrina cried out and as her climax ripped through her. Ranek grabbed her hips and held her tight as his own orgasm approached.

Katrina climbed from his cock and nestled herself between his thighs.

He stroked her warm cheek. "What are you doing, my love?"

Her grin was mischievous. "What I've been dying to do for days." Her soft voice was filled with love. She sheathed his cock in her palms and drew it into her mouth.

Ranek gripped the sheets and, within seconds of feeling her hot tongue, came in a fiery release.

Katrina lifted her chin, met his gaze and licked him from her lips.

He chuckled. "You are most undisciplined, Katrina." He gathered her into his arms and smoothed her hair from her forehead.

"Yes, I know," she whispered into his ear.

Ranek threw his head back and laughed. "And I wouldn't have it any other way."

Also by Cathryn Fox
&

Unleashed

About the Author
&

If you're looking for Cathryn Fox you'd never find her living in Eastern Canada with a husband, two young children and a chocolate Labrador retriever. Nor would you ever find her in a small corner office, writing all day in her pajamas. Oh no, if you're looking for Cathryn you might find her gracing the Hollywood elite with her presence, sunbathing naked on an exotic beach in Southern France, or mingling with the rich and famous as she sips champagne on a luxury yacht in the Caribbean. Perhaps you can catch her before she slips between the sheets with a man who is as handsome as he is wealthy, a man who promises her the world.

Cathryn Fox is no ordinary woman. Men love her. Women want to be her.

Cathryn is bold, sensuous and sophisticated. And she is my alter ego.

Cathryn Fox welcomes mail from readers. You can write to her c/o Ellora's Cave Publishing at 1056 Home Avenue Akron, OH 44310-3502.

DOLPHIN'S PLAYGROUND
Jaci Burton

ഔ

Dedication

ॐ

To my wonderful editor, Briana St. James, for taking the time to brainstorm this idea of an undersea civilization. Thank you for always lending an ear and helping bring life to the thoughts running through my head. Your guidance and your friendship are the best.

To Desiré, for your thorough and extensive research on dolphin life. Your keen insights and valuable information brought validity to my writing, and I'll be forever grateful for the time you took to read this book.

To Sandra Webb, the best proofreader an author could ask for. Your enthusiasm and comments make me smile. Thank you for reading my books.

To Mel and Jodi, my friends and critique partners who walk through this process with me, who give their unending support and who manage to keep up with my frenzied writing—You know I could never do this without you. Love and hugs to you both.

And, as always, to Charlie…the man who brings me joy every day. Without your love, none of this would make sense. There would be no fantasy, no magic, and no happily ever after. I love you.

Chapter One

ಬ

Dr. Jasmine "Jaz" Quinlan peered out the window of her office inside southern California's *California Bay Aquarium*. The sun fought to break through the early morning fog, a gray wall so thick she could barely see the water.

Distinctive shapes lay at the water's edge. Her pulse picked up a rapid pace as she willed the sun to breach the last of the chilling summer fog.

Please don't let it be She hoped she was wrong, she hoped what lay in the sand was some washed up driftwood, not the living, breathing creatures she loved.

As if in miraculous answer to her fervent prayers, the mist lifted just enough to showcase at least a dozen bottlenose dolphins.

They'd beached themselves, which meant they came to the shore to die.

Shit! She offered up a desperate wish that these dolphins weren't suffering from the morbillivirus, which could wipe out entire pods. Knowing time was of the essence here, she called for a rescue crew. Dressing quickly, she grabbed for her medical kit as she was running out the door. There were no people on the beach yet, so the dolphins hadn't been discovered.

The last thing she wanted was a crowd to gather. It made her work so much more difficult when both the good intentioned and the downright curious got in the way.

In a few adrenaline-filled seconds, she'd flown down the back stairs, her shoes filling with sand as she raced the short distance from the beach to the water line.

Her heart broke at the sight of the struggling dolphins. She grabbed her kit and examined the first few she came upon, breathing a sigh of relief when she detected their heartbeats.

"They're still alive. Let's get these hoists going!" she shouted to the approaching staff members. Trucks with hoists were brought onto the beach so they could get the dolphins lifted and taken inside.

They worked tirelessly through the morning, loading the struggling dolphins one by one while volunteers poured water on the sick mammals to prevent dehydration and overheating.

Jaz wiped the sweat from her forehead, pushing away the annoying curly red strands of hair that flew in her face from the stiff ocean breeze. She'd long ago discarded her jacket and sweatshirt, her body soaked with the efforts of maneuvering dolphins weighing several hundred pounds. Thankfully, there were enough hands available. They turned each mammal enough to slip the hoist lines underneath them.

The last of the dolphins were loaded up and delivered to one of the aquarium's tanks by nightfall.

But her work wasn't finished. Now she had to figure out what was wrong with them, and how to keep them alive. Simply returning them to the ocean would have done no good. Dolphins beached themselves when they were too sick to remain in the water. They'd just end up on the shore again tomorrow.

Crowds had gathered around the beach and watched the process. News crews hovered nearby, reporters begging for an interview. Talking to the press was not her forte. She looked frantically for Mandy Daniels, the aquarium's PR representative. Unfortunately she was nowhere to be found.

That left her to tell the press something, anything to get the cameras out of her face.

"Dr. Quinlan, do you have any idea what's wrong with the dolphins?" asked one reporter, shoving a microphone under her nose.

"Not yet, but we'll start tests right away." She headed toward the aquarium, knowing that the media couldn't follow beyond the gates.

"Do you think it's pollution? Perhaps an oil spill?"

"Doubtful. There's no record of a spill and the ocean around the aquarium is tested regularly since we pump sea water into our tanks."

"How long do you think before—"

"No more questions." Jaz reached the gate, swiped her ID card and slid through without listening to the tail-end of the reporter's question. She'd never before appreciated the sound of the lock automatically clicking the gates shut, but now she was glad they kept the hungry reporters at bay.

With a sigh of relief, she hurried up the back stairs and changed into her wetsuit, then rushed to the pool. Her staff were already busily taking blood samples and monitoring the vital signs of the ailing dolphins.

"Skin temperature and tone on this one seem within normal ranges." Bob Pine, one of her assistants, looked up as she entered the shallow part of the water, then bent his head to his work again. She waded over to one of the dolphins and immediately started taking temperatures and extracting blood samples, shouting out data to one of the other assistants standing beside the pool.

They worked systematically on all the dolphins, who seemed to exhibit no external symptoms of illness or injury. Which meant whatever was wrong with them was internal.

After putting identifying markers on all the dolphins, the staff hurried to the lab to process the blood work. Jaz exited the pool and stripped off her wetsuit, intent on rushing up to her apartment to change clothes and head to the lab. Unfortunately, she was blocked in her progress by the one person she did not want to see today.

"Dr. Quinlan, who authorized this rescue?"

Claude Morton, administrator of the *California Bay Aquarium*, peered at her over stylish glasses that probably cost more than she made in one year. His Armani suit was completely out of place in this environment, but to Claude, image was everything. He spared no expense, at least as it related to his own personal attire and lifestyle. But spend a dime that wasn't in the aquarium's budget, and he paled as if the money came out of his own bank account.

"I authorized the rescue. Did you want me to stand by and watch a dozen dolphins die on the beach while a marine mammal center stood less than fifty feet away?"

He wrinkled his nose, no doubt protesting the smell of the water and mammals. Good. She hoped the smell made him nauseous.

"We are not responsible for what occurs outside the aquarium's property, Dr. Quinlan."

"Now's not a good time to get into this, Claude," she said, knowing calling him by his first name would irritate the piss out of him. Claude preferred to throw around his own PhD as if it were a Nobel Prize and insisted the staff call him "Dr. Morton." In fact, it was well known he came from old money, the colleges he attended practically bought and paid for by his family.

Typically, she ignored him. Today wasn't typical. She started to push past him but he blocked her exit.

"We need to talk about this. You have to move these dolphins out of here, now."

Refusing to let him intimidate her, she said, "They're ill. They need medical attention. I'm not moving them."

His face reddened. "You *will* move them. We do not have the funds for this kind of rescue."

"No, Claude. They're staying."

With a glaring look, he pulled his cell phone from his pocket. "Fine, I'll just have them removed if you won't."

Jaz breathed deeply to keep herself from kicking her moronic boss in the balls. Then an idea struck. "Fine. You do that. In the meantime, I'll go talk to the reporters currently drooling at the gate for a juicy story. I think I'll tell them the administrator of the aquarium would rather a dozen dolphins die because it might cost his multi-millionaire family a few thousand bucks of pocket change to save their lives."

The redness left his face in a second as he peered around the corner of the building, finally noticing the camera crews and photographers. Straightening his jacket, he turned away from the crowd and sent her a scathing look that didn't scare her in the least.

"You've won this round, Dr. Quinlan, but I can assure you as soon as possible I will be relocating those dolphins."

"You do that, Claude, and I *will* go to the press. Only it won't be the kind of public relations you're looking for."

They stood practically nose to nose. Jaz was mindful of the reporters behind her. Thankfully they were out of earshot.

"Why do you care so much?" he asked. "They're just animals."

This was one of those days when she wished she could dive in the ocean and live with the creatures she loved so much, instead of imbeciles like Claude.

"They're mammals, Claude. Not animals. Mammals. Just like you and me. Only they're smarter than a lot of humans I know," she finished, hoping he'd grab the insult.

"They are a lower level life form. At the aquarium, they're here for the entertainment of our paying customers. Hardly the same as humans."

His comment brought her blood pressure up another notch, as if she hadn't already struggled to hold in the ire which rose by the second. The only reason she stayed on at this circus fest was her fear that Claude would stop caring for the dolphins if she left.

"If I had my way we'd free them all, or close the stupid shows you insisted on bringing on board. This place used to be for study and research. Paying guests were more than pleased to simply observe the dolphins and other mammals without having them jump through a stupid hula-hoop to entertain them."

Claude sniffed. "The aquarium's income has increased dramatically since I instituted the shows two years ago."

Two years ago. Two years of a living hell. More for the dolphins than for her. Why couldn't things go back to the way they were before?

"You don't need the shows, Claude. Why don't you let me help you put a program together that's educational instead?"

He crossed his arms and peered at her over his glasses. "You? I think not. Go back to your lab, Dr. Quinlan. I'll speak to the reporters about our rescue mission."

And when exactly did the rescue mission become *his* rescue mission? Jaz shook her head and brushed past him without another word. Before she did something stupid, like call him a dickhead.

Somehow, some day, she'd get Claude Morton out of this aquarium and get all their lives back to normal.

Until then, she had dolphins to save.

* * * * *

"Dammit! Five more minutes and I'd have been there."

Triton paced in front of the monitors. The sick dolphins now resided in an aquarium. He'd heard their cries of distress and raced to the shore, only to find the aquarium's doctor had already arrived, as had her crew. What a fucking disaster.

For a month they'd been sick, and all of Oceana's medical advances had been unable to help them. Triton had watched them all, waiting to see if they'd beach, only they'd gotten to the shore without him knowing.

"She seems to care about them."

Triton nodded in response to Ronan's voice. "True, but she's a land human. I want the dolphins away from her and out of that zoo."

"Nothing you can do about it now. You know as well as I do that we can't just make twelve dolphins disappear from the aquarium."

He blew out a frustrated breath. "Yeah, I know." Oceana's rules forbade calling attention to their civilization. Removing the dolphins would be impossible. At least right now. "Let's just hope the female knows what she's doing. If she further harms the dolphins, I'll—"

"You'll do what?" Ronan interrupted. "You can't do anything to a land human. Our laws do not allow interference."

"Tell me something I don't already know."

"Trey," Ronan said, using his nickname. "You have a warped view of land females. You can't blame every woman for the pain Leelia caused you."

Trey ignored Ronan, concentrating instead on scanning the dolphins' vital signs. "It's strange. Whatever made them ill isn't showing up on our scanners. None of the common ailments are causing their distress."

Ronan sighed. "Probably something man-made, or a pollutant we haven't come across yet."

"Fucking great. Just what we need. A mystery we can't solve." And in the meantime, they could lose twelve of their dolphins. Unacceptable. But what could he do? They were in the hands of Dr. Jasmine Quinlan now. He knew of her, had heard she was a brilliant marine mammalian veterinarian, but she was still a land human and ignorant of the extensive knowledge available in Oceana.

"Go up there and work with her. See if you can't speed her along, or at least find out the cause so we can work on a cure down here."

No way had he heard Ronan correctly. He turned and arched a brow at the tall, imposing figure who was his brother and the leader of the guardians of the sea. "Wanna tell me that again?"

Ronan crossed his arms. "You heard me. Go up there. We'll set up impressive credentials for you. You can be another marine mammal veterinarian like Dr. Quinlan. I'll make sure that the land humans believe you've been assigned to assist her."

"Get someone else to do it, Ronan. You know I hate land."

"You're the guardian of the dolphins, Trey. Who else would you suggest I send?"

"Let Dane do it."

"Dane may have some of your dolphin skills, but he doesn't have the same scientific knowledge."

Shit. He knew he'd have to be the one to go. The safety and care of the dolphins was his responsibility. "I guess it'll be me, then. But I hate this and you damn well know it."

Ronan smiled. "I also know you don't want anyone else messing with your dolphins."

He had a point. "Fine. Get me a background and I'm outta here."

Ronan disappeared, leaving Trey to ponder the hundreds of reasons why he didn't want to go on land. None of which had to do with Dr. Jaz Quinlan. Impressive credentials, seemed to be genuinely concerned for the dolphins' welfare. But all he really knew about her read like a resume. What he did know was she was bound by land, something he simply didn't understand.

The lure of land. What was it about living above the water that was so appealing? Leelia had found terra irresistible, and had chosen a new life as a land human rather than spending the rest of hers in Oceana.

With him.

Women. They never knew what they wanted. Trey knew, though. They wanted whatever they couldn't have and no matter what they got they were never satisfied.

He stayed as far away from land humans as he could, preferring a quick fuck with one of the water sprites who wanted nothing more than to get him and themselves off in the process.

That's all women were good for. On land or under the sea.

So, he'd go and play undercover guardian and figure out what was happening with the dolphins. No better way to find out what was going on than to go directly to the source and get as close as possible to the doctor.

First, he wanted to check on the dolphins.

And he knew exactly how he was going to do it.

Chapter Two

රෝ

"Another dolphin has beached."

Jaz's gaze snapped to Tricia, the heavily panting assistant leaning against the doorway to the lab.

"Another one? Just one? Where?"

Tricia nodded, bent over and rested her hands on her knees. "Just one. Same place as yesterday. I ran as soon as I spotted it."

"Grab the hoist and let's get it up here, stat!"

Three hours later, they had the dolphin in the tank with the others.

"Wow, this one's huge, isn't he?" Tricia asked.

She nodded. "Yes. Has to be at least thirteen, fourteen feet."

He was beautiful. Long, sleek, clearly irritated as hell that he was ill. Funny enough, this one had no scarring. Most dolphins were riddled with scars and markings, but he was nearly perfect. And he didn't exhibit any of the symptoms of the others.

"I don't think this one is sick," Jaz said, extracting a blood sample and stroking the dolphin's back. "I think he's looking for the others and beached himself to find them. He must be the dominant male in the pod."

"Then he's one hellaciously brave guy to follow them to the beach." Tricia looked over at the tank and smiled.

"Yes, he is." Something about this one struck her. Perhaps his willingness to throw himself onto the beach in an effort to stay with his pod?

He certainly was a sight to behold. Strong, muscular, and healthy, too. After checking his vitals, she was convinced he did not have the same illness as the others.

"Hey there, pal," she said, rubbing her palms over his back. "You just wanted to be near your clan, didn't you?"

He responded to her touch by swimming closer to her hand.

"You like attention, don't you?" When she bent over and kissed his snout, his eyes followed her movements. Then he stared at her in a way she could only describe as…unusual. Almost like some intelligence lurked inside him, and if she willed it hard enough, he'd speak to her.

If only he could. She'd think she had died and gone to heaven. The dolphins had ten times the personality of any man she'd ever dated, and more charisma, too.

How bizarre to compare a dolphin to a man. And yet, considering the men she'd been with in her lifetime, she'd rather spend time with the dolphins. At least they had a personality, unlike the boring scientists she'd had relationships with. No wonder she preferred her vibrators to real sex.

It was a good thing her work kept her so busy. No time to ponder the fact she was thirty-years-old and had yet to find a man who appealed to her as much as the sea and all its creatures. Perhaps she was meant to live in the ocean instead of on land.

Maybe the man of her dreams lurked under the sea.

She snorted. For a scientist, she sure had some foolish notions. She should have left her childish dreams in her youth, where they belonged.

The dolphin raised its head against her hand as if seeking her touch.

She grinned at him. "I'll bet you have lots of things you'd like to tell me, don't you, pal?"

"Dr. Quinlan, what's going on here?"

The sound of Claude's voice made her wish she could morph into a dolphin and swim away with the perfect bottlenose here. If only wishes could come true.

"I'm working." She heard his footsteps on the wet cement and hoped his expensive Italian shoes warped in the salty water.

"Are the dolphins cured yet?"

"No."

"When will they be?"

"I have no idea."

"I need a timetable, now."

Jaz resisted the urge to tell him to shove his timetable up his ass. But the dolphins needed her more than she needed to tell off her boss. "As soon as I know something, you'll know something."

It was apparent he drew closer because his cologne overpowered the air. Amazing that a hundred bucks an ounce could smell so revolting. She preferred the saltwater scent of the ocean and the creatures inhabiting it to human males like Claude.

Apparently the dolphin felt the same way because he made a loud exhaling sound as Claude approached, his fins whipping from side to side. Clearly he was agitated at the administrator's arrival.

"I know exactly how you feel, pal," she whispered to the dolphin.

To further irritate Claude, she took out a piece of squid from the bucket at her feet and hand fed the dolphin. After he swallowed, she stroked his soft tongue.

"Tell me that isn't another dolphin," Claude said, wrinkling his nose as he eyed the squid pieces.

Well, she at least had to give him credit for recognizing that this bottlenose was slightly different in appearance than the others. "It's not another dolphin. It's a humpback whale."

She really wanted to add a *duh* to her answer. She didn't. But, damn, she really wanted to.

"And I suppose you rescued *this* one off the beach, too."

No, he swam up the beach and tossed himself into the tank, you moron. "Yes, as a matter of fact we did."

"Do you realize what it's costing us to house, feed and treat these dolphins?"

She moved her hand absently over the dolphin's snout. "Considering they haven't eaten and we don't know what's wrong with them, I'd say it hasn't cost much."

"Yet."

She shrugged. Whatever it took.

"You're playing fast and loose with the aquarium's budget, Dr. Quinlan. We're going to have to do something about this."

"Like what?" Maybe he'd fire himself. That would sure save money on the budget, considering the outlandish sum of money he made. Now that idea held a great appeal to her. Probably would to the board, too. If he didn't have family connections, Claude Morton wouldn't be in the position he was in now. As it was, he had no earthly idea how to run an aquarium. All he wanted to do was look good in front of his daddy by saving them money. As if the aquarium wasn't strapped for cash already because of his tightwad ways.

He tipped his chin down so he could peer at her over his glasses, a movement designed to intimidate. Jaz tried to hide her smirk. She'd been frowned upon by better people than him.

"They have to go. I'm going to have to discuss this with the board."

"You do that, Claude. In the meantime, I'll be treating these dolphins." She turned away but he grabbed her arm, his fingers digging into her skin. Before she could pull away, the bottlenose made a series of squeaking noises and soundly drenched Claude with a huge shot of water from his snout.

The scathing retort she wanted to give died on her lips as she gazed at a now soaked Claude. Jaz couldn't help the giggle that escaped her throat, just imagining the cost of Claude's dry-clean-only suit, now ruined by salt water. She turned to the dolphin and winked. "Way to go, pal."

Claude sputtered, rage evident on his face. For once, though, he seemed at a loss for words.

"You'd better change before you catch your death." On the other hand…

"We're not finished, Dr. Quinlan. I'll have you up for a board review within days."

"Give it your best shot, Claude."

He stormed off and she turned away. "Arrogant prick," she muttered, then stroked the dolphin again. "I owe you one, pal."

* * * * *

Arrogant prick was right. If Trey had his way he'd have morphed into his human form and soundly kicked that milquetoast's ass from here to the other side of the earth.

Dickhead. Angry welts circled Jaz's arm where Claude had grabbed her. There was nothing worse than a male who got off on hurting females. They were the lowest of life forms, in Trey's opinion.

Someday, Claude Morton would pay for hurting Jaz.

Not that Trey had any feelings for her. She was simply female and therefore needed protection.

Okay, maybe he'd been surprised at the way he'd reacted to her touch, her soft voice, the caring way she'd examined him. If he'd been in his human form, he'd have been hard pressed not to take her in his arms and taste her.

And that didn't sit well with him at all. He didn't have cravings. Not for a particular woman, anyway. If he wanted a fuck, he knew where to get one. And not once had he given a water sprite a second glance afterwards. Not that they cared, anyway, since pleasure was their primary focus, too.

"You seem as irritated as I am," Jaz said, petting his dolphin skin in a way that made him want to feel her touch on his human body.

Her green eyes mesmerized him, pools the color of the deep sea. Bright, round, with dark lashes that spiked against her brow despite the fact she wore none of the makeup land females were fond of. Her skin was tanned, her body lithe and athletic, showcasing very long legs and the most perfect ass he'd ever seen.

She was nothing like Leelia, who was dark and voluptuous, with eyes and hair like a midnight sky. And he'd loved Leelia's body, every inch of it. Jaz was like a sleek mermaid, her red hair flying behind her in the ocean breeze.

Her hands were perfection. Long fingers that he could well imagine wrapped around his—

Not good. Not at all. With a quick swish of his tail, he swam to the other side of the tank, searching for some distance from the woman he had no business feeling a spark of attraction for.

Merlin lay listless there.

"No progress?" he asked the ancient dolphin.

"Still about the same. How's the good doctor doing?"

"Can't tell."

"Then you need to resume your human shape and find out. We're getting more ill by the day, Triton."

"I know." Impotent frustration raged through him. He knew they were sick, and yet no one in Oceana could help them. What made any of them think a human could?

"She's special, that Dr. Quinlan."

"Why do you say that?" Trey peered over at her, watching the way Jaz handled one of the dolphins. Her low, sultry voice drifted toward him, permeating his senses and bringing thoughts to mind he had no business thinking.

"Because I know, Triton. I can feel her. She seems one of us."

"Ridiculous. She's a land human."

"Which means what, exactly? That she can't love the sea as much as you do?"

No one who lived on land could love the sea as much as the people and creatures of Oceana. "Yes, that's what it means."

"You just harbor resentment toward all females because of Leelia."

Would everyone continually remind him about his disastrous relationship with her? "This has nothing to do with her."

"Every move you make has to do with Leelia. You need to let it go, Triton. Let *her* go. Start living in the present and looking ahead. You never know when your future will be standing right in front of you." Merlin inclined his snout toward the other side of the tank.

Matchmakers wherever he went. "Why is it that all of you think that unless someone is mated for life they're not happy? I'm perfectly content with my life as it is. Which means I don't need to add anyone to it."

"Yes, you do."

"No, I don't."

Merlin coughed, ending their friendly argument.

"I'm going to the surface, will transform. See what I can find out. Maybe give the doctor a nudge in the right direction once I figure out what she's doing."

He watched her tend to the dolphins and wished he could be doing anything but what he had to do. He telepathically sent a message to Dane to come take his place as a dolphin tonight. Once the switch was made, he'd reintroduce himself to Dr. Jaz Quinlan.

And he'd bet all the treasures in the Afrendi shipwreck that she wouldn't be happy about meeting him.

Chapter Three

ജ

"Excuse me, but who are you again?" Jaz asked, eyeing the tall stranger who'd just stepped into Claude's office. Bad enough she had to be summoned away from her work so late in the evening, but then Claude quickly rattled off the guy's credentials and she barely heard a word of what he said.

Probably because she was busy picking her tongue up off the floor where it had dropped when she'd gazed into eyes the color of the Caribbean Sea. And those stunning eyes were framed by raven hair that fell across his forehead in a way that was sexy as hell.

Okay, maybe every damn thing about him was sexy, from the way his worn jeans fit snugly against his lean, muscled body, to the T-shirt that hugged his chest and shoulders.

Only one thought rolled through her mind then.

Sex. Hot, sweaty sex that went on for hours. She never had thoughts like that about men. Well, she did, but not lately. There were reasons she owned a dozen vibrators of varying shapes and textures. One was her complete lack of a social life, the other was the corresponding lack of a sex life.

Oh shit, and now he was talking and she hadn't heard a word he said.

"Sorry. My mind is elsewhere. Run that by me again?"

Claude interrupted with a heavy sigh. "Really, Dr. Quinlan, couldn't you at least try to pay attention?"

She shot Claude a scathing look and turned her attention to the dark hunk of gorgeous man before her. "My apologies. I'm working out some complex formulas in my head and they pull at my concentration."

His skin crinkled at the corners of his eyes when he offered her a half grin. "No problem. I do the same thing."

She arched a brow. "You do?"

"Yeah. I'm Triton Sanders." He extended his hand and she slid her fingers into his palm, instantly feeling the shock of sexual awareness. Her body warmed and flooded with desire, her panties dampening and her mind whirling with visions of the two of them tangled together in an intimate kiss.

Holy shit. She was way past the point of teenage fantasies, but man did she just have a humdinger of one.

"Triton?" she said, clearing her throat and hoping for some moisture on her dry-as-a-desert tongue. She looked around for water, anything.

"Most people call me Trey."

Claude had no trouble clearing *his* throat. Loudly. Jaz turned, her body flushing with embarrassment. Great. She did not need to be caught ogling a strange man in front of her idiot boss.

"As I was saying, Dr. Quinlan, Dr. Sanders here has been retained by the board of directors to…ah…assist you in your research."

"Assist me?" The warmth left her body in an instant, replaced by cold dread.

"Yes." The smirk on Claude's face told her she wasn't going to like what he had to say.

"Care to enlighten me as to what kind of assisting the board thinks I need?"

"Dr. Sanders is a marine mammalian specialist. His forte is the diseases prevalent in marine mammals. He's going to help you find a cure for the poor, sick dolphins."

Poor, sick dolphins her ass. If Claude had his way, they'd be rotting carcasses on the beach right now.

"I don't need any help, Claude, and you know that." She tried to keep her tone polite and professional, but she knew it came out sounding tight and irritated.

"Doesn't really concern me whether you think you need help or not, Dr. Quinlan. Dr. Sanders is here and he's staying until the dolphins are cured."

Claude stood, his way of dismissing her from his office. Jaz refused to budge, wanting to get Dr. Trey Sanders out of her hair before she left. "No offense to Dr. Sanders, but I work better alone."

"I'll try not to get in your way," Trey said, forcing her to look over at him again.

Would it appear unseemly if she both groaned and drooled over him? Really, she'd never get any work done with him underfoot Or under anything. Or over anything. Or next to—

Good God, she was experiencing some kind of libido-gone-wild episode! What was wrong with her, anyway? "I appreciate you making the trip from…where exactly are you from, Dr. Sanders?"

"It's Trey, and I'm from Philadelphia."

"I see." Philadelphia. Old money. Probably a friend of Claude's family. "And you know the Morton family?"

"Indirectly. My family is connected to theirs in many philanthropic ventures."

Ugh. Another preppie, rich-boy know-it-all. Just what she needed. Too bad her knowledge of his background didn't douse the flame burning hot and tight inside her right now. He'd opened some kind of portal to her sleeping sexuality and there'd be no closing it until she got a release. Which she planned to do as soon as she finished here.

Seeing that she clearly had no choice about working with him, she nodded. "Fine. Meet me in the lab in the morning and we'll get started. Just remember to stay the hell out of my way. The more you interfere," she said, making sure to cast a pointed look in Claude's direction, "the longer it'll take to figure out what's ailing the dolphins."

On her way out of Claude's office, she glanced at her watch. The realization struck that she hadn't had a break or any food yet today. She hurried back to her apartment and slammed the door with a resounding thud.

Her heart pounded against her ribs, her body bathed in sweat despite the cool weather outside.

Never in her life had she experienced such a fast and furious physical reaction to a man. And never had her body fired, moistened and practically sent her into the throes of orgasm just by standing next to a man.

But she was nearly there right now. Irritated, shaky, and craving a climax like she'd been denied far too long. She had to get back to work, she had no time for this.

Then again, she'd never be able to concentrate on her work until she released the tension inside. Ignoring the fact that she should get something to eat, she bypassed the kitchen and headed straight to her bedroom. Satisfying her libido seemed much more important than her hunger right now.

Rummaging quickly through her nightstand, she found the small bullet vibrator and turned it on, the whirring sound heightening her anticipation. She lay on the bed and slipped her sweats and panties down to her knees, spreading her legs as wide as she could.

The mere thought of Trey Sanders sent her spiraling into arousal. She closed her eyes, settling the egg against her throbbing clit. It slid easily against her skin, mixing with the juices of her desire.

He struck her as someone who spent a great deal of time in the sun. No tanning bed gave his skin that sun-kissed look. His jet-black hair and sea-blue eyes lent him a movie star appearance. The laid-back kind of star, the one that drove women crazy with his sultry looks. His body was perfectly shaped, wide at the shoulders, narrow at the waist and hips, his thighs muscular but not too beefy. She hated beefy.

A whimper escaped as she moved the bullet against a particularly sensitive area along her slit.

Was his cock as big as he was? He had to stand six three or four, easy. She wasn't short, either, and he was a giant next to her.

Big, tanned, gorgeous, sexy. "Oh, yes," she whispered, sliding the bullet into her pussy, teasing herself by withdrawing it, holding the whirring egg over her throbbing clit before slipping it down and over the folds again.

She raised her hips and shoved the bullet inside, thrumming her clit with the fingers of her other hand while she fucked herself with the vibrator.

It built up inside her, the heightened tension, the excitement, the anticipation of a much needed release. Her mind conjured up wicked images of what she and Trey could have done together if Claude hadn't been standing there.

What would Trey taste like? Sweet or salty? And would his cock fit in her mouth? Would he want to lick her pussy, suck on her clit until she flooded his tongue and face with her come? Would he jettison his own inside her eager mouth, letting her suck him until he had nothing left to give?

Oh, yes, there. She imagined him climbing on top of her, slipping his heavy cock deep into her pussy, then ramming it hard and fast until she screamed in ecstasy.

The sensations intensified. Soon, very soon. Jaz squeezed her legs together, letting the magical vibrator do its thing, feeling the waves crash over her as it built to a frenzied pace. She reached between her legs and circled her clit, rubbing fast and furious until the sudden rush of her orgasm flooded her pussy.

She bit her lip to keep from screaming out loud, but couldn't help the whimpers that escaped. Her hips bucked off the bed as her orgasm poured through every pore, every muscle and organ until she was drenched in sweat and her own juices.

When the waves subsided, she reached inside her still-quivering body and pulled the bullet out.

Jaz panted, trying to catch her breath. Good lord, that had been intense. How long had it been since she'd come? Days? Weeks maybe? Or had it been only yesterday?

She could hardly remember masturbating to such a furious crescendo. This one had seemed more intense than anything she had experienced recently.

Her mind drifted back to Trey Sanders, and her pussy spasmed, warming and opening. Her nipples beaded against her thin T-shirt, begging for his touch, his mouth, his hands on them.

She was ready for more.

She was ready for him.

She was in deep trouble.

* * * * *

Trey had known the minute she'd looked at him that he was in deep trouble with Dr. Jaz Quinlan. Her green eyes had darkened, pupils dilating. Her breath came in quick pants, her breasts rising and falling rapidly.

He'd caught her scent, a curious mixture of vanilla and an essence unique to a female. The scent of arousal. Her arousal.

And then he'd hardened instantly, shocking himself and forcing him to place the envelope containing his bogus portfolio in front of his erection so no one would see.

Thankfully she'd been too busy staring at his face and sneering at her boss to notice.

Damn, she was a spitfire. Hot, passionate and didn't want anyone to fuck with her or get in her way. And at the same time she oozed sexuality as if she carried it around with her like an extra skin. He'd felt her—all of her, vibrating against him, touching him in ways he hadn't been touched in a very long time. His senses tuned in to her scent, the way she moved, the way she kept fiddling with her hair until all he wanted to do was block out that moronic Claude, throw her on top of the desk and fuck her until they both screamed their release.

If his senses were any indication, she'd been thinking the same thing. She'd certainly scurried out of there as quickly as she could. Curious, as soon as she left he'd excused himself, found the apartment he'd been assigned to, and discovered it was next door to Jaz's.

He'd heard her, his sonar finely tuned, for some strange reason his body psychically connected to hers. Her breathing whispered to him through the walls, her quiet pants and moans driving him insane.

Granted, he couldn't see her, but he could well imagine what she was doing in there.

Lying on the bed, no doubt, her pants pulled down and her fingers strumming rapidly against her clit.

He wondered if she had a red thatch of hair on her mound that matched the beautiful curls on her head, or if she went bare. Either way, the thought enticed him, hardened him, made his balls pull up tight against his body.

Thoughts of masturbating along with her had entered his mind, but he stopped himself. Okay, maybe he had rubbed his cock through his jeans, but that only made the ache worse.

Then he'd heard her muffled cries, as if she were trying to hold back. He'd bet she was a screamer. He loved it when a woman screamed her orgasm out, letting it fly through her like the rush of an oncoming wave.

When she went quiet, he imagined her lying there, her body flush with her orgasm, her skin pink and vibrant, her pussy damp.

His cock strained against his jeans, begging for the chance to slide into her wet cunt. Too bad she wasn't there.

Nevertheless, why should he deny himself a little pleasure? She certainly hadn't.

He sat on the bed and unzipped his jeans, allowing his rigid cock to spring free. He closed his eyes and leaned back against the headboard, imagining her.

Her scent surrounded him and he placed his fingers over his shaft, lightly stroking. A visual entered his mind of Jaz standing at the foot of his bed, showing him how and where she touched herself, teaching him the secrets of her body so that he could please her the same way she pleased herself.

And then his hand became hers as she crawled up the bed and grasped his erection, her fingers tightening around the base and slowly slipping upward to the tip. She'd bend down and lick away his salty fluid, then put her lips on him, taking him deep inside the warm recesses of her mouth.

He groaned, unable to hold back, not caring at this moment if she banged on the wall and asked him what the fuck he was doing in here. Maybe if she did, he'd invite her over and ask her to watch him come.

And that thought tightened his balls into hard knots. They rested snug against his body, readying for release.

Release which wasn't going to take long. He quickened his strokes, visualizing her pussy beaded with moisture, knowing she'd taste like her scent...sweet, intoxicating, arousing. He'd want her to beg him to lick her pussy, then he'd want her to demand he make her come.

Her soft whimpers as she climaxed rang through his ears as he pumped his cock faster, tightening his grip on the shaft. Would her cunt be as tight as this? Would she wring out an orgasm so intense it would make him dizzy?

The sensations spiraled out of control. He let loose a low growl as his climax shot upward, wetting his own hand as he pumped his cock furiously, imagining that it was Jaz's pussy gripping him so tightly.

He panted, relaxed, slowly stroking until there was nothing left to give. He righted his clothing and went to wash up, not nearly satiated enough from his release.

A temporary release, unfortunately. His body was still on fire for Jasmine. But he refused to be swayed by the red-haired siren who'd seemed to capture him. No, he may have eavesdropped on her little escape into masturbation, but no way did that mean he wanted to fuck her In his fantasies, maybe. In reality, not a chance. He was tougher than that and could easily resist whatever temptation she threw at him.

In fact, it was still early and he'd be damned if he was going to wait to join her in the lab, knowing she'd put him off until tomorrow to purposely avoid him. Besides, Dane hadn't seemed all that pleased to have to while away the days in the aquarium tank. Truthfully, right now he wished he could trade places with his brother. The aquarium seemed much safer than here on land.

He waited for the sound of Jaz's door, then decided to fix himself a cool drink to douse the fire raging within him.

Hopefully, his desire for her would subside by the time he arrived at the lab.

Chapter Four

80

Jaz knew the minute Triton Sanders walked through the door. Her senses perked up, her body tuned into him like some weird radio frequency.

Damn. And just when she'd managed to get her thoughts under control. As it was, she was certain she still wore the stupid I-just-had-an-orgasm-and-damn-it-was-great grin on her face. The heat of a blush crept over her cheeks. Sometimes she hated being a redhead. Every freckle, every blush showed on her body like a damn blinking beacon.

She turned, intending to question him about why he ignored her request to meet in the morning, when his grin stopped her mouth from opening.

He looked at her with his brow arched and a knowing smile on his face as if he was aware of what she'd been doing twenty minutes ago.

No way could he know.

"I thought I told you we'd meet in the morning."

He shrugged and approached her. "I didn't want to wait. What are you doing?"

Trying to work alone and get thoughts of you out of my head. "Running the blood samples against some of the known toxins caused by pollution."

"Do you think a pollutant is the cause?"

"I don't know. Maybe. Frankly, it's too early to tell."

Trey stopped next to her, ignoring the way her cheeks reddened the closer he got. He avoided inhaling so he wouldn't breathe in her sultry scent. "Have you considered poisoning?"

She examined the data on the computer. "Yes. It's on my list to test. I'm hoping that's not it." She looked up at him. "Why would someone want to poison the dolphins?"

"Who knows? There are a lot of sick humans out there."

Tendrils of hair escaped her haphazard ponytail and curled along her cheek. He wanted to grab one and slide his fingers through the silken mass, then free the rest of it and bury his hands in her hair.

Damn. A rush of heat settled in his groin. He forced his thoughts to Oceanic formulas and away from sweet-smelling redheads.

Blood samples whirred softly in the analyzer. Trey took the opportunity to familiarize himself with the lab. All the latest technology, much of it state of the art.

"You have very impressive equipment," he stated, stifling his grin when she turned and gave him a wide-eyed look.

"Excuse me?"

"You know. Analyzers, chromatographs, microscopes. Lab equipment?"

"Oh! Oh, yes of course." She hurriedly turned away, but not before he caught her face turning pink again.

"I got the impression from Claude that your funding is somewhat limited."

"That's an understatement. He gives me very little to work with." She busied herself with one of the analyzers, continuing to avoid looking at him.

Trey peered into one of the microscopes, adjusting the viewer to clarify the image. "Where did you get the expensive equipment?"

"I do a lot of begging to big companies with money to burn and a cause to identify with."

Could she move any further from him? Whenever Trey sidled closer to view what she was working on, she'd move to a different analyzer or pick up a chart and make notes while she was walking away.

"Do I make you nervous?"

Her hand stilled on the clipboard but she didn't look up at him. "No, of course not. Why would you think that?"

"Because you keep blushing, and moving away from me whenever I get close."

"I do not."

He approached her, knowing he had no business challenging her this way, but he couldn't seem to help himself. "Prove it."

Then she did look at him, her gaze wary. "What?"

It had to be the way she seemed terrified of any contact with him that made him want to push her just a little bit. "I said prove it. We're going to be working closely together. If you run to the other side of the room every time I get close, this project is going to take twice as long."

In an obvious attempt at bravery, she lifted her chin. "I don't care where you stand. I'm simply used to working alone and don't need someone hovering over my shoulder."

"I wasn't hovering. I was looking."

"Well, quit looking and do some work." She thrust a clipboard at him. "Those are the notations from the first round of tests. The blood samples are over in the refrigerator."

They worked side by side through the evening, neither saying much other than calling out data or asking questions. Trey settled into a rhythm, studying the notes and tests that Jaz had run so far.

He had to admit, she was thorough. Most everything he would have thought of, she'd already done. Which didn't leave him much room for suggestion, but at least he knew now that she wasn't incompetent. In fact, she'd even thought of some angles that hadn't occurred to him. Grudgingly, he realized she wasn't inept. For a land human, that is.

By the time they'd run through all the tests, Trey realized they'd been up almost the entire night. Jaz yawned and covered her mouth, then rested her hands on her lower back and stretched. The movement thrust her breasts forward, her nipples straining against her tight T-shirt.

His cock responded, twitching and reminding him that the short relief he'd had earlier hadn't done nearly enough to dampen his arousal. With water sprites always available and willing, he rarely had to resort to masturbation for release.

"Muscles sore?" he asked.

She turned and shook her head. "I'm fine."

He caught her wince and the way she tried to stretch her neck.

"No, you're not. Nothing worse than lab work to tighten up your shoulders." He approached and stopped in front of her. "Turn around."

Her eyes narrowed. "Why?"

"So I can massage the kinks out."

From her expression of horror one would think he'd just offered to cut her throat.

"I can do that myself."

"You can rub your own shoulder blades? Now, this I'd like to see."

"Not what I meant. I'll take a hot bath when I get to my apartment."

Her statement conjured up visuals he'd just as soon not be having. "Turn around. I won't bite you." Although he'd like it, and he'd bet she would, too.

"No, really, I—"

"Just turn around!" He hadn't meant for it to come out so forceful, but she quickly turned her back to him, surprising him once again. She sure was hard to figure out.

Taking a deep breath, Trey laid his hands on her shoulders and closed his eyes as the feel of her silky skin shot through him like a bolt of lightning. When he pressed in on her muscles, she quickly inhaled, then let out a soft moan.

Oh, hell, whose brilliant idea was this? Every time he bore down against the tight muscles in her shoulders, she arched her back and let loose little whimpers and moans that sounded like whispered words of passion.

His cock responded by hardening, lengthening and being generally in his way. He didn't want to desire this woman. He didn't want to have images of sliding his shaft into her pussy and feeling her vaginal walls squeeze him until he spurted deep inside her. He didn't want to taste her lips to see if that scent of vanilla lingered on her mouth.

What was even worse was now that he'd started touching her, he didn't want to stop.

"That feels great," she said, sweeping her hair away from her neck. He wound his fingers slowly up toward the nape, brushing the silken tendrils aside, desperately wanting to place his lips there and see if she shivered when he kissed her.

He supposed groaning would be inappropriate right now, but damn if he found it difficult to keep from voicing his frustration. His hard-on pressed painfully against his jeans, pulsing and pounding from tip to base. Now he wished he hadn't listened in to Jaz's impromptu masturbation noises earlier.

"Um, Triton?"

"Call me Trey." He ran his fingers up the nape of her neck, gently massaging the base of her scalp.

"Trey?"

"Yes."

"I think that's good enough now."

"Is it?" He didn't want to stop. What would she do if he turned her around, swept her into his arms and took what he wanted so desperately to take? "Are you sure it's good enough, or do you want more?"

She stilled. All he heard was her breathing—rapid inhales and exhales. Her scent floated around him, that curious mix again of vanilla and aroused female. He took a chance and pressed closer, feeling her tense when his erection brushed against her buttocks.

But she didn't move away, didn't turn around, didn't slap him or tell him to stop.

She stiffened, then sighed. A long, shuddering breath that tore away the last vestiges of self-control he possessed. He turned her around and gazed at her face. Her eyes were dark green pools of desire. Her tongue swept out and licked across her bottom lip.

Oh no. He wanted to be the one to lick her lips. He bent toward her and brushed his tongue along the seam of her lips, tasting where she had just tasted. She gasped in a feather light whisper.

"What are you doing?" she asked.

"I'm kissing you. Do you mind?"

Confusion furrowed her brow. "Um, no, I guess not. But I should mind."

"Why?"

The question hung suspended between them for a few seconds. Then she shook her head, her hair falling toward her face. "I have no idea."

When she wound her arms around his neck and pressed her lithe body against his, he lost it completely. Any hold he had on what was right or wrong disappeared when she touched him.

He pulled her roughly against him until every inch of her body that was able to touched his. Her mound pressed against his erection and he rocked against her, rewarded with her whimper of pleasure.

Then he did what he'd wanted to do from the moment he'd met her—he tasted her mouth, his tongue diving inside as soon as he pressed his lips against hers.

What was she doing? Jaz tried to clear her head, unable to believe she'd just willingly stepped into the embrace of a virtual stranger. And yet since the moment she'd met him she'd felt connected to him.

This contact seemed preordained, as if she'd been meant to touch him, kiss him, feel his hands roaming over her body. She welcomed it despite the fact her behavior was totally insane and completely unlike her.

His lips were full and warm. His mouth tasted of coffee and some kind of minty flavor. Peppermints, that was it. One of her favorite candies. She licked the flavor off his tongue and he groaned, his fingers digging into her hips as he ground his sizeable erection against her. The heat of his shaft burned through his clothes and hers. She wanted nothing more at that moment than to feel him buried deep inside her.

She tilted her head back, allowing him access to her neck. His lips seared her skin as he traveled from her chin to her collarbone, licking the hollowed spot there. She shivered, wanting more than she dare ask for.

But he instinctively seemed to know what she craved. He turned her again so her back was to him, then snaked his hand down over her collarbone and across her shoulder, leaving a hot trail down her arm. When he crossed over and palmed her abdomen, her belly quivered. His hand hovered close to the waistband of her pants. Would he slip his fingers inside and plunge them into her pussy?

Did she want him to? Oh, hell yes she wanted him to.

He didn't. Instead, he reached under her top and moved his hand upward, flaming her desire with every touch of his palm against her bare skin. When he reached her ribcage and swept his hand up over her breast, her knees nearly buckled. He wrapped one arm around her middle and teased first one, then the other breast, thrumming her nipples until they stood hard and rigid under his questing fingers.

He pulled her shirt up and over her breasts, freeing them for his touch. The rise and fall of her chest thrust her breasts deeper into his hands. She looked down and watched him roll a nipple between his thumb and forefinger. The spark of his touch shot between her legs, wetting her, readying her for him.

She bit her lip to keep from begging him to touch her clit, to send her over the edge. Her episode earlier with the bullet vibrator did nothing to assuage her hunger for release. If anything, it only heightened her sexual senses to the point where the slightest movement of his hand against her pussy would shoot her off like a rocket.

"Do you enjoy my touch?"

His words, whispered against her ear, were like a soft caress. She shivered.

"Yes."

"Do you want more?"

"Yes."

"Then touch me, Jaz. Reach behind you and touch me."

She did, gladly, eager to palm his hard shaft. He rocked forward, pressing his erection against her hand. She cupped him, sliding her fingers over denim and wishing it would magically disappear so she could feel his hot, hard length in her hand.

"Do you want my cock in your pussy?"

She closed her eyes, her mind awash in images of just that. Trey hovering over her, spreading her legs wide and lifting her hips. His gaze would be glued to hers. She'd want to watch his eyes, watch them darken when he slid inside her.

"Yes."

"Yes, what?"

"Yes, I want you."

"No. Tell me what you want, Jaz. Tell me exactly what you want."

He tortured her, making her say it when he knew damn well what she wanted. She'd never been vocal during sex. The men she'd been with previously hadn't wanted to hear what she liked.

Sex had been quiet, in and out, she thought with a laugh. No talking, nothing like this burning inferno of heat that Trey had conjured up inside her.

His desire for her frightened her and excited her at the same time. She shouldn't do this with a stranger. Definitely not with a professional colleague.

But she wanted it. Now, here, just like this. And she wanted to tell him exactly how.

"I want your cock in my pussy, Trey. Fuck me."

He laughed then, a husky rumble that tripped through her senses, making her shiver, making her want, making her need him.

She turned, ready to face him, ready to beg him to take her right here, right now.

Then she froze at the sound of footsteps outside.

"Shit!" was Trey's whispered response to the sound.

She quickly moved away, righting her clothes and hoping like hell she didn't wear a telltale blush on her cheeks. Her lips felt swollen from his deep kisses, her body on fire and so near completion she could finish herself off in seconds.

She quickly glanced his way, only to find him sitting on a stool, his face buried in the microscope.

By the time four of her lab assistants entered the room, she was head down in her own research. She just hoped she looked more innocent than she felt.

"Wow, you two are at it early this morning," Bob, one of her lab assistants said as he strolled in.

He had no idea how close they'd come to really being at it. She nodded and tried for a smile. "Thought we'd get a head start."

Head start? Hell, she hadn't been to sleep yet. She glanced at the clock and realized it was already five in the morning.

She'd just spent the night with Trey Sanders, only not in the way she'd wanted to.

Chapter Five

ဢ

"Are you insane?" Dane flapped his fin and communicated in the squeaks and sounds of dolphin language. Trey really needed a friendly ear, and one of his guardian brothers was as friendly as it was going to get in this hostile land environment.

He couldn't believe what he'd almost done with Jaz. "Yes, apparently I am. I don't know what I was thinking."

"So, you're telling me you had a chance to have sex with the hot redhead and you blew it?"

Not quite the kind of ear he wanted. "No. I'm telling you I almost fucked her and that's why I'm insane."

"Okay, I'm a little confused here. The bad thing is you almost fucked her. Meaning you're glad you didn't finish what you'd started?"

Sometimes Dane irritated the hell out of him. "The bad thing is that I almost fucked her. I shouldn't have touched her."

"Why the hell not? From what you told me, she was more than eager to do it."

"She was."

"Then, what's the problem?"

Trey rolled his eyes. "The problem is I don't want to fuck her."

"Why not?"

"You're supposed to be helping me!"

"How can I help you if you don't make sense?" Dane dove down and came back up, spraying water in Trey's face.

"Cut that out, dammit!"

"Hey, I have a solution," Dane said.

"What?"

"Trade places with me. You swim around in the aquarium, and I'll go fuck the nice doctor."

He leveled a glare at the dolphin. "You're an asshole, Dane."

"So you've told me." He winked at Trey, then chattered noisily.

"Would you stop that? Someone will hear you."

"Who are you talking to?"

Someone *had* heard. Jaz. Damn. He whirled around and offered an innocent smile. "Just talking to the dolphin."

She crossed her arms and lifted a brow, then approached him, her tennis-shoed feet squishing in the water-clogged walkway. "You were talking, the dolphin was chattering. You make a habit of having conversations with mammals?"

"As often as I can. They typically provide more intelligent responses than humans."

Her lips quirked. "I don't disagree with you there. I'd much rather talk to them than the people around here. However, they usually don't talk back."

"Sure they do. You're just not listening."

Jaz tilted her head as if she seriously considered his words. He really needed to be more careful with what he said around her.

She brushed past him and grabbed the bucket, tossing a squid piece to Dane, who greedily ate and then put his snout under her hand.

With gentle strokes, she caressed Dane's back. Trey followed the movements of her hand, mesmerized by her gentle touch, remembering what it felt like when she petted him that way. He had a sudden urge to switch places with Dane.

"Have you studied dolphin language?" she asked.

He tore his gaze away from her hands and met her curious sea-green eyes. "Actually I have."

"They have a syntactic or hierarchic communication system. I've done a bit of studying myself. It's quite easy to communicate with dolphins, in a crude fashion, of course. Mainly hand signals and learning their vocal responses to certain stimuli."

Uh huh. He had no idea what she was saying, because his mind was elsewhere. The morning sun hadn't yet broken through, leaving a distinct chill in the fog-enshrouded air. She hadn't zipped her jacket. And he already knew she wore no bra under that flimsy top. Her nipples peaked hard underneath the shirt. His cock still ached from their near-encounter in the lab a couple hours ago.

"Am I boring you?"

He cleared his head of thoughts of her naked and lying on one of the lab tables, and said, "Sorry. My brain is a little fuzzy. Add lack of sleep to the jet lag from the trip yesterday."

She blushed at his mention of lack of sleep. Obviously, she was thinking the same thing he was—exactly what they'd been doing while neither of them were sleeping. "No, I'm sorry. I should have forced you to go to bed last night."

"So, you like to dominate?"

"Not at all! Oh…oh, you meant…"

She sucked in her bottom lip. He traced that lip with his thumb. "You're going to have to quit blushing if you're going to work around me, Jaz. I always say what's on my mind."

She took a quick step back. "I'm not blushing. It's the wind."

He looked toward the ocean. "There's no breeze."

"It's cold."

"I can tell." He made a point of looking down at her chest, causing her cheeks to pinken further. "Like I said, I always say what I think."

"Want to know what I think?" she asked.

"Sure."

"I think you're dangerous. And I think I need to go take a shower and get a little sleep. See you later, Dr. Sanders."

"It's Trey," he said, but she was already walking swiftly away.

"Smooth move there, Casanova."

"Fuck off, Dane." Trey stormed away, intent on getting a little sleep himself. Dane's dolphin laughter resounded in the quiet morning.

* * * * *

Jaz stretched and looked at the clock, grimacing at the red numbers glaring back at her.

Noon. She'd gotten five hours of sleep. At least they were five good hours. She'd crashed and slept like the dead, refusing to let her mind dwell on the dolphins or on Trey and what she'd almost done with him last night.

Almost? Hell, if her assistants hadn't gotten an early start and walked in on them, she'd have gladly dropped her pants and spread her legs. She'd been so damned eager to feel his cock inside her she'd have begged if necessary.

Rolling over and stretching, the cool sheets scraped against her sensitive nipples. Her mind wandered to remembrances of Trey's fingers on her breasts. Her pussy dampened and she longed to reach down and massage away the throbbing arousal building there.

But not now. She had no time to while away extra minutes pleasuring herself. But she'd damn well do that later to take the edge off. The last thing she needed right now was to drool on Trey while they were trying to work together.

She stepped into the shower, hoping the hot water would rinse away any desire she felt for him.

Unfortunately, the water in the apartment next door turned on at the same time.

Trey was in his shower, too. Oh, God, why couldn't she screw her head on straight about him? She barely knew him, and yet almost had sex with him. That kind of behavior wasn't her at all. She rarely had time for men and relationships, and she sure didn't want one with Trey Sanders.

But thoughts of him standing in his shower shot through her mind. Naked, his body glistening with soap and droplets of water. Would he touch himself? Stroke that fabulous cock until it got hard, pumping faster and faster until he shot a hard stream of come against the tile wall? Would he think of her as he did it?

He was probably thinking about blood poisons and possible bacterial infections related to the dolphins. Surely not about her. Sometimes her own stupidity astounded her. She poured soap into her hands, determined to wash away every image of him.

How would his hands feel running down her legs, feeling her calves, the soles of her feet?

No! Stop, stop, stop! She rinsed off and then lathered her hair, breaking into song to keep her dirty little mind occupied elsewhere and off visuals of a certain doctor's sexy, naked ass.

By the time she'd dried her hair and put it up on top of her head, she felt much more assured that she could, in fact, handle working around Trey. After all, she had all those vibrators that gave her such pleasure. She could anticipate their touch, not his.

She had just slipped into her shorts and tank top when a knock sounded at her door. She opened it to find the man who occupied her mind standing there with a grin on his face. His clean, just-showered scent blew in with the breeze, making her mouth water. His hair was still damp, one wavy, raven lock falling over her forehead. She balled her hands into fists to keep from reaching out and sweeping it away from his face.

"I heard your shower going , so figured you were up and moving about. Ready to get started?"

"Sure," she said with as confident an air as she could muster. Bound and determined to think only about her job, she said, "I want to check on the dolphins first. I'll meet you at the lab."

"I'll come with you. I want to check their appearance, temperature and skin tone today."

Great. He was like a leech, sucking onto her and tagging along wherever she went. How was she supposed to think about having sex with her vibrators when a living, breathing man with a cock followed her around?

She'd just ignore him. When they arrived at the tank, she slid into her wetsuit and climbed into the pool, checking all the dolphins.

"No change here. No improvement, but at least they haven't gotten worse."

Trey had donned his wetsuit and stood over one of the dolphins, petting its skin. "Same here. So whatever the problem, it's slow acting."

"I wonder how long they've shown symptoms?"

"About a month before they beached."

She stilled and looked up at him. "How would you know that?"

He stared back at her for a few long seconds, then said, "Just a guess. From the looks of their skin and the level of toxins in their bodies, I'd say whatever it is has been working on their internal systems for about that long."

"Oh." He'd seemed so assured about the time frame. How odd.

"Maybe we should take some coral samples," he said.

"Coral samples? Why?"

"Because if the coral is affected somehow, they may emit a toxin. It's been known to happen."

"I haven't seen any evidence of pollutants in the area or bleaching of the coral."

"Nevertheless, it bears a sample or two. I'll go collect some and meet you at the lab."

She nodded and he took off quickly toward the supply station to grab a sample kit. Funny, he didn't take a mask, fins or tank. How close did he think the coral was? She was about to try and catch up with him, but then figured he'd end up coming back when he remembered he didn't have a tank.

Jaz turned back to the dolphins, expecting to hear the gate open any second. But when she didn't, she stood on the edge of the aquarium rim, looking over the fence toward the beach.

Trey was gone. Not on his way back, either.

That's odd. She stepped out of the tank and headed down to the beach, searching for him.

She must have stood there a good half hour. No sight of him. Now she was beginning to worry. Surely he wouldn't dive without a tank. The water was murky, the coral located quite a distance down. No way he could get there, grab samples and get back up without needing a breath.

He must have changed his mind and gone to the lab or his apartment. Maybe he was going to dive later in the day. Feeling more than a little stupid, she was about to turn and head back to the lab when something bobbed out of the water.

It was Trey. A chill shivered up her spine as she watched him walk out of the surf.

He paused when he saw her, then smiled. "Success. Got a few samples. There's a bit of bleaching on a crop of coral down there."

"How far down there?"

"A ways."

He started to walk past her but she grabbed his arm, noting how warm his skin below the short-sleeved wetsuit felt to the touch. She'd been in these waters a lot. They were cold. Her teeth usually chattered by the time she surfaced. His body temperature was normal, which wasn't…normal.

"Wait a second. Do you realize how long you were down there?"

"No. I didn't have a watch on."

"Over a half hour."

He rolled his eyes at her. "I think you're wrong. I couldn't have been down there that long."

"Why not?"

"Because I'm not wearing a tank."

"And why is that?"

He shrugged, the wetsuit clinging tight against his broad chest. She ignored the pull of attraction.

"Because I didn't need one. I looked at the underwater maps of the area. I knew how far down I had to go and I was in a hurry. Didn't need a tank."

"That's ridiculous, Trey," she said, walking quickly beside him as he headed toward the aquarium. "No one goes into those waters without an air tank. How could you even see without a mask?"

"I've got great underwater vision. And I can hold my breath for a long time."

"Not that long. Not for a half hour. No human can."

He paused and turned to her, his blue-eyed gaze focused on her face. She squirmed a bit, but held her ground, waiting for him to say something. "Okay, you got me. I'm an underwater superman, posing as a mild mannered marine scientist."

"You're full of shit."

"So I've been told." He walked away, hollering something about changing before meeting her in the lab.

She stood there, her mind whirling with questions and feeling stupid for even thinking the things she was thinking.

There was something strange about Triton Sanders. Something that didn't sit right with her sense of logic. Damned if she knew whether it was the scientist in her, or the woman in her, that found him so compelling and enigmatic.

But she was determined to find out more about him. Starting tonight.

Chapter Six

⅋

"Would you like to have dinner at my place tonight?"

Trey looked up from the printouts of yesterday's lab results, certain he'd heard Jaz wrong. "Dinner? At your place?"

She offered a half smile that he wanted to lick from her lips. "Did I not say it loud enough?"

"I heard you. But why?"

"Why what?"

"Why dinner?"

She shrugged and turned away. "Just thought it would give us a chance to get better acquainted. Maybe go over some of the tests we ran today."

They were alone in the lab, the rest of the staff already gone for the day. Trey had worked diligently, forcing his mind to focus on research instead of on Jaz, where it sure as hell didn't belong.

And now she wanted him over for dinner? Considering the chemistry between them, that could only spell disaster.

"I *can* cook, you know."

He'd bet she could, in more ways than one. He shifted against the heaviness pulling in his groin. Unable to come up with a reasonable enough excuse to say no, he nodded and smiled. "Sure. Dinner at your place. What time?"

Jaz glanced up at the clock. "It's five-thirty now. How about eight? I have a few things to finish up here and then I'll go start dinner."

Several hours later, Trey stood at the door to Jaz's apartment, a bottle of wine and a bouquet of wildflowers in his hand.

"Idiot," he mumbled. "Flowers and wine. This isn't a date. She's going to think you're a fucking moron."

What possessed him to go to the market and buy wine and flowers was beyond his ability to understand. But impulse drove him, and he typically followed his instincts.

He was fairly certain that this time, his instincts had led him astray. Nevertheless, he was here. He knocked.

"Door's open!" she yelled. "Come on in!"

He stepped in, the smell of something incredible permeating the room of her small apartment. It looked similar to his in design, but definitely better decorated. Small plants littered every table and windowsill, and the couch in front of the fireplace was draped in afghans and colorful blankets, an open book sitting on the center cushion.

It was warm and comfortable. Nothing like his apartment.

He followed the delicious spicy scent into the small kitchen. Jaz's hair was piled high on her head, loose ringlets of red curls draping down. Her neck was exposed and Trey was pummeled by a burning desire to kiss the soft skin exposed at her nape.

She wore shorts and a sweatshirt, her long legs tantalizing him and making him wonder how they'd feel wrapped tight around him. His jeans tightened uncomfortably.

"I put the lab results on the table over there," she said without turning around, pointing toward a chrome and glass round table nestled in the breakfast nook. "Go ahead and get started. I'm almost finished here."

He set the wine and flowers on the empty counter, feeling stupid for bringing them. Clearly, this was a business dinner. He wondered if she'd notice if he grabbed them and left, then returned with his business head screwed on straight.

"You're awfully quiet tonight." She turned and smiled.

When she spied the bottle and flowers, her smile died. She met his gaze, curiosity etched on her features. "You brought those for me?"

He nodded, feeling every bit the idiot.

Jaz fingered the petals of the daisies intermixed with purple freesia. She picked up the bundle and held them to her nose, closed her eyes and inhaled.

Time stopped as he watched her, fascinated with the look of pleasure on her face.

"They're beautiful and smell heavenly. Thank you, Trey."

Her whispered voice was like a soft caress over his skin. "You're welcome."

"Would you open the wine? I haven't had wine in ages." She pulled a corkscrew out of the drawer and handed it to him, then reached in her cabinet for two glasses.

Trey studied the way her shorts lifted and tightened against her buttocks. He was experiencing some tightening of his own.

Focus. Work. Dolphins. Lab Results.

By the time he'd opened and poured the wine, Jaz had dinner on the table.

A vegetable lasagna that melted in his mouth had him wolfing down the food.

"This is fabulous," he said between mouthfuls.

Her eyes sparkled. "Thanks. I like to cook."

Being single, he didn't spend a lot of time thinking about or preparing food. The ocean was filled with things to eat. He hadn't realized before what he was missing.

After consuming two platefuls of food and a few glasses of wine, he finally pushed back from the table and looked over at Jaz.

She watched him, toying with her half-eaten plate of food.

"What?" he asked.

"I've just never seen someone eat so much. Were you starving?"

He laughed. "Probably. Sometimes I forget I'm supposed to eat."

She nodded. "I know the feeling."

They cleaned up the dishes, then spread the lab reports out on the table. Jaz finished her wine and absently held her glass out for Trey to refill while she kept her focus on the results.

"It has to be some kind of bacteria," she murmured.

He handed the glass back to her. Their fingers touched and she met his gaze, her eyes curious and confused. Probably the same as his. What was it about this woman that sizzled his insides and made him want her?

She was a land female, of average looks and decent intelligence. Nothing like the raving beauty of the sea sprites, nothing like the charismatic mermaids, nothing like any of the women in Oceana.

And yet, suddenly every Oceanic female species paled in comparison to this alluring redhead with eyes like the green hills near his home in the sea.

Sex. It had to be sex. He hadn't had any in awhile, clearly he was physically attracted to Jaz, and he hadn't had a decent release in too long. She'd fired up his libido, and it wasn't going to dampen until he'd doused the fire.

"What do you think?" she asked.

He had no idea, since he hadn't heard her question. "What do I think about what?"

Jaz looked up from her paperwork. "Bacteria. I said I think the problem is bacterial."

Focus, Trey, focus. "Could be. But if it is, it's no bacteria I've ever encountered."

She nodded. "That has to be what it is. It can't be viral or a communicable infection, because not all the dolphins have it. The Bottlenose who washed up the day after the rest of them shows no signs of infection. As far as the symptoms, fever, elevated white blood cell count, all points to bacterial. But the tests we've run so far indicate no known bacterial elements present in any of the dolphins' blood. And all their blood counts are nearly similar."

He poured another glass of wine for them both, hoping the alcohol would dull his senses and make him immune to her. So far, no success. He barely listened to what she said, his thoughts wrapped around undressing her with his teeth.

Fortunately, she barely noticed, so intent on her charts and graphs and analysis and rattling off data. Analysis he'd poured over hours ago, coming to the same conclusions she was telling him about now.

"What about gastroscopy?" he suggested.

She looked up. "You think it may have a gastrointestinal cause?"

He shrugged. "It's a possibility. Although there are no sponges adhering to the intestinal wall, causing infection."

"Palpation. Typically, infection by sponge adherence is palpable in swollen abdominal cavity. You can run ultrasound if you'd like, but I doubt that's the cause."

"Well, they haven't exhibited any vomiting or gastrointestinal distress. I think you're off base here."

Of course, she had no idea how much of an expert he really was. "It's a waste of money to run ultrasound. Try lavage instead," he suggested.

She arched a brow. "This is my lab, Dr. Sanders. I think I know what's best for my dolphins."

"Your dolphins, are they? Do they know that you've claimed ownership of them?"

"You know what I meant. I'll order the ultrasounds in the morning."

"Are you always so obstinate, or are you really convinced you're always right?"

"What makes you think your theory is correct?"

"I don't have a theory," he said, swallowing the last of the wine. He stood and stretched. "I just know what it isn't."

"I'm not willing to gamble on the dolphins' lives just to save a few bucks. Frankly, I'm surprised you would be."

She had no idea what lengths he was going to in order to save the dolphins. He wished he could tell her, but he couldn't. So, she thought him uncaring. Didn't bother him one bit.

"Go for it. Waste the aquarium's money. You'll find no evidence of sponges."

She approached him, stopping inches away, suspicion evident in her narrowed eyes. "Did Claude hire you to keep watch over my spending?"

"Huh?"

"You heard me. I know how much that penny-pinching sonofabitch wants to save a buck or two. You sound just like him. Willing to sacrifice the lives of the dolphins to save money. Money he and his family have plenty of."

"I have nothing to do with Claude Morton or his money. My concern lies with the dolphins, and they're the only thing I'm interested in." He meant that in more ways than one, the least of which was his ever-growing attraction to her.

And she must have caught on to that, because she glanced at the flowers sitting in a vase on the kitchen table. "Really? And here I thought you were wining and dining me to get me into bed."

"Whatever gave you that idea?"

"The wine, the flowers, the lab yesterday. You were all over me."

"The wine and the flowers were nothing more than a thank you for cooking me dinner. As far as what happened in the lab yesterday, you know as well as I do that's simply biology. We're both healthy, sexual beings and got carried away, but it's not personal. I'm sorry if you thought I was interested in you personally, Dr. Quinlan. You're way off base here."

She flushed, and he felt like an asshole. She was closer to the mark than even he wanted to admit to himself.

"I see. Thanks for coming and going over the paperwork with me. If you don't mind, I have work I'd like to do tonight, so I'm going to excuse myself and head to the lab."

Thank God. He'd finally be able to get away from her and focus on making the dolphins well. "Fine. Thank you for dinner."

He made his exit as quickly as he could, shutting and locking the door to his apartment.

He heard her door open and close again no more than five minutes later.

Trey paced for a while, knowing he should go down there and help her, but also aware that wouldn't be the smartest move right now.

They couldn't see eye to eye on anything, he knew things he couldn't tell her about, and as a result they'd delay analysis of the real problem with the dolphins.

He'd have done better to just take the dolphins out of the aquarium and let the land humans wonder what the fuck had happened. At least he'd have them in the ocean where he could test them in his own way, find out what was wrong and hopefully cure them.

Not that they'd had any luck doing that before they beached themselves. He scrubbed his hand over his face.

Goddamn Ronan and his brilliant ideas.

He needed a swim, to cool off and clear his head.

Mainly, he needed to stay as far away from Jaz as possible.

He stormed out of the apartment and headed to the beach, shedding his clothes on the sand and diving into the water.

He swam fast and deep, down past where humans could safely travel.

Toward Oceana, its lights and transparent structures calming him.

Home. Where he needed to be. Where he was supposed to be. The place that always made him feel good.

Except right now his thoughts focused on the surface, on land. On the dolphins, and on Jaz. He pictured her in the lab, working alone this late at night. Her hair would escape her ponytail and frame her face. Her beautiful, creamy face.

She'd stretch, her breasts pressing up against the little shirts she wore, her nipples hardening as they rubbed against the material.

Trey closed his eyes and willed her out of his thoughts, but they persisted. He should just go fuck a sea sprite, let loose of some of his pent up anxiety and sexual frustration.

Except for the first time, the thought of release from one of the sprites did nothing for him. Where they'd always appealed to him before, now they couldn't hold a candle to the flame sparked within him by a certain land female.

Ah, hell.

He left his sanctuary and soared toward the surface.

Chapter Seven

ဢ

"Don't know what I'm doing, my ass," Jaz mumbled, still angry as hell at Trey's condescending tone.

She'd never been questioned about her work before, by any colleague. The only one who'd ever challenged her was Claude, and his interest was mainly financial. At a cost of over two thousand dollars a day, taking on an additional dozen or so dolphins was a burden for the aquarium. She knew that, but it still didn't deter from her determination to care for them until they could be released.

And damn Triton Sanders for making her feel incompetent. She knew what she was doing. She was one of the best in her field, and she'd be damned if she'd allow him to make her second guess herself.

He certainly knew how to piss her off. Now if she could just work her frustration into some productivity, maybe she'd be able to figure out this whole mystery in short order.

But her thoughts kept drifting back to Trey. How he'd looked standing in her kitchen tonight, his jeans snug against his thighs and cupping his near perfect ass. The way his dark hair accentuated the crystal blue of his eyes. The wine and the flowers.

Had anyone ever brought her wine and flowers before? Not that she could recall. She'd been so touched, she was speechless. Of course, she'd taken it personally and she shouldn't have. He'd just been brought up to bring thank you gifts to dinner. It had nothing to do with her.

But then again, the way he looked at her sometimes, like he wanted to strip her naked and devour her on the spot, sent thoughts of doing dark and wicked things with him soaring through her mind.

Triton Sanders was a confusing mix of potent, sexual male and irritating as hell man. He intrigued and at the same time infuriated her.

And she'd never desired a man more than she did him.

She leaned away from the microscope, seeing nothing in the smears she'd taken earlier that would give her any clue as to the bacteria causing the dolphins' illness.

Frustration on so many levels hammered at her, the least of which was her conversation with Trey tonight.

She thought back over the handful of relationships she'd had in the past. Mainly other biologists like her. One in college, the rest as she'd moved through her education and work life. Boring. None gave her a spark. Sex had been biological, and at that not even great biology.

No man had ever made her come. And she wasn't difficult. With her vibrator she came like a wild woman, so why did a man's touch fail to take her over the edge?

Easy answer. Wrong men. Men who didn't care whether she was pleasured or not, or who were so completely inept they couldn't bring her to orgasm with their hands or their mouths.

She sighed, wrapping her arms around herself to ward off the sudden chill of loneliness that crept around her. Was she doomed to spend the rest of her life alone?

Since Trey walked into her life, she'd felt more heat, more life, than she'd felt...ever. But they were completely wrong for each other. He was old money and rich lifestyle. She was the child of California hippies, poor on money but rich on love.

Her parents were happy. Why wasn't she? Because they'd found a love she could never hope to duplicate?

She'd certainly never find anything like that with someone like Trey. There was a cold wariness to him that chilled her.

Yet at the same time, a fire burned within him that she connected to on many levels. Just thinking about his internal heat shot sparks of arousal deep in her belly.

She massaged the tense ache in her neck, resigned to working alone through the night.

That is, until she heard the creak of the lab door opening.

Quickly turning around, she saw the one person she didn't want to see again tonight.

"Trey."

His hair was wet. Had he showered?

His clothes clung to his wet body.

"Where've you been? In the aquarium?"

"I went for a swim in the ocean."

Her jaw nearly dropped. "Now? It's freezing out there."

He ignored her comment and approached her slowly. His jaw was clenched tight, his lips a straight line.

"Is there something wrong?" she asked.

"Hell yes there's something wrong."

Not again. She couldn't handle another altercation with him tonight.

"What is it?"

With each of his determined, agonizingly slow steps across the room, she grew more and more nervous. He seemed really agitated. Her heart pummeled her ribs and her palms began to sweat.

Despite the fact he was scaring the living hell out of her, she couldn't be more aroused. Something elemental passed between them, some unspoken language that told her exactly what it was that irritated him.

The same thing causing her to lose her focus and think only of him.

By the time he reached her, she was more than ready. He grabbed her, pulling her roughly into his arms, his mouth crashing down on hers without a single word spoken between them.

She met his assault eagerly, her passions ignited before the first touch of his lips on hers. He thrust his tongue inside, devouring her with his none-too-tender mouth.

His hands were everywhere, roaming along her back, grabbing her buttocks and pulling her against his erection. She whimpered and ground against his cock, desperately wanting him inside her.

Jaz inhaled his scent, fresh and tangy. She tore her mouth away from his to kiss his neck, licking at the salty ocean drops that still lingered on his skin. He groaned and dug his hands into her hips, then reached up, pulling her tank top off.

Her breasts filled his hands, his thumbs finding and flicking her already hardened nipples. He bent his head and tasted first one, then the other, licking her over and over again until she feared she would faint.

"Trey," she gasped, "please."

He lifted his head and met her gaze, his eyes dark with passion. "Yes. Beg me for it, Jasmine."

Oh, God. She couldn't, wouldn't, had never begged a man to fuck her. But Trey wasn't any man. He was the one she wanted right now, right here, like she'd never wanted anyone before.

Who was this woman in the arms of a stranger? Certainly not Dr. Jasmine Quinlan. Jaz never acted this way. Her life was all about control. A boring, mundane, everyday controlled existence. She'd never make love with someone she barely knew, especially in her lab, where they could be discovered any minute.

She searched Trey's face, his expression tight, barely leashed control evident in his clenched jaw and nearly trembling hands.

Right. Her life had been so satisfying up to this point. Never before had she felt volcanic eruptions deep inside her. Trey would make her erupt—that much she already knew.

"Fuck me, Trey. Here, now and do it quick. I need to feel your cock inside me."

With a low growl, he swept her into his arms and sat her on top of the laboratory counter. None too gently, he shoved the beakers and microscopes to the side to make room for her.

"Let me tell you how this is going to work," he said.

She watched him pull his T-shirt off, revealing an impressively bronzed chest.

A tattoo of a dolphin on his left bicep caught her eye. Well, surprise of all surprises. The Ivy League rich man had a tattoo.

He'd surprised her again. She traced the outline of the swimming dolphin with something akin to awe spreading inside her.

Triton Sanders was a mystery.

But at least one part of the mystery was about to be solved. She focused once more on his incredible body. Muscles rippled in the harsh light and she reached for him, but he stepped back. When his thumb grazed the top button on his jeans, her throat went dry. Did she really have any idea what she was doing?

No. And strangely enough, she didn't care.

The button flipped open, followed by the zipper. He quickly pushed his jeans off and stood gloriously, magnificently naked. His erection sprang forward, thick and pulsating. She licked her lips, dying for a taste of him.

His gaze caught and followed the sweep of her tongue across her lips. He shook his head and smiled. "No, little siren, that's not what's going to happen." He pushed her down and reached for the waistband of her shorts, making quick work of pulling them off. "First, I'm going to taste you and find out if that sweet vanilla scent that seems to be a part of you extends to that luscious pussy."

She was going to die. Her lab assistants would find her tomorrow, sprawled naked and lifeless on the counter. She was going to have a heart attack from being so turned on. Her juices flowed against her panties and she arched her hips, silently begging for his tongue.

As if he heard her mental pleas, he tore the flimsy silk panties from her and buried his face between her legs.

Jaz gasped at the first contact of his lips on her clit. He licked softly along her slit, tasting her, teasing her, until she closed her eyes and reveled in the wicked things he was doing to her. Already, release was imminent.

When he thrust his tongue inside her pussy, she covered the loud moans escaping her lips with her hand, still cognizant of the fact they were in a semi-public place.

She could almost laugh. Semi-public, and she was naked and spread-eagled on the laboratory counter. With a man whose tongue sparked a magic she'd never known before.

"Yes, lick me there," she cried, shocked at her bold request. He complied, eliciting her wet response. She squeezed her legs together, intending to capture his mouth in that special spot for as long as she could.

Then she felt cool air as he pulled away. "No, Trey, don't stop." Was that her voice, so breathy and low?

"I have to stop, Jasmine. When you come, it'll be when I'm inside you. I want to feel your cunt squeezing my cock. I want to taste your cries when you climax."

"Oh yes. Yes, I want that. Now, Trey. Now."

She'd never been more demanding. Or more needy. Desperately, she clung to his arms, not wanting to let go of him for a second lest he disappear.

He stepped to the edge of the counter and grabbed her legs, pulling her toward the edge. She propped herself up on her elbows so she could watch.

A wickedly sensual half-smile curled his lips. With one thrust, he embedded his thick shaft to the hilt.

Jaz let out a scream of pleasure, no longer caring where she was or who might come in and find them. Her entire being was focused on the feel of Trey's cock inside her. Her sex surrounded him, moistening them both with wet desire.

Trey pulled back and plunged again, harder. She groaned and reached for his arms, needing to touch him more than she needed to breathe.

"Your pussy was made for me, Jaz. Feel how snug I fit inside you? How your body grabs onto me?"

"Yes," she whispered, her gaze fixated on the lines of intense concentration on his face. He studied where their bodies met and she studied his reaction.

He grabbed her legs and threw them over his shoulders, lifting her hips in the air and sliding his hands underneath her buttocks. With slow, measured strokes he took her deeper and further into a place she'd never been before...a place no man had ever taken her.

Closer and closer she swam toward a culmination she'd waited a lifetime to experience. Part of her couldn't believe this was happening. But it was going to. It was inevitable, it was meant to happen. And soon.

When he reached between them and applied gentle pressure to her clit, she tensed and cried out. An orgasm so intense it brought tears to her eyes rushed through her body. Sweat poured from her, her limbs trembled and whimpers of ecstasy escaped her lips.

Trey stilled inside her, letting her ride out the waves of her climax until she settled back, her body no longer wracked with spasms. And then he began to move again, pulling her legs off his shoulders and leaning over her so she could wrap them around his waist.

She pulled his cock in deeper and he plunged repeatedly against the boundaries of her body. He was relentless, his body taut, his muscles a heated steel. When he bent down and captured her lips in a carnal kiss, she felt the response build within her again, shock and pleasure like nothing she'd been prepared for.

"Again, Jasmine. Come on me again."

She couldn't. It wasn't possible. And yet, it was. Trey's tongue tangled with hers, licking her lips, her mouth, taking in her cries of delight when her electrifying orgasm took her over the edge a second time.

"Oh God, Trey, oh God," was all she could mumble. Her climax sparked, holding her prisoner as wave after wave crashed within her.

This time, he went with her and it was her turn to take in his groans as his lips ground against hers and his seed shot deep within her. He held her tightly clasped to his body, cradling her head against his chest, shuddering until the last of his climax subsided.

She couldn't move, couldn't breathe, couldn't even lift her hands.

Never had it been like this. So intensely physical, and yet so deeply emotional that she shed tears of joy.

Trey pulled away and stared down at her while she tried to climb back to reality. Then he reached for their clothes, handing her shorts and tank top without looking at her.

The warmth that had filled her only seconds ago was suddenly replaced by a chilled dread as she realized that whatever she may have felt was one sided. Clearly, Trey felt no emotional bond between them. To him, it had been sex. It was written all over his blank face. He'd climaxed and that meant it was over. No emotion, no involvement, just a fuck.

That's all she'd been—just a fuck.

"We'd better hurry and get dressed before someone comes in," he said, turning away from her.

Jaz fought back the welling tears, embarrassed by her foolish fantasies of finding the man of her dreams. She quickly dressed, grabbed her shoes and headed out the door.

There was no point in attempting to have a conversation. They'd fucked, purely and simply, and that's all there'd been to it. The sooner she grabbed that concept of cold, hard reality, the better off she'd be.

* * * * *

"So what you're telling me is that you're still a dumbass."

Trey wondered sometimes why he even bothered to have conversations with Dane. Clearly, the only thing he ever got from his brother was insults. "No, that's not what I said at all. I said I made a huge mistake with Jaz."

"Because you had sex with her."

Trey inhaled the pre-dawn foggy air and turned to Dane, who had taken human form to converse with him. They were alike in so many ways, down to the dolphin tattoo all guardians wore. Dane wasn't quite as tall as he was, and his hair not as dark, but they had the same mannerisms. A few similarities in their shapeshifting abilities, and a few differences, too. As with all the guardians, each of them was unique.

Dane's eyes sparkled with mirth. "So, you had sex with her and you think that's a mistake."

"Yeah."

"In what universe, Trey? C'mon. She wanted it, you wanted it, I assume you both enjoyed it, so what's the big deal?"

"Dane, you do realize that under no circumstances are we to fraternize with land humans other than what is absolutely necessary."

Dane winked. "I'd say getting a good fuck is an absolute necessity."

"You're an idiot."

"And you're a dumbass."

Trey was about to say something else to Dane when his brother suddenly morphed back into his dolphin form. Which could only mean one thing.

"What the hell is going on here?"

Jaz. He turned and shrugged. "Just checking on the dolphins."

"It's five in the morning."

"I'm aware of the time." Even in the darkness, he could see the pain on her face, the confusion that he'd put there. He'd been hot and all over her one minute, then cold and walking out on her the next.

How could he explain to her, when he couldn't figure it out himself?

She was just a woman, no different than the sea sprites he fucked. He'd been horny and so had she. They'd engaged in steamy sex that was fulfilling for both of them. He shouldn't have to treat her differently than the other women.

But she *was* different from the other women. He *felt* differently about her. Yes, he was attracted to her physically, but there was more. And that was the crux of the problem, and the reason for his horrible behavior.

"And why were you yelling at my dolphins?"

Shit. "Because that one annoys me."

She crooked a brow. "Annoys you? How so?"

He's a pain in my ass, that's how so. "Non-cooperative."

"It's because you don't talk nice to him."

Talk nice to him? Trey would like to kick his ass! He glared at Dane, who chattered noisily. What Jaz couldn't hear was Dane's maniacal laughter. *Dickhead.*

"They're just dumb animals, Jaz. You don't have to talk nice to them."

"Dumb animals? How dare you!" She pushed him aside and leaned over the tank, petting Dane's snout. "Don't listen to him, baby."

Trey rolled his eyes. "Give me a break. He's not your baby."

"Is too, aren't you sweetie?"

When she pressed her lips to Dane's face and Dane responded with a wet lick to Jaz's mouth, Trey had had enough. He pulled Jaz away from his brother, his anger growing by the second. Dane's snicker wasn't helping one bit.

"Grow up, Jaz. Quit treating these creatures like babies. They don't want or need your help."

"And you have become an expert in reading their minds since when?"

Since the day he was born. "I just know. They're not intelligent like you and me. They're...stupid."

Of course he was simply trying to get back at Dane. Dane responded by shooting a snout full of water at Trey's face.

Jaz laughed and patted Dane on the head. "That should tell you what they think of your opinion."

Trey wiped his face, making a mental note to kick Dane's ass later. "Don't you have work to do in the lab?"

At the mention of the lab, her face colored. She pulled her sweater around her chest and lifted her chin. "Don't *you* have work to do in the lab?"

"Yes. I was on my way before you wasted my time with this moronic conversation about dolphins."

"Just what size pole is stuck up your ass this morning, Triton?"

"I'm fine. You're the one who showed up here in a pissed off mood, ready to attack me. What wrong? Didn't I calm your nerves enough last night?"

Her eyes widened. "I don't want to talk about last night."

"Good. Because it was a huge mistake anyway." One he'd known better than to make. Now he'd be sure never to make it again.

"Sorry I wasn't good enough for you. I'm sure you're used to much better than me." She turned on her heel and stormed off. Trey followed her movements, feeling worse now than he did before she showed up.

"Like I said. You're a dumbass."

He didn't say a word in response to Dane's insult. This time, his brother was absolutely right.

Chapter Eight

ဢ

Jaz did her best to avoid Trey over the next two days. Thankfully, the tests they'd run had yielded some promising results. They were close to figuring out the culprit responsible for the dolphins' illness.

Isolating bacteria found in one of the samples, she and her staff busily set about attempting to identify it amongst millions of potential suspects.

Trey worked with the assistants, all of them as tirelessly devoted to finding the cause as she was. She had to admire Trey's work ethic, even if she still bristled at his odd behavior.

Their night together in the lab had been magical. Hot, powerful, sensual and more than she had ever expected. He touched her in ways that went beyond the physical, both frightening and enticing at the same time.

But he was all wrong for her. He was surly, unpleasant, insulting, and way out of her league on the social scale. Clearly, he wanted nothing to do with her after their encounter.

Which was fine with her, except for one small problem— she still wanted him. Her body craved him. He was like a single lick of her favorite ice cream. One taste wasn't nearly enough. She wanted all of it. All of him.

And she was angry as hell for that wanting.

Casting surreptitious glances in his direction, she scrunched her nose in self-irritation at even watching him, wondering what he was thinking.

She'd been so much better off with her vibrators. At least with those, she didn't have to worry about what they thought about her, whether she was good enough. They gave her the release she needed, and then were perfectly happy to be shoved back in her nightstand drawer until the next time.

Men were much more complex. No wonder she had little use for them.

"Bob, what about those serum levels?" she asked, forcing her mind back on work, where it belonged.

"I think I might have something here."

The answer came from Trey, not from Bob.

She rushed over and peered at the data on the computer, conscious of the fact she was closer to him right now than she'd been for two days. She couldn't help but take a deep breath, his crisp, ocean scent reminding her what she loved the most about the sea.

"This looks like a new bacterium," she said, lifting her head and meeting his gaze. "Have you ever run across it before?"

Trey shook his head. "No. I'd like to do a little more analysis on it. More in-depth. Looks like something that might originate in the digestive tract, which would explain their lack of appetite and symptoms similar to sponge ingestion."

She nodded. "Go ahead. Pull whatever resources you need from the staff."

He stared at her and she stared back. The blue of his eyes, so like the turquoise waters off the Caribbean, held her. She could almost hear his voice in her head, deep, husky, filled with the promise of hot nights and passion.

They weren't even alone in the room and yet the pull of attraction made her forget everything around her. She licked her lips, remembering how Trey's felt against her mouth and on her pussy.

Her body trembled as he inched closer.

Was he going to kiss her? Right here in front of the staff?

Lord, she hoped so.

"Dr. Quinlan, come quick! It's one of the dolphins!"

Trey pulled back and Jaz turned to Tricia, who stood in the doorway signaling for them to follow.

The sun was shining this afternoon, but a cold chill crept over her as she spotted one of the dolphins floating on the surface of the pool.

"Shit!"

Her mind barely registered Trey's curse as she jumped into the water. Hurrying toward the dolphin, she pulled the stethoscope from around her neck and placed it against the dolphin's heart.

Nothing. The bottlenose dolphin's lifeless eyes told her the truth. He was gone.

Pain rifled through her. She wanted to sit down right where she was and wail at the injustice of it all, but there were other things that had to be done. She instructed the staff to remove the dolphin from the tank and take him into the necropsy room for examination. The other dolphins were loudly distressed, each of their laments like a knife in her heart. Jaz fought back tears, needing to remain stoic and professional in front of everyone.

She knew how they felt when they lost one of the mammals. It tore them up as much as it did her, and they looked to her for strength. She had to pull it together, despite wanting to run upstairs, fling herself on her bed and weep for about a day.

Trey's expression was blank. Tight, controlled, revealing nothing. He helped remove the dolphin, but never said a word.

Did he even care? Did his heart bleed for these magnificent creatures, or did he look upon them the same way as Claude? She really had no idea how he felt about the dolphins. He masked his emotions well.

Frankly, she didn't want to think about Trey right now. Now was the time to look on the morbid, yet potentially advantageous side of a negative situation. The necropsy would at least give them an opportunity to do a more thorough investigation of the bacterium present in the dolphins and what type of systemic damage it had been doing.

That could provide a clue as to its origin.

They worked through the evening. Trey assisted, giving her no inkling as to his feelings about the dolphin's death. Tissue samples, morphometrics and photos were taken, all to study later.

Jaz suppressed her emotions during the procedure, thankful when they finished and she could send her assistants home for the night. Trey walked out with a few of the staff without even looking at her, still not speaking.

Guilt wrapped itself around her, pounding away at her already miserable headache. She should have worked harder to save the dolphins. Instead, she'd been playing sex games with Trey. A complete waste of time that she could have used on research.

Why did she suddenly feel so alone, so miserably unhappy? She'd suffered through the deaths of sea mammals before. Some she could save, many she couldn't.

Still, it frustrated her to lose any of them. She pulled off her examination gloves and mask, then went upstairs to her apartment and showered. After two glasses of wine she was still unsettled, anxiety keeping her energy level too high to even think about sleeping. She threw on a jacket, grabbed a blanket and headed to the beach.

The moon cast a silver glow over the ocean, the whitecaps sparkling like blue diamonds.

The cool night air wrapped itself around her, but she hardly felt the chill. She stared out over the water, feeling helpless against the mystery of the dolphins' disease.

Every time one of the sweet creatures died, a little of her died along with them.

She could no more stop the tears rolling down her cheeks than she could stem the tide from coming in each day.

Mourning the way she couldn't in front of everyone earlier, she let loose of the sorrow that had gripped her since she first sighted the floating dolphin. Her shoulders slumped and she buried her chin against her chest, grieving for the magnificent creature who would never again skip gaily over the ocean's crests, who would never chirp with joy or dance about on its tail.

* * * * *

Trey stood at the sidewalk, watching Jaz's shoulders heave with what he knew had to be crying.

Pain knifed through him. Pain at the loss of one of his friends. Lednor had been one of Oceana's oldest dolphins, but despite his advanced age, he didn't deserve to die this way, stripped of even the barest decency and being cut open for examination.

The scientist in him knew that the necropsy would be beneficial. The Oceanic in him railed at the injustice of being held at the mercy of the land humans' rituals.

And yet he'd stood mutely by, even assisting Jaz while she sliced into one of his best friends. Because he knew they might learn something.

Tonight he'd sat at the edge of the aquarium with the other dolphins. Their grief was palpable, their illness only making it worse. Dane did what he could to help them, to be there for them, and for that Trey was grateful.

Didn't matter anyway. Nothing anyone said or did would take away the pain of the loss of one of their own.

Trey heaved a sigh, frustrated and feeling more miserably powerless than he ever had before. What made it worse was knowing he'd been wrong about Jasmine. She cared, truly cared for the dolphins, more so than she let on. She may have professionally carried out her job today, but she'd been struck hard by Lednor's death. Almost as hard as he'd been, and she didn't even know his dolphin friend.

And now she sat alone in the sand, the cool night air whipping around her, and sobbed out her grief.

Despite his need to keep his distance from her, he could no more turn his back on a land human in pain than he could on his own kind. It didn't matter that it was Jaz, only that she was hurting. She really didn't matter to him on a personal level.

Right. And neither had Lednor. Sometimes he was amazed at his ability to rationalize his feelings, to discount them as if they didn't matter, as if people didn't matter.

He stepped off the walkway and into the sand, stopping at her back. Her sniffles stabbed at him, making him want to draw her against him and hold her until she hurt no more.

"It's cold out here," he finally said, at a loss for any words that would offer her comfort.

She turned and glanced up at him, swiping at the tears that had left tracks on her cheeks. She sniffed and looked away, staring at the water. "I hadn't noticed."

"You have a blanket."

"I'm not cold."

He sat on the sand next to her, taking the blanket and wrapping it around her shoulders. She shivered so hard her teeth chattered.

"What do you want, Trey?"

"I don't want anything."

When he offered her a handkerchief, she mumbled her thanks. "Then why are you here?"

He gazed out over the waters of his home, unable to bear her red-rimmed eyes and tear-streaked face. Her pain swept through him. He felt her anguish, her rage at being unable to stop the ravages of the disease. "Maybe I just needed to sit out here, too Makes me feel close to them."

"To the dolphins?"

"Yeah."

She nodded. "Sometimes I wish I could just dive down there, live among the creatures of the sea, be one of them."

For a fraction of a second, his heart stopped beating. "Why?"

"Because I love it. I've always loved the ocean. The colors, the creatures, the complete feeling of weightlessness and a freedom like nothing I could ever experience here."

All the things he loved most about Oceana. All the things Leelia hated. "You'd get tired of it."

"Wanna bet? I was practically born with my feet in the water. My parents were marine photographers. I was swimming in the ocean before I could even walk. And I've never felt more at peace, more complete, than when I'm diving."

Shit. He didn't want her to love the ocean, didn't want her to have dreams about living there. She was a land human, and land was where she belonged.

"What about you?" she asked. "What about the ocean compels you?"

He chose his words carefully. "There's a beauty down there incomparable to anything on land. Clear, pristine, visions like nothing I've seen anywhere else. It's a quiet peacefulness that relaxes my mind and makes me feel a part of the great undersea universe."

When she didn't answer, he turned to her. Her eyes filled again with tears.

"I had no idea you felt that way," she said, sniffling.

Oh, hell. He should learn to keep his mouth shut. "It's nice down there. And people don't bug me."

Then she giggled, something he hadn't expected. "I agree. I'd prefer to spend all my time with dolphins and the other sea creatures. I'm not much of a people person. At least that's what I've been told."

They were more alike than Trey wanted to acknowledge.

"I should have saved him," she added.

"Who?"

"The dolphin who died today. I wasn't focused on my work like I should have been. I should have worked harder, faster, done something to make sure that we saved them all."

The tremble in her voice told him the tears had begun to flow again. "What could you do? You're only one person, Jaz. Even you can't save them all." And neither could he, much as he hated to admit it.

"I know the answer is staring me right in the face and I just can't see it. I have to get back to work."

She moved to stand, but Trey grabbed her arm and kept her seated. "You're exhausted. It's been a rough day for everyone."

"I'm fine." She tugged at his hand, but he wouldn't let her loose. "Let me go, Trey."

"No."

He wanted to think it was because she'd make a mistake if she went back to work in her emotional state. He wanted to think it was because he cared for the dolphins and didn't want her to miss a vital clue.

He wanted to think he didn't care about her.

But that was a lie.

"Stay here with me, Jaz."

"Why?"

Good question. He knew the answer, but didn't want to lend it a voice. Yet he couldn't help the words that spilled. "Let me make love to you tonight."

Her eyes widened, her lashes spiked with the moisture of her tears. "Wh…What? Here? Now?"

"Yes. Maybe we both need a little comfort tonight. Maybe it's lame, I don't know. I just need to hold someone in my arms."

"Someone?" she asked.

He closed his eyes for a second, realizing he was doing this all wrong. And reminding himself that this was a huge mistake. They were a mistake.

But he couldn't stay away from her.

He opened his eyes and met her curious, teary gaze. "No. Not someone. You. I need *you*, Jasmine."

Jaz stared at Trey, not sure how to respond. His suggestion to make love was the last thing she thought she'd hear from him after the last time they'd been intimate. He'd made it clear he didn't want anything more to do with her.

She shouldn't trust him. He'd crushed her earlier, treated her like dirt, fucked her and then left her without a word. She should spit in his face and walk away.

A small part of her really wanted to do that. She still hurt over his callous abandonment of her the other night. She should get up right now and walk away.

But she didn't. For some reason, his pain emanated from his body to hers, maybe even from his soul to hers.

She didn't want to believe they had that kind of connection. She wanted to hate him.

She couldn't hate him.

Despite her reservations, she was touched. Beyond touched. Stunned was more like it. Of all nights for him to tell her he needed her, that he wanted to be with her, tonight was perfect.

Perfect, and all wrong.

She shouldn't be with him. Not after what happened the other night. What guarantee did she have that he wouldn't use her again, then discard her as callously as he had then?

Yet, somewhere from deep inside she knew he wouldn't do that. That this time, it would be different.

Besides, she desperately needed to hold on to someone, to feel alive, to feel those sparks that come from touching and being touched by someone you desire.

No, not someone. Trey.

Trey, who'd cruelly walked out on her after their lovemaking in the lab, who she was convinced didn't care one whit about her. And yet, there was a tortured soul buried deep inside him that she'd at first refused to recognize, that he hid well behind a mask of indifference. Now she saw it very clearly. Or maybe just felt it.

As if on cue, the wind died down, leaving a peaceful calm in its wake. Her body warmed at the thought of being in Trey's arms again.

Pushing her hesitation away, she reached for him.

Chapter Nine

ॐ

Jaz caressed Trey's cheek, intent on running her fingers through his dark hair. Instead, he pulled her onto his lap and settled her against his chest. Her knees brushed the sand as she straddled his legs.

The position was warm and comfortable. Her body fired to life and the chill left her bones, replaced by a heat that began deep inside her. A spark of desire flamed that had nothing to do with having body contact with just any man at this given point in time, but a man who for some reason she'd bonded with.

He wrapped his arms tighter around her, then simply held her close. She laid her head on his shoulder and took comfort from his powerful strength, his arms tightening against her back. She closed her eyes and listened to the waves crashing against the shore, felt Trey's heart beat rhythmically against her breast, listened to his even breathing as it ruffled her hair.

For the first time in as long as she could remember, she didn't feel alone.

Trey held her for what seemed like an eternity. All the stress she'd bottled up inside left her body. She grew hotter with every light caress of his hands along her back.

When he leaned back, cupped her face between his palms and pressed a soft kiss to her lips, she melted into a puddle. His gentleness was unexpected. Where she thought he'd want hot, unbridled passion, he surprised her by giving her feather-light kisses and tender caresses.

Would she ever be able to figure him out? Did she even want to?

Trey stood and pulled her up, then spread the blanket beneath them. He dropped to his knees and drew her down with him, pressing her onto her back and covering her body with his. The heat emanating from him kept her warm. Quite warm, in fact.

She couldn't read his eyes in the darkness, but she felt the tension in his body. That taut, coiled holding back, as if he was physically preventing himself from doing something.

"What's wrong?" she asked.

"Not a damn thing. Just looking at you."

Looking at her made his muscles bunch up in knots? "And?"

"You're beautiful. Sometimes I forget to breathe when I look at you."

Oh, that was so unfair. And she thought she had no more tears to shed.

"You don't have to say that." Clearly, he was being kind, complimenting her because he thought she was hurting. That's what men did, even though they did it without really feeling it.

"I don't say things I don't mean, Jaz. Trust me when I tell you you're beautiful." As if to prove it, he ran his hands over her surely messy hair, pulling the elastic ponytail holder out and fanning her hair out on the blanket.

She looked like hell, she knew it.

"I'd love to see what your hair looks like in the water."

"It looks wet."

He chuckled, deep and low. She felt it inside her, deep and low.

"I'll bet it spreads out like a fast moving fire. Your hair is like a wild blaze, Jasmine. And so soft it slides like water through my fingers."

She sucked in a breath when he tangled his fingers in her hair.

"I wonder how you'd like it if I turned you over on your knees and wound all this beautiful hair around my fist, then yanked it as I fucked you from behind."

Wet heat spread between her legs at his words, images of the two of them fucking fast and furious spiraling through her mind. She'd never had wild sex, only…regular sex. But she'd already had a preview of the fact that there was nothing *regular* about Trey.

"Would you like that?" he asked again.

His gaze bored into hers, holding her captive. A willing captive, because there was nowhere else she'd rather be right now. "I might. I don't know. I've never been…that is, I'm not the type…"

"You've never had hot, passionate sex before?" He crooked a smile as if he didn't believe her.

"No. I haven't. Well, a couple days ago in the lab."

"Really? That was the first time you've been out of control?"

He thought she'd been wild? "Yes."

"And did you like it?"

He still had hold of her hair, slowly winding it around in circles over his fingers.

"Yes."

"Wanna do it again?"

"In the lab?"

He laughed. "No. Hot and passionate, like the other night."

She wanted to ask him if he'd jump up and leave her again like he did the other night, but her courage failed her. Besides, she didn't want him to think she really cared one way or the other.

Anyway, it didn't matter. Here and now was what mattered and she wanted him. She didn't want to think about anything else.

"Yes, Trey. I want it like the other night."

He slid his arms around her back and pulled her tightly against him, crushing his mouth to hers. He plundered her lips, searching and finding her tongue.

His hands were everywhere, pulling at her clothes and yanking them off. In minutes she was naked, the cool night air raising goosebumps over her skin.

Trey closed his eyes for a moment, and in that moment the chilled night air dissipated, leaving only warmth in its wake.

She should be shivering out here in the cold. Yet she wasn't. Her body burned from a fire deep within.

When Trey stood and undressed, her breathing quickened. With every drop of clothing onto the blanket, her body flamed hotter. His erection jutted out as if reaching for her. A sudden desire overwhelmed her as she gazed at his shaft. She wanted to suck him until he spilled his hot come down her throat.

And she'd never wanted to do that before, with any other man.

She raised up onto her knees and reached for him. "Don't. Not yet."

He paused and arched a brow. "What do you want, Jaz?"

"This." She bent forward and took his shaft in her hand, softly stroking the length until droplets of moisture appeared at the tip. She licked them off, surprised at his salty sweet flavor. "You taste good, Trey."

With a groan, he tilted his head back and tangled his fingers in her hair, encouraging her to continue. She continued to caress him lightly, fascinated by his body's reaction to her touch. His cock hardened considerably under her fingers, pulsing and emitting more of the clear liquid that she eagerly licked away.

When she placed her lips around the head of his penis he sucked in a breath, his body tensing. She slowly slid her mouth down around his cock, inch by delectable inch, until she'd taken in as much of him as she could. Then she moved back, watching her saliva glisten on the ridges of his shaft as she withdrew.

In short order she discovered a rhythm he seemed to like. Slow, then rapid sucks up and down, all the time keeping her hand on him and stroking him as she sucked. She remembered the feel of his mouth on her pussy and wondered if she gave him the same kind of pleasure he'd given her.

From the sounds he made and the way his hips arched towards her mouth, she must be pleasing him. A power filled her as she realized that she could pleasure a man, something she'd never thought she could do. Her few forays into sex previously had been fast, uneventful and completely unsatisfying. The men she'd been with hadn't taken the time to engage in extended foreplay.

But Trey seemed to love it. Not only did he enjoy receiving pleasure, he sure as hell knew how to give it.

"That's good baby," he said, panting. "Like that. Faster."

His commands thrilled her and she complied, taking him rapidly between her lips and sliding her mouth over the length of his cock until his fingers dug into her hair and he pulled away.

"No more," he gasped, "or I'll come in your mouth."

Wasn't that the idea? "Go ahead."

He dropped to his knees, his eyes dark with passion. "Some other time. Now I want to fuck you."

Jaz could barely catch a breath before he'd flipped her over onto her stomach and said, "Get on your hands and knees."

His harsh command shivered through her, wetting her and readying her for him. She should hate that he ordered her, and yet she didn't. How could she know she would delight in taking a submissive role to his dominance? Hell, he knew more about what excited her than she did!

The things she did with Trey were outside her area of familiarity. And yet she embraced every one of his wicked desires.

Drawing up on her hands and knees, she waited. And waited. Then finally turned her head to find him staring between her legs.

"You have a beautiful pussy," he said, tilting his head to the side. "And so wet, too. Your lips glisten with your juices."

Hearing his description of her most intimate body part unnerved her. He was so blatantly sexual and she, until now, had never been exposed to a man like him. Part of it thrilled her, part of it scared her to death. She was way out of her league.

"Thank you," she mumbled, thoroughly embarrassed.

The blanket shifted as he drew against her, his shaft probing between the cheeks of her ass. When he rocked his penis against her buttocks, she trembled.

He reached between her legs and rubbed his fingers against her, then moved his cock between them and stroked the sensitized folds of her pussy. Jolts of pleasure flooded her. She wanted him inside her.

Boldly, she lifted her buttocks higher and pressed against him, unable to see but knowing what she wanted lay just between her legs. Trey laughed. "You want to be fucked, Jasmine?"

There he went again, asking intimate questions and talking dirty to her. Her nipples tingled as they pebbled. "Yes."

"Back into my cock, then."

She did, searching for his shaft. When it brushed her clit, she moaned at the sharp burst of desire, then mimicked her previous movements, arching her back and sliding her clit against his shaft.

"Yeah, baby, like that." He encouraged her to continue. Jaz was torn between her desire to come and her need to have him embedded deeply inside her.

He held his shaft for her and let her rub against it. She felt the buildup of tension, wanted the release desperately, craved the fulfillment that only he could give her.

But she wanted it while he fucked her. She reached down between her legs and grabbed his shaft, positioning it at the entrance to her pussy, then quickly pushed back, pulling his cock deeply inside her.

His satisfied moan told her he'd wanted the same thing. Her cunt tightened around his shaft, taking him in deeper, every inch making him a part of her.

Trey leaned against her back and reached for her breasts, petting her nipples with his thumbs. She felt it between her legs, that lightning strike of enhanced delight. His breath tickled her ear, his heart pounded against her back.

She should have thought about the fact they might be seen. After all, many of the staff apartments faced the beach. But the fog had rolled in and enshrouded them, providing a blanket cover of privacy.

At this point, nothing in this world could compel her to move away from Trey. His warmth penetrated her skin, sinking deep into her body and flushing her with a fever that only he could break.

Then he did what he'd suggested earlier. He grabbed her hair and wound it around his fist, pulling sharply back with his hand.

Tears moistened her eyes at the painful pleasure. He held on tight to her hair and rocked against her, fucking her hard. She gave back in kind, slamming against him until she thought she'd die from the rapture.

It was wild, wicked, even vicious. They both panted and groaned as their sweat-slickened bodies met and parted, met and parted.

He thrust deeply again, and pulses of ecstasy thrummed between her legs. She let out a wailing cry. Her orgasm rushed unexpectedly over her, drenching them both in her nectar. She moaned and pushed backwards, wanting all of him.

It wouldn't stop, the constant spread of such exquisite sensation she nearly collapsed from it. And yet, he continued.

"More, Jasmine," he whispered, then reached around and found her clit, stroking her once again to a fevered state. She didn't think it possible, but the tension inside her regathered with each thrum of his fingers on her sensitized flesh, each thrust of his thick cock in her.

"Come with me, baby," he said, his voice tight with arousal. He groaned and plunged ever deeper. "Come with me now."

Like a man who wouldn't take no for an answer, Trey continued to rub her clit and relentlessly stroke her cunt with his shaft. The combination was too much to bear.

"I can't…oh, God, Trey I'm coming again!" She flew over the edge, her pussy squeezing his shaft tightly until he stiffened and groaned out his climax, holding tight to her as the tremors shook his body.

She collapsed onto the blanket, Trey falling beside her and gathering her into his arms.

Tensing, she waited for his abrupt departure. But this time he stayed, pulling her close and holding onto her like he'd never let her go.

His skin was bathed with a fine sheen of sweat and she trailed her fingers over his chest, feeling the staccato beat of his heart against her palm. He kissed the top of her head and stroked her shoulder, her arm, reaching for her breasts and playing lazily with a nipple.

With a contented sigh, she watched his hands move over her body, surprised to find that yet again she could be aroused.

"We'd better get inside before you freeze to death," he said.

Reluctantly, she agreed. "Funny, I'm not cold."

He smiled and handed her clothing to her. "Neither am I. You make me hot, Jaz."

His words settled somewhere between her legs. The feminine part of her triumphed in the fact she could actually turn a man on. The scientist in her knew it was merely biology. That she was nothing special.

And yet, she wanted to be.

Trey gathered the blanket and held out his hand for her. She clasped hers in his and walked toward the apartments, wondering what was going to happen next between them.

It seemed as if a wall had crumbled. Whether he'd been the one to put it up there, or she had, it was gone now.

Trey had a magical hold on her, and if she wasn't careful she'd fall in love with him.

Somehow, she knew that loving Trey would hold disastrous consequences for them both.

Chapter Ten

ജ

"I'm going for a dive."

Trey looked up from the microscope at Jaz's determined expression. "You're gonna do what?"

"Dive. I want to examine the coral, then scoot around where the dolphins hunt."

"You taking a crew along with you?"

She shook her head. "No. I'll dive alone."

"I'll go with you."

She frowned at him. "It really isn't necessary. I'm quite experienced, Trey, you don't have to worry about me."

For some reason he didn't like that idea. Not that she could get anywhere near Oceana, but the thought of her diving alone bothered him. "Why don't you let me do it instead?"

She frowned, then smiled. "Don't be silly. It's my job."

He couldn't think of a logical reason why she shouldn't go, although he pondered it the entire day. The following morning, he watched from his apartment window as Jaz entered the water. Something didn't feel right about this dive she was going to do. Unfamiliar emotions tugged at his heart and chipped away at the iceberg surrounding it.

Ever since their night on the beach, he couldn't find it within him to keep his distance from her, even though he knew he should.

Without thinking about what he was doing or why, he ran to the beach and dove into the waves. In an instant, he shifted into dolphin form and headed out to watch Jaz's descent into the dark waters. She had a light that she shined around her to lead the way, but he knew her vision wasn't as good as his at these depths.

Trey watched, a sense of dread and impending catastrophe washing over him. He kept his distance, remaining behind her. She slowed as she reached the coral, the underwater camera she held zooming onto a whitened area of the coral field before moving off in its continued search.

But what did she hope to find down here? And especially at the depths she was traveling. Much deeper than she should, knowing a human's capacity.

And why the hell was he worried about her? He shouldn't care what she did. This obviously wasn't the first time she'd dived, and she was perfectly safe.

So what was he doing down here following her around like a devoted puppy? He should go to his sanctuary below while he had a free moment, then make sure he was back in the lab by the time she returned.

And yet the pull toward her was too strong. Something compelled him to remain near her. Every time he decided to leave, she'd change direction and he'd follow. Thoroughly disgusted with himself, he swept around the front of her, figuring he'd just blow by her and then head down toward Oceana.

Only she must have spotted him. Maybe she'd thought he was a shark, because she jerked upright and turned quickly. Veering to the right, she slammed into a jutting rock ledge.

She'd hit her head. Blood rose from the back of her head and she began to sink fast.

Damn! He shifted into his human form and swam quickly toward her, capturing her in his arms.

Jaz, can you hear me? She didn't answer the thoughts he'd put into her head.

Jaz, wake up.

Her eyes remained closed. He put two fingers to the side of her neck, and near panic set in. Her pulse was weak. He laid one hand on her chest and realized her breathing was ragged and very slow.

Glancing quickly up toward the surface, he knew there was little time. She must have hit the ledge hard because blood continued to pour from the wound on her head.

There was no other choice. He turned and headed down, swimming quickly to Oceana.

He was afraid if he didn't get her there soon, she wasn't going to make it. There was no time to take her to the surface and find a doctor. She needed help now.

If he didn't get the wound closed up soon...

That thought sent adrenaline pouring through his system. He fought back the panic choking him and concentrated on getting Jaz to the sanctuary.

He flew through the watery doorway and into his bedroom, laying Jaz on the transparent cover. Quickly he removed her mask and air tank, then felt the back of her head. A jagged wound the size of his fist and quite deep left blood pouring onto his hands.

There was no time to think. He placed his palm over her head and closed his eyes, feeling the power centering itself in his middle. Her wound began to close, her body repairing itself.

He laid his other hand over her breast and forced her heart rate to normal beats, thankful when her pulse kicked up and her breathing normalized.

For the longest time he stood over her, watching her sleep. He knew she'd recover completely, that it had only been a severe gash, but the thought of losing her was incomprehensible.

And the thought of why losing her meant so much to him was something he refused to ponder any longer. He covered her and left the room, heading into his kitchen for a drink.

She was going to be fine. He knew that. At least he had some knowledge of healing. Which unfortunately didn't transfer to eradicating their dolphins' mysterious illness. If they had been injured like Jaz had been, he could have helped them. But this disease that had grabbed hold of the dolphins was unlike anything Oceana had ever seen, and their healing powers were useless against it.

Now he had to figure out what to do next. He knew he shouldn't move her yet, but her people would expect her back. He also knew she shouldn't be here, shouldn't wake up here, but he had no other choice. What was done was done and he couldn't change it now.

He'd have to rush up to the surface and leave some message with her staff that she was going to be out of town on research. They'd buy that and it would give him a little time to get her well and back to the surface.

He'd have to erase her memory, of course, but he'd worry about the details to that later.

Right now he had to cover his tracks, and hope to hell that he hadn't just made a huge mistake in bringing Jaz to Oceana.

* * * * *

Jaz woke with a start, clawing at her throat and gasping for air. She bolted upright and opened her eyes, fighting the feeling of suffocation that surrounded her.

Only she wasn't drowning. She wasn't even in the water.

She also wasn't home.

Where was she? She blinked and looked around, never having seen a place like this before. She was in a bed. Felt normal. So did the blankets surrounding her. Except everything was nearly transparent.

She blinked again, certain her eyes deceived her, and yet it was true. She ran her palm over the mattress, which felt just like a regular mattress, except she could barely see it.

How odd.

And she was naked. Which was interesting because she certainly hadn't been naked when she was diving Where were her clothes? How had she gotten here and why couldn't she remember anything?

Fighting the pain that stabbed at her temples, she rose and wrapped the silken sheet around her body, mentally pulling forth the last thing she remembered. Her mind was wrapped in a fog, her head pounding. She felt her head for any injury, wincing when her fingers moved over a sizeable bump on the back of her head.

What the hell had happened?

The last thing she remembered was diving, then seeing a shark or something.

That was it. She'd bumped her head. She remembered the sharp pain, but after that it was all a blank. If she'd lost consciousness while diving she should be dead. She'd have sunk to the depths beyond which a human could survive.

But she obviously wasn't dead.

Or was she? This place certainly looked like nothing she'd seen before. Maybe it was heaven, or some obscure after-death place. Not like she had any experience in either of those locations.

The room was near dark, and yet the walls of whatever building housed her were transparent. Outside looked like…water.

In fact, water surrounded all the walls. She walked out into a hallway. The place was structured just like a house. The hallway led into a couple other rooms that she didn't venture into, because she headed toward the end of the hall where there was a source of light.

A living room, a kitchen and even a dining area greeted her.

Regular looking furniture, but sure as hell irregular at the same time.

She was underwater. But how? What was this place? And why was she alone?

"Hello? Is anyone here?"

No answer. She stepped to a doorway, realizing immediately there was no door handle. The sound of the currents was very strong here. She placed her hand on the clear glass.

But there was no glass. Her hand slipped right into water. Water that stayed outside the door and didn't come into the structure. She quickly pulled her hand back. It was dripping wet.

What the hell?

She did it again, sliding her hand through the open doorway, only this time she left it there. Wriggled her fingers. It *was* water. Withdrawing her hand, she licked her wet fingers.

Salty water. Ocean.

She was in the ocean. Or something nearly like it.

The water outside was as clear as standing on land, not murky like the dark ocean depths. Only there were no people walking by.

There were fish. Colorful, strange fish she had never seen before. A new species perhaps? They were smaller than a dolphin but larger than a salmon or trout, and striped with every color of the rainbow, from blues to yellows to lavenders and reds. Each of the stripes glowed like a neon sign.

And dolphins! A dolphin raced by, then turned and stopped at the doorway.

It looked amazingly similar to the Bottlenose who'd washed up on the shore the day after she'd rescued the others. Perfect skin, no scars, same markings.

"Is it you?" she asked, feeling a little ridiculous for talking to the dolphin. She reached out her hand and the dolphin approached, rubbing its snout against her palm.

"It is you!" Instinctively, she knew it to be true, even if her mind refused to believe this was anything other than a dream.

At this point, anything or anyone even remotely familiar filled her with joy.

But how could it be the same dolphin? He was in the aquarium tank, and sure as hell hadn't jumped out to join her in the ocean. Yet, she was convinced it was him. "Am I glad to see you, pal."

The dolphin hovered, seemingly watching her.

"I wish you could talk. Then maybe you could tell me what I'm doing here. And while you're at it, where I am."

But, of course he couldn't answer her. He didn't swim away, just hovered near the doorway, his tail fluke swishing. Suddenly he moved away for a few seconds, then back, then away again. Almost as if he was trying to get her to follow him.

"I'd like to, pal, but I can't breathe in the water like you can. Wrong kind of mammal here."

The dolphin shook its snout back and forth and opened its mouth. If she didn't know better, she could swear it was trying to communicate with her. She wished she'd done more in-depth research into dolphin communication. She'd been studying them for years, and yet not once had she trained any with hand signals or rudimentary communication techniques.

Knowledge like that sure would have come in handy right about now.

Then the dolphin did something remarkable. He poked his head past the watery door, allowing her to pet him. He even exhaled a fine mist of water, seemingly taking in the air in the room.

Just physical contact with another creature made her feel less lonely, less in the dark about where she was.

"Thanks, babe," she whispered, kissing the dolphin's snout. She could have sworn he grinned at her. When he wriggled a little further in, Jaz was shocked. Half in, half out of the water, the dolphin regarded her with curious…

Blue eyes? Dolphins didn't have blue eyes.

Maybe she really was dreaming, because the dolphin's eyes looked remarkably like Trey's, a clear crystal blue that seemed so unusually vibrant.

"Your eyes look just like Trey's," she said, knowing the dolphin didn't understand her, and yet needing to keep talking if for no other reason than to hear a voice. The silence surrounding her was driving her crazy.

Then the dolphin chattered, making strange sounds in a language she'd sell her soul to understand right now.

"I wish I could just step through that doorway and swim away with you. You think you'd like to take me away to your dolphin hangout, pal?"

Again he chattered, more animated this time.

"Hey, make me a credible offer and I'm yours."

She laughed then, feeling ridiculous and not caring in the least. Despite the fact she should be terrified at what was happening around her, she'd never felt freer, more at home.

Ocean surrounded her. Her ocean. Her home, the place she loved most. Sea creatures that she adored swam right outside the transparent enclosure.

"You know, pal, everything I want is right here within my reach. If only I could do that deep sea breathing without needing oxygen, I'd be in heaven. Then I could go out there and take a swim with you."

She swept the trailing edges of the bed sheet behind her and took a step closer to the wall. The dolphin backed away, completely submerged in the water once again. Jaz slipped her hand through the doorway, wriggling her fingers in the water. Then she stepped closer, watching the water slowly inch up her arm.

With a sigh, she pulled back.

"Wanna know something else?" she said to the hovering dolphin, unable to believe the feeling that had just come over her. "I wish Trey were here right now to share this with me. Isn't that the dumbest thing you've ever heard?"

Chapter Eleven

လ

Trey hadn't expected Jasmine's reaction to waking up in his sanctuary. Nor her enthusiastic curiosity about her surroundings.

Actually, he hadn't expected anything. What a mess he'd made out of this situation. And now she was inside, and he was outside, unable to reveal himself to her.

He felt her longing, her wish to step through the portal and out into the sea. He could grant her wish, too, but at what risk? Once he revealed himself, she'd know. He'd have to tell her everything, and then take her back. Already the complications were nearly insurmountable. He'd taken care of her absence at the aquarium by stating that the two of them were going on an excursion to try and find the cause of the dolphin's illness. That at least bought him a little time. And what about the dolphins there? What was their status? He needed to get back to them, needed to get her back up there.

Shit. This whole situation was a clusterfuck of epic proportions. He had to think, and quickly, of a possible solution. But instead, he hovered near the doorway like a lovesick mate worrying over its female.

Lovesick, that was a laugh. Trey didn't love anyone. No, he'd been soundly cured of that affliction by Leelia, and he'd never fall for a woman again. But his feelings for Jaz came damn close to love.

Maybe he was just half in love with her. He blew the water out his air hole in laughter, making Jasmine squeal in delight as he popped in and out of the sanctuary.

He had to figure out what the hell he was going to do.

And he really should stop hovering and drooling over how Jasmine looked wrapped up in a sheet.

But goddamn she was sexy, like a siren. Compelling, with an aura that literally glowed around her body. He wanted to discover her body again and again, beginning with the treasures hidden beneath the silken sheet which clung to her breasts and hips.

"You know, pal," she said, interrupting his lascivious thoughts, "if I wasn't convinced I was dreaming, I'd sure think I was in heaven." She turned and looked at the room, then back at him.

Her hair was a wild disarray of tangles and curls, her face flushed, giving her that sleepy, sexy look that drove him crazy. He wanted to thread his hands through it and draw her mouth into a kiss. God, he wanted that really bad right now.

"This place, this underwater home of...well, whoever it belongs to, is like a fantasy come true. This is my dream, actually. To live in the ocean, deep underwater, away from the trappings of land. What's it like down here, pal? Can you tell me?"

He wished he could. He wanted to. No—he didn't want to. He didn't want his heart to ache for her, didn't want his body to beg for her touch, didn't want his soul to connect with hers in the way it had.

"No, of course you can't tell me. But I wish you could. If it's an illusion, I don't ever want to wake. If it's not, then I don't ever want to leave."

And why did that thought fill him with hope, with a yearning he hadn't felt since—no. Impossible. He swore he'd never feel this way again. He had to get Jasmine out of there, and quickly.

"Are there other people like me down here?" She stepped toward the monitors. Fortunately, her body wasn't programmed to receive the signals, so all she saw were ocean and beach scenes. "Someone please tell me where I am. Am I a prisoner, or what?"

Her pleading voice nearly did him in. Not because she seemed anxious to get out of there. On the contrary, her avid curiosity shocked the hell out of him. And suddenly he wanted to reveal himself to her, to tell her everything, just to watch her reaction.

Which would be a very bad choice. Yet she called to him in the worst way. Nothing like he'd ever felt with Leelia. Jasmine's love for the ocean matched his. He felt her happiness, her giddy delight at being surrounded by water. Leelia had never looked upon Oceana as home. She'd longed for land her entire life, and despite the fact that Trey had loved her with all his heart, his love hadn't been enough to keep her happy. In the end, land life had won, and he had lost.

He'd sworn he would never lose like that again. For years he'd been content to do his job. When he wanted a woman, or rather, sex, he knew where to get it. And not once had his heart been in danger.

Not once.

Until now.

Damn, he was going to do something really stupid and couldn't do a thing to stop himself.

Instantly he was inside the sanctuary in human form. Jasmine had her back turned and hadn't yet noticed him. He stood watching her, listening to her hum a familiar song about life under the sea, feeling the vibrations from her body, and wanting her more than he wanted to breathe. He was near shaking with the desire to hold her, feel her heartbeat against his chest, and taste her.

"Jasmine."

She jumped and whirled at the sound of his voice, her eyes widening. "Trey! Oh my God, Trey!"

He walked toward her, loving the shocked look on her face, and the desire that instantly crept into her eyes when she saw he was naked. Naked and hard.

"I don't understand. Where are we? How did I get here? How did *you* get here?"

"Later." He reached her and without halting his stride, swept her into his arms, tearing the sheet away from her body and crushing his mouth against hers.

She met his lips with an eager whimper, threading her hands around his neck and fitting her body against his. He turned and walked through the doorway into the water.

Jasmine didn't have time to even gasp before he'd converted her to ocean breathing. She pulled her lips from his as he swam away from the sanctuary, her face registering shock.

"You can breathe in the water, just relax. And you can talk, too. Everything you can do on land, you can do here. And more."

"But how?" she asked hesitantly, as if trying her voice to be sure what he said was true.

"Later. I want to make love to you now, Jaz. I can't wait any longer." He took her to a sheltered cave, the place where light flickered in and out like a roomful of candles. Billowing seagrass and waving anemone greeted them as he swam through the entrance.

Jasmine's heart pounded against his chest, her nipples hardening as he gathered her closer in his arms. Her eyes darted everywhere, as if she couldn't get enough of all the sights.

Damn, he suddenly wanted to show her everything, tell her everything, let her ask questions for days, weeks...

Years.

No, he wouldn't think that. He wouldn't feel it. He just needed to be inside her right now. Fucking her was all that mattered. If he fucked her, maybe his need for her would go away.

He held her up in the water and touched her like he'd been dying to do, running his fingertips over her skin. His balls tightened at the thought of being sheathed inside her here in the sea, loving her on his home ground where they could hang suspended, weightless, do anything they wanted to do in any position.

Her lips parted as she wound her arms around his neck, wrapping her legs around his waist. Her cunt rocked against his erection, the heat from her body burning him, making him want her, need her, more than he should.

But he couldn't help himself. She was a fire in his blood, and not even the water surrounding them could quench the flame.

He reached between them and grabbed his shaft, probing the entrance to her sex. She lifted and impaled herself on his cock with one quick move.

Christ, she was tight, and so hot and wet he could come in an instant. She didn't speak, just lifted herself up and down on his rigid pole.

Trey moved them through the water, turning them in circles. Jaz held on tight, her eyes wide, the green orbs as dark as the ocean floor moss.

"Kiss me, Trey," she whispered, then fit her mouth against his.

He was dying, spiraling out of control with her in his arms. A need to be deeper inside her overcame him, and he pushed her torso backwards so she was lying prone, then held onto her hips and drove himself hard and fast within her.

Jasmine gasped her pleasure, her cunt tightening around his cock. Trey thrust harder each time, rewarded with a flood of her heated juices.

Locking his gaze on her body, he swept his hand over her upthrusting breasts, watching the nipples tighten and bead. He moved his hand downward, feeling the flinch of her belly as he swept over her waist, then petted the curls on her mound.

When he reached for her clit, circling it gently, tugging it, she cried out.

"Trey, I'm going to come!"

He wanted that more than he'd ever wanted anything. Watching her eyes widen, feeling her body convulse against his, drew his balls up tight and forced a release so powerful he had to hold onto her hips to control his movements.

He jerked repeatedly against her, hanging onto her as her body shuddered against his, her clenching vaginal muscles milking him.

When he emptied the last of his seed within her, he pulled her upright and laid her head on his shoulder.

What the hell had he done? He'd revealed himself to her, showed her things he had no intention of showing her.

Ronan was going to have his ass for this.

* * * * *

Jasmine sucked in a deep breath of…well, actually she sucked in a deep breath of water, the thought of which still brought a sense of wonder. The whole biology of being able to breathe in the ocean should have perplexed her.

If she had a working brain, which she hadn't since Trey had appeared. One look at his naked body, his erection gloriously jutting out, and she'd forgotten her shock and surprise at seeing him, her body taking over completely in a frantic rush of desire.

But now that her desire had been sated, temporarily at least, she had questions.

Lots of questions.

"Trey?"

He pulled her tighter against him. "Yeah."

"I have questions."

"I know."

No answer. She waited as patiently as she could, until she couldn't wait any longer. Pushing lightly against his chest, she met his gaze. "Trey, I meant I have a *lot* of questions."

His bleak expression told her he knew the answers. And quite possibly, he didn't want to give them.

Her head was spinning. Oddly enough, she wasn't afraid, despite the fact she was standing on the ocean floor, breathing water into her lungs. For that matter, so was Trey. No, the only thing she felt was a rabid curiosity that demanded satisfaction.

"Let's go back to the sanctuary."

He held her hand and propelled her along in the water, back toward the glass-like enclosure they'd left. That must be the sanctuary. He pulled her through the doorway, and instantly the water left her lungs. Not even a gasp escaped her as she easily made the transition from breathing water to breathing air again.

Where that air came from, she had no idea. She still didn't even know how she'd gotten here, or for that matter, where 'here' was.

Her body dried quickly. The ambient temperature in the room was comfortable enough not to need clothing, yet Jaz felt strange wandering around naked. Trey didn't seem to mind it at all, a fact that wasn't lost on her.

When he wandered into the kitchen and immediately opened a cabinet and pulled out two shell-like glasses, she began to wonder.

"Is this your place?" She stepped into the room, marveling at the strange dishes and appliances. If they even were appliances. More like transparent boxes that sat where a stove and a sink would sit.

"Yeah." He kept his back turned to her when he answered, then paused as if waiting for her response.

Questions bombarded her and she didn't know where to start. Instead, she stayed silent, waiting for him to start talking.

When she didn't say anything, he filled their glasses with something green and handed her one. She sniffed it and took a small sip. It was sweet, yet tangy. "This is good. What is it?"

Trey motioned her into the living area. "It's made from one of the sweeter seaweeds. It's like punch or tea."

She followed him into the living area and sat next to him on a cushiony sofa that felt soft as a cloud, still feeling strange about having a conversation while naked. Her eyes gravitated to Trey's body, mesmerized by his strength, the way his abdominal muscles rippled when he moved, the light dusting of curling, dark hair on his broad chest.

Instead of concentrating on her questions, she was memorizing every square inch of Trey's magnificent body.

And watching the way he was watching hers, resulting in her traitorous nipples puckering under his heated gaze.

"You're doing that on purpose," she accused.

He arched a brow. "Doing what?"

"You know very well what." She set the glass neatly between her legs, which afforded her no cover whatsoever. Instead, it drew his gaze down to the mound of red curls cushioning the drink.

Trey took a long swallow, then set his glass on the table in front of them. "Not my fault you're sexy."

She watched his cock lengthen and squirmed in her seat, her body quickly igniting. Ignoring her reaction to his arousal, she said, "I need answers, Trey."

"Wouldn't you rather play some more?" he asked, grazing his knuckles over her cheek.

She shivered, her body telling her that's exactly what she'd rather do. But she remained firm, needing answers right now more than she needed sex. "Yes, but later. I really need to know what's going on here."

With a sigh, he nodded. "I'll answer what I can. Start asking questions."

Chapter Twelve

80

Where to even begin? Jaz sucked in a deep breath and started with, "How can I breathe under water?"

"It's complicated."

"Try me."

With a sigh, he said, "It's an easy transformation for those of us down here. The biology isn't something I can easily explain to you, except to tell you that when the ocean water enters your lungs, they convert from air breathing to water breathing. Your lungs are able to pull the oxygen it needs from within the water you ingest."

She blinked, her mind not even beginning to assimilate the possibilities. "Where am I?"

"In the ocean."

Okay, that one was a given. "How did I get here?"

"You hit your head on a jagged rock ledge. Knocked you out. Had a nasty gash on your head, too."

"But I woke up here, in this sanctuary, as you call it. How?"

"I found you and brought you here."

She touched the tender spot on her head, but felt no cut, only a tender bump. "I don't have any stitches."

"I healed you."

Okay, that part would require some questions. Shock and a grateful warmth surrounded her at the thought of him rescuing her from what would have surely been her death. "Thank you."

"You're welcome."

Before his husky voice distracted her, she asked, "What is this place?"

"It's my sanctuary."

"What do you do here?"

"I live here, I work from here."

"In other words, you're not from a rich family in Philadelphia."

"No."

"Are you human?"

"Yes. Well, sort of. I have the same human biological makeup as you do. With a few subtle differences."

Breathing underwater was a subtle difference? No way. "Are there others like you?"

He paused, then nodded. "Yes."

"How many?"

"I can't say."

"Why can't you?"

Trey stood and walked to the glass wall. Jaz's body heated as she surveyed his perfect body, marveling at his broad shoulders, long legs and especially his well-shaped ass.

"I shouldn't have told you what I have," he said.

She stood and approached him, stopping a few feet behind him. "Why not? And you haven't told me anything, Trey."

"You shouldn't be here, you're not supposed to know about us."

"Who is 'us'?"

He turned, his smile apologetic. "I can't tell you."

Frustration began to simmer. "Dammit, Trey, if what you say is true—if you brought me here, if these wondrous things I've witnessed are real...it's more than I've ever dreamed could be possible. But I've got to know more."

He studied her for a few minutes, as if fighting some internal battle. Finally, he said, "This is Oceana, a civilization of underwater inhabitants."

She could barely form words, her mind taking in what he'd just said. "An entire…civilization?"

"Yes."

"People just like you live down here?"

His lips curled upward. "Not all like me. Some are like me, some are creatures of the sea, some are a combination of both. Everything you could imagine, Jasmine. All types of creatures."

"Mermaids, you mean?"

He nodded. "Yes, mermaids, mermen, many other types of beings you had thought were only fantasies."

"Where did you all come from?"

He led her back to the sofa. She sat, tucking her feet underneath her.

"We've always been here, just as your kind have always been here."

Her kind. Humans. This was totally unreal, and yet her entire being embraced what he said as fact. Excitement bubbled up inside her. "What else can you tell me? Can you tell me about your civilization? What about your customs? Does everyone live in a place like this? Do you have cities, states, countries?"

"One question at a time," he murmured, tucking an escaping tendril of her hair behind her ear.

She shuddered at his touch, her body warming. She needed him again, wanted him next to her, inside her, a part of her. Despite what she'd just discovered, despite the realization he wasn't quite human, she still wanted him.

Reaching for his face, she cupped his cheeks, pressing a kiss to his mouth. His generous lips curled upward in a grin. "Was that a question, or a request?"

"Just a passing thought."

"I like the way you think."

He reached for her, but she laid her palms on his chest. "Answer my questions first, Trey."

"I've already told you too much. Land humans don't belong down here."

"Land humans? That's what you call us?"

"Among other things."

The disdain in his voice was evident. "You don't care for my...species, I guess you'd call it...do you?"

"Land humans belong on land. My people belong down here. We're not meant to mix. One culture doesn't assimilate well into another."

"And has that happened before? Do your people live on land?"

He averted his eyes, but not before she caught the pain reflected in the crystal blue depths. "Some do. It's frowned upon, forbidden, actually."

Jaz shook her head, more confused than ever. Not only did she have a mountain of curiosity about Oceana, but she sensed a deep pain within Trey and she suddenly wanted to know what caused him hurt more than she wanted to know about Oceana.

"What happened, Trey?"

"Nothing."

"Did something happen to one of your people?"

"I don't want to talk about it, Jasmine."

"This has something to do with a woman, doesn't it?"

He arched a brow. "What makes you say that?"

"You have a hurt look. Someone hurt you. A woman." She reached for him, refusing to be put off when he pulled away. "I'm right, aren't I? Tell me about her."

He shrugged as if it didn't matter. She knew it did. "There's nothing to tell. There was this woman, years ago—an Oceanic woman. We were supposed to marry, had been together many years. I thought I was enough for her, but she chose to live on land. She wanted to be a land human more than she wanted to remain in Oceana."

What he didn't say was that this woman chose land over him. "That had to have hurt you."

"Nothing hurts me. I just learned that it's foolish to trust any woman, or love any woman."

"You can trust me, Trey."

"You're a woman, Jasmine. Trust isn't in my vocabulary. Now let's drop this subject."

Don't push him. Not now Setting aside the pain at his words, she nodded and said, "Okay, I won't ask you to tell me any more about your relationship with the woman who hurt you. But I do have a lot more questions."

"Start asking."

"No, don't say any more!"

A booming voice made her jump, her gaze gravitating to the source.

A man stood at the doorway. He was very tall, older than Trey, and imposing as hell. Long, dark hair was quickly drying against his neck. His sharp gaze was focused on her.

Dear God, he was beautiful. Fierce, like a warrior, with his flowing black hair and cerulean eyes that seemed to cut right through her. His body was magnificent—hard, firm and muscled. A cloth of some sort was fastened at his hips, dropping down low on one side. The result was a teasing glimpse at a nearly naked, perfect male specimen.

But he looked angry as hell. He held a trident in his hand, a vicious looking weapon that made him appear all the more imposing.

Immediately scrambling behind Trey, her body trembled at the deep timbre of the man standing just inside the watery doorway.

"You had no right to bring her here, Triton. No right to tell her the things you've told her."

"I had no choice, Ronan." Trey stood, holding out his hand for Jasmine. With great reluctance, she followed as they approached the one called Ronan, but Jaz didn't care at all for the way he was looking at her.

Looking at her. And she was stark naked! She quickly grabbed the discarded sheet near her feet, hurriedly wrapping it around her body. She looked at Trey, who smiled and shook his head.

"There is always choice, Triton," Ronan said, not even glancing in her direction. "You know better than to bring a land human here. What is it with these females? First, Dax, now you. You know the trouble we had with Isabelle.

"Isabelle and Dax turned out fine. Don't worry about this, Ronan. I'll take care of it."

Take care of it? Did that mean her? And what exactly would he take care of? "Excuse me, but who are you?"

Ronan turned a sharp gaze on her, then nodded slightly. "My apologies for being so rude, Dr. Quinlan. I am Ronan."

"Nice to meet you, Ronan. Now can you tell me what's going on?"

"I think Triton has told you enough. You aren't supposed to be here."

Like her presence in Oceana was her fault? "I realize that, but the fact of the matter is I *am* here. You might as well answer my questions."

Ronan turned his frowning gaze to Triton. "I warned you about this."

"I had no choice. What was I supposed to do? Let her die? It was my fault she got hurt in the first place."

Trey's fault? How could that be? He wasn't even there at the time. She stupidly veered into the rock ledge because she'd been trying to avoid a shark or something.

She rubbed her temples as a memory flash sailed through her mind. No, not a shark. It had been a dolphin. The dolphin from the aquarium, the one who'd been hovering outside Trey's sanctuary. But if he said it was his fault, that meant...

"The dolphin."

Trey and Ronan both turned to her.

"The perfectly formed Bottlenose had been outside the sanctuary. I swore he had almost human qualities. When you appeared, Trey, the dolphin disappeared." Putting her thoughts into words made her shiver. It couldn't be, could it?

Trey opened his mouth to speak, but Ronan spoke first. "You already know too much." Before she could object, he turned to Trey. "Triton, deal with this now."

Trey's eyes narrowed. "She deserves to know. I trust her."

A warmth crept into her soul at his words. He trusted her, with what must be an incredible secret. The very fact she was here, underwater, that Trey had already told her more than he obviously should have, touched her deeply.

"Why?" Ronan asked.

"Why do I trust her? Because she has the dolphins' interests at heart. She's made breakthroughs in the disease, Ronan. She knows what she's doing. She wants to help cure them."

Ronan laughed. "She's a land human, and doesn't have the knowledge we do. She can't help."

Okay, that was about enough. She'd stood by long enough and listened to them talk about her as if she wasn't even there. "Excuse me, but why are we discussing my dolphins?"

Ronan arched a brow and said, "Your dolphins?"

"Yes, my dolphins. I've been working my ass off trying to find a cure for their disease. And I'm close to finding the cause, which means an antidote will follow. Are you telling me you've been trying to cure them?"

"Of course we have been," Ronan said. "The dolphins are part of Oceana."

She crossed her arms and cast him a smug look. "So why did they come to me?"

Trey snorted a laugh. Ronan glared at both of them. "You seem very sure of yourself, Dr. Quinlan."

"I'm good at my job, Ronan. I've nearly isolated a new bacterium that could be the cause. In fact, the reason for my dive was to verify what I'd found. Now, you want to tell me you've found what I've found? And if so, then why haven't you cured them?" She didn't know who this guy was, but got the idea he was somebody with major influence in Oceana. Nevertheless, she found his attitude condescending and insulting.

Ronan's eyes widened. "Condescending and insulting?"

Oh, holy hell, she knew she hadn't said that out loud. "How did you do that?"

"We possess the powers of mental telepathy, Jaz," Trey answered. "Be careful what you think."

She looked at Trey. "You can read my mind?"

"Yes."

All the things she'd thought on land, all the fantasies she'd had about him. Had he heard them all?

"No, not everything. Some, yes, but not all. I try not to invade, especially those who do not know their minds are being read. Your secrets, whatever they are, Jaz, are safe."

It was damned disconcerting having someone inside her head. She'd have to be more careful what she thought.

"Enough of this," Ronan said, "Get her back on land where she belongs. And erase her memory before she goes."

"What?" She didn't know what that meant, but didn't care one bit for the sound of it. "No one is going to erase my memory without my permission. This is my body and my mind and no one is going to fuck with it."

"Cheeky little thing, isn't she?" Ronan said to Trey.

"You bet she is. Damn smart, too." Trey tried to keep his face serious, but Jaz caught his near-smile.

"And you think she can be of some help?"

Trey nodded. "With her knowledge and our laboratories, she might be able to come up with a solution to our problem."

Ronan studied her, as if trying to decipher how trustworthy she was. Really, the man was insufferable. And she didn't give a damn if he did read that comment from her mind.

Then his lips twitched. Subtle, and gone as soon as she'd noticed it. Surely the ogre wasn't trying to fight a smile, was he?

"Very well, Triton. See that it's done. But watch her. I don't want her to know more than she has to. Although it doesn't matter, anyway. Soon enough she'll forget."

"Would somebody please tell me what the hell that means?" she asked.

"It means what it means, Dr. Quinlan. But thank you for working so diligently to save our dolphins."

Oh sure. Just as she was about to tell him to kiss her ass, he had to go and say something nice. "You're welcome."

Ronan turned and walked through the doorway, completely disappearing in the water outside.

"Insufferable bastard."

Trey laughed, then. Loud and hard. "I swear, I've never seen anyone give Ronan as hard a time as you just did. Normally, our people just about fall at his feet."

"Why?" She followed him to the monitors, watching as Trey moved his hand across them. Visuals of the ocean sprang to life.

"Because of who he is."

"Who is he?"

"Land humans think of him as Neptune, or Poseidon. He is the master guardian of all the living things in the ocean."

She was certain her jaw dropped to her chest. "Neptune?"

Trey shrugged. "It's folklore, actually. But that is his official name, although he prefers to go by Ronan. Either way, he is what you would call the ruler of the oceans."

Holy hell. And she'd just insulted the hell out of him. *Nice move there, Jaz.*

"Would have been nice if one of you had told me that before I spoke to him like he was nobody."

"Ronan can take it. He gets too uppity sometimes anyway."

Jaz tilted her head. "I see you don't give him the honor he deserves."

"He's my brother and an irritating pain in the ass sometimes."

"Your brother?" Every ounce of blood dropped to her feet. She felt lightheaded, dizzy, her mind no longer able to comprehend all that she'd learned in a short period of time.

"Yeah. Don't make a big deal of it. We're just normal people. Well, normal for Oceana anyway."

All her childhood fantasies, legends of Poseidon and the creatures under the sea. All of it was true. This was just too much.

"Sit down, Jasmine," Trey said, finally noticing her distress. "You look pale."

He pulled up a chair and she plopped down. "I just can't believe all this."

"Well, you'd better get a grip on it because we have a lot of work to do."

He was right. Despite her shock, her attempts at assimilating all she'd heard, the one fact remained that dolphins were still sick and needed her attention. As soon as she isolated the cause, they'd be able to develop an antidote. And right now, that had to be her primary focus.

"You're right. The dolphins are our first priority. Where do we start?"

Chapter Thirteen

સ

Trey was impressed at Jasmine's fortitude. Not many women could go through what she'd been through in the past twenty-four hours and not be traumatized by it.

Instead, she seemed to have embraced life in Oceana as if she'd been born here.

Disconcerting thought. One that made him feel like he'd never felt before.

A woman he cared about who actually liked living in the sea.

No. He *didn't* care for her. They were simply emotionally joined because of the dolphins, not because of any feelings he had for her.

They had work to do, and they had to hurry before they lost any more dolphins. Now was not the time to think about how her skin reflected the water's light, about how her hair fell in soft waves down her back, or the way she chewed her lower lip when she was concentrating.

After Ronan left, Triton took her to the lab, careful to limit the number of Oceana residents in there. His first choice was to make them all leave, but their scientists had work of their own and needed to be there. All non-essential personnel were asked to make themselves scarce. It wouldn't do for her to see that many people besides him. The more memories she gathered, the more difficult it would be to erase them when the time came.

And when that time came, he *would* leave her life and her memories.

The thought of Jaz not being able to remember him and all they'd had together caused a sharp ache in his chest. Shouldn't it make him happy to know he'd finally be able to break free of her? That his ties to a land human would be severed?

That's what he wanted. He hadn't wanted to go topside in the first place, least of all to get involved with a woman there. A land human. Too close to Leelia, too many bad memories.

So why did he ache all over at the thought of never seeing her again?

"Your lab equipment is incredibly high-tech."

Jasmine's voice brought him back to the here and now, where he was supposed to be. "Does it help?"

She peered into their microscopes. "Hell yes it helps. This stuff is fantastic. Cuts the working time in half. Where did you get the bacterium samples, by the way?"

"From the lab topside. By the way, the aquarium staff thinks you're on a research trip to find out more about the bacterium. The dolphins are unchanged, status wise, and your crew is looking forward to your return."

"They'd never believe that I'd leave the dolphins."

"I kind of helped them along with a suggestion."

"What do you mean, you helped them along?"

"It's kind of complicated."

"And I'm kind of smart. So tell me."

"It's a psychic connection. I tap into their brains with a subliminal message. Sort of like projecting something on a movie screen. They see images in their head, putting in what I want them to know."

"I see. Like what you'll do to my memories once this is over."

"Sort of." He wondered how she felt about that. Her reaction was unclear as she kept her emotions masked. More importantly, how did he want her to feel about it?

"As long as they don't think I'm lying dead in the bottom of the ocean, I suppose that'll work. I wish you didn't have to do that to them, though."

"What would you have me tell them, Jaz? That you suffered an injury while diving and I rescued you, and you're doing a bit of research in Oceana, an underwater civilization no one is supposed to know about, and you'll be back later?"

She scrunched her nose. "I guess not. This is all just so...complicated, Trey."

Indeed, it was. More than even she could imagine. "I know. I'm sorry, but that's the way it has to be. We've survived down here forever without land human intervention because we've managed to keep our existence a secret. With the media as it is today, can you imagine what would happen if your people found out about our existence?"

"I wouldn't tell them."

"We can't afford to take the chance it might slip out. One of the primary reasons we keep Oceana undiscovered by land humans."

"So everything I know about this place, the incredible things I've seen, will all be erased from my memories."

"Yes. There's no other choice."

She hesitated, then nodded. "I guess I understand the necessity. Shall we get back to work?"

Just like that, she'd shut him off, as if she didn't care.

He rolled his eyes and went back to work, disgusted with himself. Here he was mooning about how Jaz felt, when he didn't want her around in the first place. And he sure as hell didn't want any attachments, especially to a land human.

It was best this way. Do their jobs, bring the dolphins back to health and return Jasmine to land, where she belonged.

Without memories of him or Oceana.

* * * * *

Jaz's eyes widened as a man with a human torso and a fish tail swam to the entrance of the lab. His lower body gleamed an aqua blue color. As he swam through the watery doorway, his lower half transformed into a human male. Thankfully, he wore the same kind of loincloth some of the men wore here.

Oceana was amazing. Different species from human to merman to sprites and so many others she couldn't even name them all. Many ran around naked, a fact she found quite interesting, and yet not shocking in the least. Some wore the loincloth or toga-like shifts.

She looked around for Trey, but didn't see him.

"Hey," the man said, nodding and moving over to one of the tables.

"Hey," she mumbled in response, shocked to her toes.

She couldn't help but stare at him, and heated from forehead to her knees when he looked up at her with a questioning look on his face.

"Are you new here?" he asked.

"You could say that." Was she even supposed to tell him she was from topside?

His aqua eyes widened. "Oh, you're the land human."

"Yes."

He walked over to her and held out his hand. Webbing spread wide as he opened his fingers. "I am Zaren."

"Hello, Zaren," she said. "I'm Jasmine."

His smile gleamed white against his dark skin. "Welcome to Oceana."

A shock of awareness spread through her as he squeezed her fingers. Such heat emanated from his body. It was almost like touching Trey, but with Trey there was more of a passionate connection. With Zaren, it was different. "You're a merman?"

He nodded. "Bet you don't see my kind up on land very often."

His smile was infectious, and her wariness began to dissipate. When he motioned her onto a stool next to his, she sat, thankful for someone to talk to. Trey had been disconcertingly silent lately. "No, I don't see mermen of any kind topside."

"Kind of hard for us to occupy your labs in this condition."

"Yet you assumed nearly human form when you came in here."

He nodded. "True. Can't flood the lab with water because of our experiments, so we shapeshift to accommodate the lack of ocean."

More things to amaze her. "Are all of Oceana's people shapeshifters?"

"No, just the guardians."

"Guardians?"

"Don't you have work to do, Zaren?"

Jasmine turned at the sound of Trey's voice, surprised to find him glaring at them. She looked at Zaren, who shrugged and smiled. "I'm talking to Jasmine right now."

"Jasmine's busy and doesn't need to waste time making idle talk with you."

Zaren arched a brow. "If I didn't know you better, Triton, I'd think you want to keep her all to yourself."

"I think you're full of shit, Zar. Now go fuck around somewhere else and leave us to our work."

Zaren laughed, picked up Jasmine's hand and pressed a soft kiss to her palm. She shivered when sexual heat instantly trickled down her body. When she looked up at Zaren, he winked. "A little psychic gift from me to you."

She supposed *whoa* wouldn't be an appropriate response. "Umm, thank you."

"Trust me, Jasmine," he said as he stood and headed to the door. "It was my pleasure."

She watched him leave, marveling at the instant transformation from human male to merman as he stepped through the watery doorway, then swam away. She looked at Trey's angry face.

"He sent you a sexual connection, didn't he?" he asked, his voice dark and accusatory.

"I guess so." She rubbed her palm against her thigh, still feeling the tingle.

"Prick," he mumbled.

Jasmine fought a smile. Trey was jealous!

Now why did that thought thrill her so much? And why did she suddenly want to see what she could do with that jealousy?

"It was amazing. Like nothing I've ever felt before," she said as matter-of-factly as she could, moving back to the microscope she'd been working at before Zaren's arrival.

"Really. Never felt anything like that before, huh?"

"Nope, nothing that intense. My body still tingles."

She waited, poised for his response, some perverse side of her wanting to see if he even cared that another man had shot her a sexual zinger. But he didn't say a word. So she decided to push a little harder, and let out a dreamy sigh.

"All right, that's enough!"

She jumped at the sound of his voice, and looked up to find him storming toward her. Instead of fear, her body came alive with a sensual tremor of excitement.

He didn't stop when he reached her side, just pulled her against him and ground his hips against hers.

Pinning her hands at her sides, his fingers dug into her flesh. But it didn't hurt. Instead, her cunt moistened, instantly ready for him. These little shifts the women of Oceana wore didn't include underwear, which stimulated her to know that nothing separated his cock from her pussy.

And she'd bet Trey already knew that.

"Is this exciting to you, Jasmine?" he asked, the husk in his voice thrilling her.

"Yes," she managed in a whisper. Her throat was dry. All moisture in her body had gathered between her legs.

"Better than Zaren's little psychic fuck?"

"Yes." She'd pushed him too hard, had no idea he'd react this way. But still, she was incredibly turned on, especially when he dragged her into a narrow passage, not quite outside the main lab but away from the viewing area to anyone outside.

His eyes had darkened to a stormy blue, his gaze so intense the heat between them was palpable. Her nipples brushed his bare chest and instantly hardened, the peaks extending as if desperately searching for contact with his body.

Just like his cock, which grew insistently against her. She let out a whimper and pushed against the hands holding her arms down. Trey released her and she threaded her fingers into his lush hair, pulling his face towards hers.

His lips crashed down over hers, his tongue plunging inside. The torture was merciless.

Heedless of their surroundings, she lifted one leg and wrapped it around his hip. The thin cloth he wore was no barrier to his burgeoning shaft, and he brushed the material aside.

Jasmine reached for his rigid heat, cupping it in her palm, sliding her hand over his length until he uttered a harsh curse against her ear.

"Yes, Jasmine, stroke my cock, make it ready. I'm going to fuck you. Right here, right now."

Part of her wanted to pull away, to beg for privacy. The other part of her didn't care where they were, as long as Trey drove his shaft deep inside her. She ached for him, craved a release that felt too long denied. Pent-up anxiety coursed through her, demanding relief.

She grazed the tip of his penis with her index finger, rewarded with drops of his silken fluid. Catching his heated gaze with her own, she lifted her finger to her mouth and licked his essence.

Trey groaned and raised her shift over her hips, slipping his cock between her legs. Her moisture seeped over his shaft and she slid against him, sparks of pleasure stabbing her core as her clit rode the velvety softness of his penis.

He held her leg poised over his hip, backed her against the wall, then lifted her off the ground and drove his cock hard into her cunt.

He captured her cries with his eager mouth. She wrapped her legs around his waist and he grabbed her buttocks, his fingers digging into the tender flesh, massaging her, pulling her closer.

She loved the feel of him, the sweet ocean scent of his neck when she buried her face against it. His pulse pounded against her lips and she nipped at it, rewarded with his guttural groan.

"Tell me what pleases you, Jasmine," he said through panting breaths. "Do you like a long cock?"

She lifted and met his teasing gaze, not sure what he meant by that question. She was about to ask when his cock elongated inside her. Subtly, so that she barely felt it at first, and then...wow. Oh, God did she feel it, inch by lengthening inch until the tip bumped against her womb.

"Or maybe long and thick."

She hadn't been imagining it. As he said the words, his thickening cock stretched her walls, filling her so completely he could barely slide it back and forth.

"Oh my God," she whispered, unable to believe what he'd just done.

"Tell me what you like, and I'll make it happen."

She couldn't wrap her mind around the delicious sensations of being so totally filled, let alone make any suggestions.

"Maybe you'd like me to have longer arms, so I can do this."

Despite their positions, she felt his fingers probing her cunt, felt him swipe at her seeping juices, then teasing the entrance to her anus. Shocks of pleasure made her pussy tighten around him as he teased her puckered hole. When he slipped his finger inside her, she cried out.

No way could he do that unless he grew longer arms.

"Holy shit, Trey!"

He laughed then, removing his fingers and returning his cock to normal size.

"I can give it to you huge like that, baby, but right now I just want to drive it up into you hard and fast until you scream sweet pleasure in my ear."

The mere thought of him doing just that had her teetering on the edge of reason. She held on tight as he once again rocked her close against him, then thrust upwards, impaling her on his thick shaft until she was near delirious with the sensations.

A spiraling, sweet tightening formed inside her core, starting at her belly and spreading outward like white heat. It was too intense, she couldn't take the pleasure.

"Hang on, Jasmine, we're almost there."

Trey clutched her close, then stroked her, his pelvis brushing lightly against her clit as he leisurely took her to the pinnacle.

The contractions pulsed within her and she dug her nails into his back. "Hard now, Trey, fuck me harder!"

With a dark laugh, he did just that, plunging deeply, so deep she felt the pinpricks of delight all the way to her womb. Then she toppled over the cliff, indeed doing exactly what he'd asked for. She screamed her climax into his ear, riding him hard and fast until she took him along with her. He tensed, then poured his seed inside her.

Jasmine kept her eyes closed tight, using her sense of smell and hearing to breathe in the scent of sex that permeated the air around them, the sweet smell of satisfaction that made her tremble in Trey's arms. She listened to the rush of blood pounding in her ears as she fought for even breathing, and heard Trey's panting breaths as he ruffled the hair against her cheek.

God help her, nothing could compare to loving this man. She'd fallen hard for a man who wasn't even human.

A man she knew she would never have a future with.

Chapter Fourteen

ॐ

"I think I've found it!" Jaz looked up excitedly and searched the lab for Trey. He came out of a storage room, arching a brow.

"You have?"

"Yes. Come look!"

For two days they'd been working tirelessly to isolate the bacterium. They'd come close so many times, only to suffer disappointment when their trials didn't equal the bacteria they'd found in the digestive tracts of the ailing dolphins.

They'd pushed on, eating and sleeping very little, barely even speaking to each other unless one of them felt close to uncovering the mystery.

In the back of her mind dwelled the fact that the closer they came to discovering the cause and developing an antidote, the sooner she'd be leaving Oceana. And when that happened, her memories would be washed of any knowledge of this beautiful place.

And of Trey.

"Tell me what you've found."

She inhaled his scent, always like a fresh ocean breeze. "Remember we talked about the dolphins ingesting sponges and that possibly being the culprit?"

"Yeah."

"Well, I took another sampling and discovered a new strain of bacteria. This one from diseased coral which the sponges must have come into contact with."

"Go on."

"I've never seen this strain before. It's almost like it's deep sea based, because I've never come across it on land. And I've never seen it on any of the coral found in the shallow waters."

"Let me see."

She scooted to the side, allowing him access to the viewing bar. His arm brushed against hers, and her entire body tingled. It still amazed her that the slightest touch of his skin against her could cause such a combustible reaction.

"That's interesting. It looks like a new strain, all right. A combination of the B and C strains we'd looked at earlier."

"Exactly. And that's why we couldn't identify it. So I'm thinking if we mix the antibiotic antidotes that separately cure both the B and C samples, then combine them into the right dosage amounts, we've got our cure."

He looked up and nodded. "Sounds like it. That's why our scientists couldn't figure it out. What it looks like to me is something that's based on both a land bacterium and one indigenous to the sea. Rare as hell."

"Exactly. I'll get to work testing the antidotes right away."

"Good." He paused, then added, "How long do you think before you'll have the antidote?"

"About two days, maximum. I'm really anxious to get this finished so we can administer it to the dolphins."

"Okay. I'll let you work on it, then."

His gaze lingered, compelling her to reach for him. She ran her palm across his cheek, her toes curling when he pressed a soft kiss to her palm.

Two days. If this worked, that's all they'd have left together.

And he didn't even know she loved him. Would it matter if she told him? Would it complicate things? Did he even care?

No. Don't think about it, and for God's sake don't tell him. She'd only end up hurting herself when she found out her love for him didn't change anything. She'd still have to leave Oceana.

* * * * *

True to her word, in less than two days, Jasmine had an antidote to the dolphins' infection. Now it was up to Trey to administer it, and if it worked, bring her back to land.

Where she belonged.

He stood over her in the darkness, watching her sleep. She'd long ago discarded the light blanket on his bed, and her body glowed in the natural ocean light.

She slept on her stomach, her hair in wild disarray around her shoulders.

The most perfect body he'd ever seen. Hell, the most perfect woman he'd ever known. And she would soon leave him.

When he looked down at her sleeping in his bed, he knew she belonged there. There, and in his sanctuary, in the lab, working side by side with him, and swimming next to him in the waters. Why did the thought of her leaving make his stomach ache with a burning pain of loss?

With a longing he hadn't expected, he wanted to crawl back into bed with her, wrap her in his arms and never let her go.

But she didn't belong with him, or in Oceana.

And he had no business loving her. But he did, had stupidly allowed his emotions to interfere with his vow not to get involved, not to love again.

This time, when she left, it would hurt much worse than when Leelia left. He realized now that his love for Jasmine was so much more than what he'd felt for Leelia.

Leelia had been an unattainable beauty, convinced that she belonged on land. He'd been more determined to convince her that she belonged with him, competing with the land for her affections. That elusive quality about her that he'd never been able to reach had been the attraction. It hadn't been love.

Not like what he felt for Jasmine.

When Leelia had left, his ego had been bruised. When Jasmine left, part of his soul would go with her.

Bending down next to the bed, he whispered in her ear. "Jasmine, I'm leaving."

She shifted and let out a soft moan. "Mmm hmm."

Trey smiled in the darkness. "I'm going topside now to deliver the antibiotics to the dolphins."

"Okay."

She was exhausted, hadn't slept at all the past two nights. No wonder she wouldn't stir.

That, and the fact he'd kept her up last night making love to her over and over again until they'd both fallen into a spent slumber.

Each time he held her in his arms, he knew that in a short period of time she'd be out of his life forever. A thought that a few weeks ago he would have welcomed with a sigh of relief.

But not any longer.

No sense in delaying the inevitable. He swept his hand over her silken hair and pressed a kiss to her lips. She murmured and sighed, offering him a sleepy smile, but didn't wake.

"Sleep well, my little siren. I'll be back soon."

He swam out the door armed with the vials necessary to treat the dolphins, hopeful that the serum would work, and at the same time dreading what would happen when he returned to Oceana.

With his lightning fast swimming, the trip topside took only a few minutes. He walked out of the water, clothing immediately appearing on his now dry body, and smiled, thinking how Jasmine would love to be able to do something like that.

So many things he had yet to show her, so many things she would be capable of if she were a resident of Oceana.

But he'd never be able to tell her, or show her, any of the miracles of their civilization.

Enough. Quit thinking about it. She isn't staying, so deal with it. With renewed determination, he slipped inside the lab, grateful it was before daybreak. He could administer the antidote, hang around a day or so and watch for results, then hopefully swim back down to Oceana with good news for Jasmine.

If the antidote worked. That was his first task. Before any of Jasmine's assistants arrived, he'd administered the serum to every one of the sick dolphins. He charted their progress, including the dates and times and dosage levels for each dolphin, knowing Jasmine would want to have access to the information when she returned.

He explained Jasmine's continued absence by indicating she was offsite gathering more information on the cause of the illness, and thought he could handle administering the antidotes. The staff seemed to buy it with no problem, their excitement over a possible cure taking precedence over any other thoughts.

And everyone at the aquarium seemed to trust him, which helped his explanation. Throughout the day, he and the staff monitored the dolphins' vital signs. Finally, the sun began its descent into the waiting horizon and the staff had gone home for the night. He had a minute in the tanks without anyone else around and a chance to talk to Dane.

"They were holding steady for a few days, but just yesterday it started to get bad. I was about to alert you."

Trey nodded. "We worked as quickly as we could. I just hope we're in time."

Dane morphed into human form and sat on the edge of the tank with Trey. "How are things going down there?"

"I just told you. We worked like demons getting the antidote ready."

Dane shook his head, his hair falling over his brow. He quickly brushed it away. "Not what I'm talking about. I mean with you and the sexy doctor."

"Nothing's happening there. We're just working."

"Uh huh. And I'm really a dolphin. Now give, brother. Tell me what's going on. I can feel the power between the two of you. It's strong. Ronan's worried."

"Ronan worries like an old woman."

"With good reason."

His life would be a lot simpler if the other guardians quit riding his ass. First they wanted him to find a woman so he'd quit thinking about Leelia. Then when he did find a woman, they told him he couldn't have her. "Ronan has nothing to be concerned about. Jasmine will be brought back up here as soon as we're confident the antidote works."

"Which doesn't tell me a damn thing about how you feel about her."

"It doesn't matter how I feel." He turned away and looked out over the ocean. The sun won the battle against the fog today, giving him a clear view of the dark sea. The orange fireball lowered faster and faster toward the water.

Jasmine was down there, waiting for him. Was she as anxious as he was about being together again?

Damn, he hated feeling this way. He'd been happier when he didn't give a shit about anyone.

"You're in love!"

Trey spun back to Dane and immediately wanted to knock the smirk off his face. "I am not in love."

"How quickly you forget that we're bonded psychically, moron. I know what you feel. Well goddamn if the little professor didn't bite you in the ass with the love bug."

"Fuck off, Dane." He'd sell his soul to keep his thoughts to himself for just one freakin' day. Why did everyone always have to know what he was thinking? Damn brothers of his anyway.

The grin on Dane's face widened. "Okay, so you love her. It's no crime, is it?"

"Crime? No. Inconvenient? Hell yeah."

"So make it work."

"Easier said than done You know damn well she belongs up here and I belong in Oceana. We are the proverbial couple from two different worlds."

"Like I said, so what? Just make it work. Does she seem like she wants to live in Oceana?"

As if she'd been born there. He'd never known a land human to take so readily to their civilization. Without batting an eye, she'd assimilated to their way of life, and seemed to love it. But that didn't matter. "Won't make any difference. She isn't staying down there with me and that's that."

"I see. You're afraid."

Trey stood and walked away, gazing out toward the ocean. Irritation bubbled up inside him, slowly heating to eruption level. "You know damn well I'm not afraid of anything."

"Except love. Leelia wins again, doesn't she?"

He whirled around, intent on giving his brother a piece of his mind, and quite possibly a piece of his fist. "This has nothing to do with Leelia. It has to do with two people who are wrong for each other."

Dane didn't seem the least bit concerned about Trey's advancement toward him. He merely shrugged and said, "You're a coward, Trey. You're so afraid of loving a woman again and losing her to the land that you won't even allow yourself to feel it."

He stopped inches from Dane, so angry he could feel the tremors coursing through his body. He grasped Dane's arms, ready to fling him into the water. "Stay out of my personal business, Dane."

Dane didn't flinch. "Why? Somebody's got to knock some sense into you. And I love you just enough to be the one to do it." He pushed back so hard that Trey had to fight for balance.

Shock rendered him still, and speechless. Dane had never fought him before. Hell, they were closer than any of the brothers. He'd never seen Dane so angry. "Why does this matter to you?" he finally asked.

"Because I've been watching this downward spiral of yours for years, Trey. Ever since Leelia chose land over you, you've had this goddamn chip on your shoulder. You shut out everyone and hid behind this wall of hurt you built so high. You shut out women, and you shut us all out, too."

"I did not."

"Yeah, you did. And the funny thing is, losing Leelia was the best thing that could have happened to you. She wasn't worth your effort, Trey, only you were too blinded by the fact that you "lost" to even see that what you lost wasn't worth keeping."

Was Dane right? Had he erected a wall around his emotions when Leelia left? He sat again on the edge of the tank and thought about it.

"Leelia never loved you. She used you, strung you along until it was time for her to leave. Only she was your first love and you were blind to all her faults. All you could see was this beautiful, exotic and wonderful woman who left you, when in fact she was a spoiled, manipulative, evil bitch and everyone in Oceana breathed a sigh of relief the day she relinquished her rights as a citizen."

Trey searched Dane's eyes, discovering a truth he hadn't been willing to see for too long.

"The real beauty, the incredibly wonderful woman who is your true life mate, waits for you in Oceana. You gonna fuck up twice in your lifetime, Trey, and let the one go that you really *should* fight to keep?"

"She doesn't belong down there with us, Dane. I have to bring her back here."

Dane shrugged and threw up his hands. "Then I'm finished with this conversation. I'll go check on the dolphins."

He watched Dane change back into dolphin form and swim away, feeling as if he'd lost his best friend. Scrubbing his hand behind his neck, he fought the headache beginning there.

He wanted to believe things could work out, but letting go of the past wasn't as easy as realizing how foolish he'd been about that past.

He wouldn't ask Jasmine to stay. It wasn't fair to her. She had a life up here on land. She was a land human, and he wouldn't take her way of life from her.

A few days later, Trey was resigned to the inevitable. The good news was that the antidote had worked. The dolphins were making steady progress toward recovery, and if all went well they'd be released within the next couple days.

A true celebration would take place in Oceana when the dolphins returned to their homes.

During those days, all Trey could think about was his conversation that night with Dane. Some of what Dane had said made sense. He *had* closed himself off, and it was probably time to start living again.

But that didn't mean making a life with Jasmine. He wouldn't compete with her life on land. He wanted a woman willing to live in Oceana, and a land human wasn't that woman.

First things first. He had to go back down and tell Jasmine the good news. Then he'd erase her memory and return her back to the aquarium, where she belonged.

How he felt about her was irrelevant. Some things simply weren't meant to be. But he was determined to get his life in order, and that meant it was well past time he found a mate.

As soon as the dolphins were returned and life got back to normal, he'd work on that.

Except every time he closed his eyes and imagined his ideal mate, the only woman who came to mind was Jasmine.

Chapter Fifteen

೫

The waiting was killing her.

Jasmine paced the sanctuary, noticing for the first time that there were no clocks in Oceana. She had no idea how long Trey had been gone, other than it had been several sleeping cycles.

She still remembered his touch, his kiss, that early morning he had left.

They'd argued about him going up and administering the antidote. It was her job, her responsibility, and she'd demanded that she be allowed to go up there and take care of the dolphins. Eventually he'd won, saying if the cure didn't work he didn't want to drag her back down again. He'd deliver the antidote, and if the dolphins started to get better, then he'd come back for her.

Come back, wipe out her memories and return her to land.

Trouble was, she didn't want to go back. She wanted to stay in Oceana.

This was her home now. Trey's sanctuary was warm, comfortable, and in his bed was where she belonged.

Only she didn't belong here, at least not according to Trey.

But who said he was the be-all, end-all decision maker around here? Didn't her wants and wishes count?

What if she wanted to stay in Oceana? Would he let her? More importantly, would he want her to? Would Ronan even let her stay?

She wrung her hands and looked outside at the blue world surrounding her. Approaching the door, she lifted her hand and slipped it through the doorway, loving the feel of rushing ocean water tickling her palm.

What if she walked through there without Trey? Would she be able to breathe, or could she only do that with Trey's magic touch?

Worry peppered her thoughts. Worry about the dolphins and whether the antidote worked, about the aquarium and how they were dealing in her absence, and mostly about what was going to happen when Trey returned.

She walked over to the monitors, reaching up and touching them as if they could give her some clue as to Trey's whereabouts. Or even his state of mind.

"You agonize too much, Dr. Quinlan."

She turned to see Ronan stepping through the door. Her heart raced, pounding against her chest. Was he here to erase her memories?

Not yet, please not yet. I need to see Trey one more time before my memories of him are wiped away. "I'm not worried."

He smiled, revealing white, even teeth. "You forget I can read your emotions."

She wrinkled her nose at him. "And that's damned irritating, too."

His eyes widened and he laughed. "So Triton tells me."

He approached her, and waved his hands over the monitors. They came to life, pictures of ocean scenes in vibrant blues and greens spread out over the screens. "Would you like to see him?"

She gazed at his face, wondering if this was some kind of joke. "You can do that?"

Another wave over a monitor screen and Trey appeared. He was at the aquarium, in one of the tanks with some man she didn't know. She frowned, wondering who else would have access to the dolphins, when suddenly the unknown man changed before her eyes, becoming a Bottlenose dolphin. She sucked in a gasp and looked to Ronan.

"That's Dane, another one of the guardians and our brother," he explained. "And in answer to your unasked questions, the dolphins are recovering."

Relief washed over her. She closed her eyes and sent up a silent prayer of thanks. "I'm glad. Once they are healthy again, we can return them to the ocean."

"Good. We are anxious to have them back with us."

Jaz shook her head. "There's so much I don't know. Your world is so magical."

"Yes, it is. You seem to have taken to Oceana quite well."

"I love it here. It's like nothing I could have imagined, and yet it's everything I have wished for."

"Your love for the ocean is unusual. Most land humans would be frightened to find themselves in your position."

She shrugged and clenched her fingers into her palm, desperately wanting to reach out and trace Trey's outline on the monitor, but unable to do so with Ronan there. "I've always loved the sea. I was practically born in it. This is home to me." Then she turned to him and said, "Why can't I stay here, Ronan?"

His eyes widened. "It's simply not done. You are human and belong on land."

"That's pretty narrow minded. Obviously my physical makeup can be altered so I can breathe down here. Are you telling me that no land human has ever made the transition to life in Oceana?"

He opened his mouth to speak, then closed it again. "It is not for me to explain these things. You will have to ask Triton."

But Triton didn't want her there. She already knew that. Asking Ronan about it was pointless.

"Some things we need to leave to destiny, Dr. Quinlan."

She nodded, misery surrounding her like an early morning fog. She wrapped herself up in a blanket of despair and resigned herself to waiting for the inevitable.

"Trey is returning," Ronan said.

She glanced at the doorway, then looked up at Ronan. "When?"

"Very soon. I will leave you now." He walked away, then stopped as he reached the doorway and turned to look at her. "Dr. Quinlan?"

"Call me Jasmine."

"Jasmine, then. On behalf of all of us in Oceana, we thank you for the work you did to heal our dolphins. You are a very talented doctor."

Somehow she sensed that a compliment from Ronan wasn't an everyday thing. "Truly, it was my pleasure. I love them all very much. When one dies, a part of me dies along with them."

"Yes, in that we agree."

"Ronan?"

"Yes."

"Thank you for allowing me this glimpse into your world."

He was silent for a second, then nodded. "You're welcome."

She looked away, not wanting Ronan to see the tears welling in her eyes. She swiped them away with her fingers, then looked back to the doorway.

Ronan was gone. Instead, Trey stood there, smiling up at her.

"Trey!" Without hesitation, she ran to him, catapulting herself into his arms.

He wound his arms around her and lifted her off the ground, nearly crushing her in a tight hug. She threaded her fingers through his hair and pulled him close, then kissed him with all the longing she'd held inside the past few days.

He groaned his response into her mouth, his tongue delving inside to slide against hers. Jaz wrapped her legs around his waist, refusing to let go of the delicious contact of her body around his.

She hadn't realized until the moment he returned how much a part of her life he'd become in such a short period of time.

She loved him. God help her, she loved him, and no matter if they had one hour, one day or one minute left together, she'd show him how much she cared about him.

"Make love to me, Trey. Right now," she urged, needing him inside her, desperate for that ultimate joining with him.

Without words, he turned and walked through the doorway. By now she was familiar with the rushing sensation of water entering her lungs, and she breathed it in, happy to be back in the ocean.

They swam together, Trey leading her by the hand toward the darkened cove she'd grown to love. A school of brightly colored fish no bigger than her hand surrounded them and followed along, swimming beside her. She laughed, reaching out to pet the small creatures as they wriggled by.

In the water she wasn't a strange human, she was one of them. She sensed no fear or skittishness from any of the fish and wished for a lifetime to get to know and study all the wonderful ocean creatures.

But a lifetime down here wasn't her destiny, so instead she'd concentrate on right now. With Trey.

He led her into the cave and set her down. Soft seagrass tickled her back and buttocks, but she welcomed his weight as he settled against her. Her body warmed and readied itself for him, opening like a flower spreads out for the heat of the summer sun.

It had been too many long days without him. She refused to think about what the rest of her life would be without Trey to hold onto, to make love to, to share her life with.

When had he become so important to her? He infuriated her, challenged her, and opened up a world to her that she'd never dreamed was possible.

And she loved him. That she wouldn't try to analyze, because there was no way to decipher the workings of one's heart. She just accepted it, determined to love him for as long as he'd allow her to remember him.

"There's a depth in those gorgeous green eyes of yours that tells me you're thinking about something. Something important."

She smiled up at him. "I'm thinking how much I've missed you, how much I've missed this." Arching her hips, she brushed his swollen cock, rewarded with his swift intake of breath.

"And what is my sweet little siren's pleasure, today?" he asked. "Would you like to make love to a merman?"

Before her eyes his body shifted, from the waist down spouting a gorgeous tail of cerulean blue. He swished it back and forth, stirring the water around them.

"Or perhaps you'd like to have a water dragon lick you all over with his sizeable tongue." In an instant, he stood before her like a great medieval dragon, a long tail swiping at the grassy floor. He tilted his dragon's head to the sky and roared, flicking his tongue out.

Her eyes widened. And what a tongue that was! Imagining a tongue like that pleasuring her had pulsing shots of pleasure melting her pussy. "Mmm, perhaps I'd like to have a dragon for a pet. I can imagine you'd keep me entertained for a very long time with that talented tongue of yours."

Surprisingly, she didn't fear his ability to shift shapes. She accepted that this was a wonderland of magic. Oceana held secrets that she knew it would take her a lifetime to discover.

She wished with all her heart she could have that lifetime with Trey.

In an instant, he shifted back to his human form. "I think I'd like to make love to you this way, unless you have some other preference."

Wrapping her legs around him, she pulled him inside her, letting out a gasp of pure delight as he buried his cock deep. "Oh yes, this is the Trey I want to make love to me."

His lips captured hers in a kiss that she swore spoke volumes to her. A kiss of desire, of longing…of love?

Surely she was transferring her own emotions into Trey's kiss. He didn't love her — if he did, he'd ask her to stay. Wishful thinking on her part wasn't going to change his mind.

And she'd never beg a man to love her, would never plead with Trey to be allowed to stay. Instead, when it was time to go, she'd go.

Maybe it was a good thing he was going to erase her memories. She'd die knowing she was missing this for the rest of her life.

He thrust deeper, then moved them off the mossy bank until they floated in the water. Trey swiftly flipped them over and she found herself straddling his thighs, her cunt impaled on his cock. The position allowed her to slide forward and back, brushing her clit against his pelvis.

"Lord, Trey," she murmured, the unbelievable sensations sending her into a frenzy of movements. Her pussy tightened around his shaft, squeezing him hard.

"You're so tight, Jasmine. Your body was made for mine." He reached for her breasts, gently squeezing them together and sliding his thumbs over her erect nipples. She tilted her head back and rode him hard.

The wild colors of Oceana floated above her, around her, her mind and body one with Trey and the exquisite beauty of the sea. She couldn't take much more. Tears blurred her vision as the intensity of feelings overpowered her.

This was the last time she'd make love with Trey. She knew it, and so did he. He poured out his feelings in his movements, in the way he lightly brushed her breasts with his fingertips, then leaned up to capture her mouth in a devastating kiss.

Her climax roared through her body. She stiffened and clutched Trey's shoulders as she rode out the sweet sensations arching inside her. With a loud groan, Trey came with her, spilling his seed in quick, short thrusts.

Jasmine collapsed on top of him, feeling them move as they slowly floated back down to the sea floor. She couldn't keep her hands still, wanting to memorize every plane and angle of his body, knowing that no matter what kind of spell he put on her to take her memory away, her heart would always be his.

"The antidote worked, Jaz. The dolphins are gaining strength every day."

She heard the sadness in his voice, and knew it equaled her own. She also knew what he was trying to tell her. Reaching for his face, she slid her palm over his jaw. "I'm glad."

She wanted to say more. *Tell him you love him, tell him you want to stay!* But the logical part of her refused to listen to her heart. If he wanted her to stay he would have asked. His feelings didn't mirror hers.

He turned her over onto her back and hovered above her, his smile gentle.

"It's time," he said.

"I know." She fought back the tears, refusing to let him see how much this was going to hurt her. She wished she could tell him she loved him. She wished she was strong enough to face the rejection afterwards, but she couldn't bring herself to open her mouth and say the words.

Kissing her lips lightly, Trey whispered, "I love you, Jasmine."

Shock silenced her. Had he said what she thought he'd just said? Before she could respond, he brushed his thumb over her forehead, and darkness began to descend upon her.

"No Trey, wait!" she cried, but her words came out slurred. She struggled against the heaviness forcing her eyelids closed, but she knew it was futile.

She wanted to tell him she loved him, and now she'd never get that chance. Her hesitation had cost her the man of her dreams.

The tears flowed freely as she sailed into unconsciousness.

Chapter Sixteen

ജ

Dear God, Jasmine had the worst hangover of her life, and she couldn't even remember drinking the night before.

She massaged her temples, reluctant to open her eyes against the morning light streaming in through the mini-blinds in her bedroom.

Her brain felt like it was covered in fuzz. For the life of her she couldn't recall what she'd done last night that would make her head pound like this.

Gradually she squinted open her eyes, then groaned and forced herself out of bed. A shower and some very strong coffee were in order. She wondered what day it was. From the location of the sun radiating into her window, it had to be mid-morning, so she hoped like hell it was the weekend.

Or else she was very, very late to work.

By the time she showered and ate she felt a lot better, except for the weird gaps in her memory. She'd just go down to the lab and read through her notes. That should help clear her mind.

Okay, so it was definitely Saturday. Friday's date on the calendar had been crossed out and there were only one or two of the weekend staff on hand. She smiled and greeted them. They waved, everyone grinning because the dolphins were all going to pull through.

Elation soared through her as she scoured her notes and reviewed the latest blood test results on the dolphins. The bacteria had been eradicated, the dolphins were eating again and showing signs of energy and playfulness. They were about ready to be returned to the ocean.

Stepping outside into the beautiful day, she squinted as she peered through the gates towards the ocean. Something pulled at her when she looked at water, a force so strong it tightened inside her stomach and caused her physical pain.

Brushing off the weird feeling, she headed out to the aquarium tanks, grinning when she saw the dolphins swimming and playing. She breathed out a sigh of relief, thankful they'd managed to come up with the antidote to the new strain of bacteria.

She sat on the edge of the tank and dangled her feet in the water, laughing as the dolphins came up and 'spoke' to her. Even they seemed happy, and she was certain they were anxious to get back to the ocean.

"Soon, my friends, you'll be back home where you belong."

That nagging sense of longing hit her again, and she found her gaze drifting toward the sandy beach and beyond. Thrilled by the impending release of the dolphins, she couldn't seem to shake the melancholy that had been with her since she woke up this morning. Tears formed and she sniffed them back, thinking she must be having some massive PMS attack to be feeling so sad over nothing.

"Well, well, well, Dr. Quinlan. Very soon the dolphins will be back where they belong."

Rolling her eyes heavenward in a silent plea for mercy, she turned to Claude. "Yes, they will be."

He sniffed, pulling the cuffs down on his starched shirt. It was Saturday, for God's sake. Didn't the man ever put on a pair of sweats and get comfortable? Probably not. She bet he starched his underwear too, the stuffy prick.

"Perhaps we can get back to training our own dolphins for the upcoming shows, then. God knows these creatures have been a horrible financial drain."

Jaz couldn't bite back the retort that hovered on her lips. "Yeah, it's a shame they didn't die the first few days. Look at all the money you'd have saved."

"I didn't say that."

"You didn't have to, Claude." She stood and brushed by him, fed up with his penny-pinching, uncaring treatment of animals. She stopped in front of him. "I'm going to petition the board to return this aquarium to a research facility. I'm turning in my paper on the antidote for the new bacterium we discovered, and going to request it be printed in the Journal for Mammalian Medicine. Hopefully we'll get enough grants and interested parties to make this place what it should have been all along—a research facility, not a theme park."

"You have no say in the matter, doctor."

He had no idea. "Watch me, Claude."

"I'll have you fired."

She laughed at his sneer, no longer caring what he did or said he was going to do. "Would probably be the best thing you could ever do for me."

She walked away without another word, determined that she wouldn't sit by and let this happen. The first thing she'd do is email some of her colleagues and get them down here to start running the show. She was a good mammalian veterinarian, but this place needed to be staffed by the bigwigs in research.

Once she got the ball rolling on that, there wouldn't be a damn thing Claude could do. The snowball effect would take over and he'd have to remove the sideshow circus and focus on research.

Back in the lab, she made notes on her observations, then planned for the release of the dolphins. Once she finished up at the lab, she went back to her apartment.

She should feel a great elation and sense of satisfaction, but she couldn't seem to shake the depression that had grabbed hold of her today. The thought she was supposed to be somewhere else stayed with her well into the evening. She tried reading a book, then doing some research, finally settling on a glass of wine while she sat outside on her balcony.

Listening to the waves crashing into the shore seemed to offer the only comfort.

What was wrong with her, anyway? Why did she feel a compelling need to kick off her shoes and run headlong into the ocean?

What was down there that she wanted so damn badly?

She wished she knew, because these feelings were driving her crazy.

* * * * *

"You've managed to irritate just about everyone in your sector of Oceana, Triton."

Trey ignored Ronan and concentrated on monitoring. "So?"

"So I think it's time we have a talk."

"I don't feel like talking." He didn't feel like doing much of anything except watching Jasmine. Of course he did it under the guise of watching the preparations for the dolphins' release today.

He couldn't take his eyes off her, hadn't been able to stop watching her since he'd erased her memories and took her back to land. God, he missed her so much it was like a knife permanently wedged in his heart.

Trey felt Ronan's hand on his shoulder. "You love her."

Denial sat poised on his lips, but what was the use? "Yes, I love her."

"What do you plan to do about that?"

"Nothing."

"Because of Leelia?"

No way would he answer that.

"You can't deny yourself the pleasures of a life mate simply because one woman hurt you, Triton. Leelia and Jasmine are two different women. Besides, Leelia never loved you."

He knew that now. Leelia no longer mattered to him.

"Jasmine, however, does love you."

Trey turned to Ronan. "How do you know that?"

Ronan smiled. "Because she looks upon you the same way Isabelle did with Dax. I may not know a lot about love, Triton, but I'm smart enough to see it when it brightens a woman's face."

She loved him? Had he been so convinced they didn't belong together that he'd been blind to the fact she loved him?

"I don't approve of land humans living down here, Triton, and you know that. But it seems my guardians have a habit of falling in love with them. First Dax, and now you. And I must admit, Isabelle has been quite an incredible find. She has assimilated into Oceana better than I thought a land human could."

"I've never heard you say anything positive about Isabelle being here."

Ronan shrugged. "I was withholding judgment until I saw how things worked out between them. After a year, it's going very well and they seem in love, but what do I know of such things?"

Trey laughed, knowing how cynical Ronan was about anything having to do with matters of the heart. Then again, not too long ago he'd been just as cynical. Until he'd met Jasmine. "Your day will come, Ronan."

"Sooner than I'd like it to, I'm certain," he said, looking for all the world like he'd just eaten something that didn't agree with him.

"Love happens to all of us at some point. With me, I just didn't recognize what wasn't love, and what was." And he couldn't believe he'd just admitted that to Ronan, or to himself. For too long he'd denied his feelings for her. Hell, he'd denied the feelings she obviously had for him. Maybe he didn't feel worthy of love after Leelia. Maybe he felt that if he pushed love away, it could never hurt him again.

Maybe during this whole process he'd had no idea what the hell he was doing. And he'd handled things with Jasmine badly, because he couldn't just reach out and accept the love she gave.

Even Ronan knew how Jasmine felt. And how he felt. It was time to stop denying what was so clear to everyone. Time to bury the past. He *was* worthy of Jasmine's love.

"Your Jasmine is special, Triton. Even I can see that. She loves the sea — it shows in her eyes, her heart, it courses through her blood as if she was born in Oceana. Her soul belongs here…with you."

"You're the one who was so adamant about getting her out of here without her memories, Ronan. Why the change of heart?"

Ronan shrugged and looked at the monitors. "Maybe I'm just getting old."

Trey snorted. Ronan was as ageless as time itself.

"And maybe I just can't fight destiny. Maybe you shouldn't try to fight it, either." He laid his hand on Trey's shoulder and squeezed, then turned and walked out.

After Ronan left, Trey looked at the monitor, watching Jasmine yelling at her crew as they hoisted the dolphins into the boat that would take them to the water.

A part of him still refused to hope that what Ronan said was true. Did she love him?

He flicked his hand across the monitor and drew closer to Jasmine's face.

She had tears streaming down her cheeks. Closing his eyes and tuning in to her, he felt a slam of emotions that he hadn't expected. Loneliness, sadness, a melancholy that tore him apart.

No, she didn't remember him, but some part of her felt a loss of something that had been monumental to her.

She did love him!

Emotion so powerful it took his breath away and nearly knocked him off his feet. He stepped backward and ran his hands through his hair. Never had he felt such a connection to a woman.

Never had he felt such love soaring through him at the thought of a woman.

He realized now how juvenile his attraction to Leelia had been. Her face was no more than a distant memory now.

The woman he loved, the woman he needed, stood on a boat silently crying out for him.

His woman. His Jasmine.

Their souls were connected. She belonged in Oceana, with him, and by God he was going right now to claim her.

* * * * *

Jasmine watched the last of the dolphins being lowered into the sea. Her heart flew along with the quickly swimming dolphin.

She'd miss them. That's why tears ran unchecked down her cheeks. They'd come to her near death and now they were returning to their homes healthy again. A part of her traveled with them, envious of their ability to explore the oceans.

When she could no longer spot them swimming around the surface of the water, she motioned the boat to head to dock. Suddenly, her friend, the perfect Bottlenose, popped its head up near the port side. She leaned over and smiled. "Well, hi there, pal. Your friends are free now. Go on, go play with them."

But the dolphin stayed near the boat, following along as it began the slow trek to shore. Why wouldn't he swim off with his pod? "Go on, pal, you can go home now!"

Still, it followed, all the way to the dock. Unusual for a dolphin to hang out around the other boats in the harbor, yet this one seemed reluctant to leave. The rest of the crew had long since disembarked, yet Jaz couldn't bring herself to walk away just yet.

She climbed down the ladder and sat on the diving ledge. The dolphin swam up to her and she reached out her hand, running her fingers over its ridged spine.

"Yeah, I'm gonna miss you too, pal. I'll miss all of you."

It chattered noisily as if in response. Jasmine splashed water back at it and hung around awhile longer, content to just sit with the dolphin swimming nearby. But finally she knew it was time to go.

When she stood, the dolphin swam off, heading out to sea.

That feeling of loss surrounded her again as she watched the dolphin disappear under the water.

With a sigh, Jasmine headed back to shore.

Her work with the sick dolphins finished, she tidied up the lab and filed her notes, then sent out emails to some of the most prominent mammalian specialists in the country. Several had already responded saying they'd love to take over research duties at the aquarium.

It was all going to work out perfectly. By the time the specialists finished with Claude, he'd have no choice but to convert the aquarium to research only. Her dolphins would be safe.

And she'd be leaving. Where she'd go, she had no idea, but there was something more for her out there.

Something called to her. She didn't know what it was, but she knew she no longer belonged at the aquarium. She just wished she knew where she did belong.

After she showered she fixed a glass of wine and watched the sun sink into the water. Its bright orange glow held off the fog, allowing Jasmine to watch the brilliant colors spread out over the ocean's surface like a fiery blanket.

The sight was breathtakingly beautiful. But Jasmine felt no joy over it, nor was she happy about the dolphins' release today.

What was wrong with her, anyway? Why did she feel so incomplete, so lost?

A knock at the door had her shaking off the sadness. She opened it, surprised to see Dr. Triton Sanders standing there.

He looked delectable in jeans and a T-shirt that showed off his sexy physique. Her heart lurched in her chest, surprising her. They'd only worked together briefly and he'd long ago left—why would his reappearance have such a profound effect on her?

"Dr. Sanders, what are you doing here?"

His grin had her thinking decidedly unscientific thoughts. "You're supposed to call me Trey, remember?"

No, she didn't remember at all. Then again, she didn't remember a lot of things lately. Maybe she needed a vacation. "Sorry, Trey. Come in, please."

He stepped inside and she motioned him into the kitchen. "Care for some wine?"

"Sounds great. How did the dolphin release go today?"

"Oh it went very well." She handed him a glass and watched his lips caress the edge. She found herself licking her own lips, wondering what he'd taste like.

Wondering, or was it remembering? Something about him struck her as familiar. Intimately familiar, which was impossible since they'd been nothing more than working colleagues at the lab. But an awareness of him on a male/female level stabbed at her. Desire flooded her body as she watched his long legs stroll through her living room and out onto the patio. She was shocked at her reaction to a man she barely knew.

And what was he doing here anyway? "I thought you'd left already."

He took a long swallow of wine. Her gaze gravitated to his Adam's apple. She shivered, but it was warm outside.

"I'll be leaving tomorrow. I just came by to check on the dolphins. You did well, Jasmine."

"Thank you for your help with this, Trey." That much, at least, she remembered. Other than that, the time he'd spent at the aquarium was pretty much a blur.

"Glad I could help. We worked well together."

His husky voice intimated something more than a professional relationship. Ridiculous. Having sex with a man like Triton Sanders was certainly something she'd never forget.

"So now what are you going to do?" he asked.

She shrugged. "Don't know. I'm quitting my job here."

He arched a brow. "Really? Why?"

"It doesn't hold the appeal it used to."

"I see. What are you going to do instead?"

"I have no idea. This is going to sound strange, but I feel as if I need to be somewhere else, doing something else, but I can't for the life of me figure out what that 'something else' is."

His enigmatic smile unnerved her.

"Are you happy, Jasmine?"

What a strange question, and yet she found herself wanting to answer him. Maybe if she voiced her concerns, they'd go away. "Frankly, I'm miserable. Ever since I woke up a few days ago I've been unable to shake this weird melancholy. Maybe it's post dolphin recovery letdown or something. This weird depression hit me like a virus and won't let go."

And now he'd think she was an idiot. *Good move there, Jasmine. Blurt out your psycho problems to a virtual stranger.*

"I know exactly what's wrong with you."

Her gaze met his. "You do?"

"Yeah."

"Well, I'm all ears. Tell me."

"You're in love."

She rolled her eyes at him, wondering which of them was more delusional. "Hardly. I'm not even dating anyone."

"You don't have to be dating to love someone."

He put his glass on the table and stood, approaching her. She put her glass down and backed away from him, but not from fear.

No, there was a familiarity in his approach that made her shiver with a sense of déjà vu. She should ask him to leave. He made her feel things she had no business feeling.

But when he gathered her into his arms, she could no more push him away than she could stop breathing. Her breasts brushed his hard chest and her nipples fired to life, puckering with a powerful need to be touched. Her panties moistened, her legs trembled.

Good God almighty, what was happening to her?

He bent his head toward hers. When his lips slid across her mouth, sparks shot between her legs and she let out a low moan. Then he took her mouth in an overpowering kiss that nearly took her legs out from under her.

She was dying in a maelstrom of emotions she wasn't prepared to handle.

And the worst part was that it all seemed achingly familiar to her.

"Trey, please," she said, pushing at him, not wanting these strange and yet familiar sensations pummeling at her.

"As you wish, my siren." He brushed his thumb across her forehead and a white heat flashed inside her head. She clutched her temples as a searing pain stabbed at her, then immediately dissipated.

Clarity came rushing back like a tidal wave. Trey stood in front of her! Her Trey, the man she loved!

"Oh God, I remember everything!" Every second of the past few weeks hit her full force.

"Of course you do. I just restored your memories completely."

Joy at seeing him again fought with the million questions running through her head. "Why? Why are you here? Why did you give me my memories back?"

"Do you remember what I said to you before I took your memory away?"

She thought about that moment in Oceana after he'd made love to her. Then she looked up at him and nodded, in awe of the words she remembered. "Yes, I do."

"Then let me say them again. I love you, Jasmine."

She nodded and smiled through the tears streaming freely down her face. No longer hesitant, she didn't want another second to pass before she told him how she felt.

"I love you too, Trey. You took my memories away that day before I could tell you that. I love you. I want to live in Oceana with you. It's already my home. I belong there, so don't tell me I can't. From the moment you brought me there it became home to me. I'm supposed to be there with you."

He laughed lightly and kissed her. "Of course you're supposed to be there with me."

The words she thought she'd never hear, the man she thought she'd never be allowed to remember, all of it was real.

"I'm living in a dream, Trey," she said as he gathered her close and pressed a kiss to her forehead.

"So am I. I never dreamed I could love someone again. Until you made me realize that I'm in love for the first time in my life. Let's go home, Jasmine."

She walked out with him, leaving everything behind. She'd already written her letter of resignation. She wouldn't need any of her things—not in Oceana.

When she stepped into the water with him holding tight to her hand, she smiled, anxious to return to the place she called home.

To Oceana.

About the Author

∽

Jaci Burton has been a dreamer and lover of romance her entire life. Consumed with stories of passion, love and happily ever afters, she finally pulled her fantasy characters out of her head and put them on paper. Writing allows her to showcase the rainbow of emotions that result from falling in love.

Jaci lives in Oklahoma with her husband (her fiercest writing critic and sexy inspiration), stepdaughter and three wild and crazy dogs. Her sons are grown and live on opposite coasts and don't bother her nearly as often as she'd like them to. When she isn't writing stories of passion and romance, she can usually be found at the gym, reading a great book, or working on her computer, trying to figure out how she can pull more than twenty-four hours out of a single day.

Jaci welcomes mail from readers. You can write to her c/o Ellora's Cave Publishing at 1056 Home Avenue Akron, OH 44310-3502.

Also by Jaci Burton

ഇ

Why an electronic book?

We live in the Information Age—an exciting time in the history of human civilization in which technology rules supreme and continues to progress in leaps and bounds every minute of every hour of every day. For a multitude of reasons, more and more avid literary fans are opting to purchase e-books instead of paperbacks. The question to those not yet initiated to the world of electronic reading is simply: *why?*

1. *Price*. An electronic title at Ellora's Cave Publishing and Cerridwen Press runs anywhere from 40-75% less than the cover price of the <u>exact same title</u> in paperback format. Why? Cold mathematics. It is less expensive to publish an e-book than it is to publish a paperback, so the savings are passed along to the consumer.

2. *Space*. Running out of room to house your paperback books? That is one worry you will never have with electronic novels. For a low one-time cost, you can purchase a handheld computer designed specifically for e-reading purposes. Many e-readers are larger than the average handheld, giving you plenty of screen room. Better yet, hundreds of titles can be stored within your new library—a single microchip. (Please note that Ellora's Cave and Cerridwen Press does not endorse any specific brands. You can check our website at www.ellorascave.com or

www.cerridwenpress.com for customer recommendations we make available to new consumers.)

3. *Mobility.* Because your new library now consists of only a microchip, your entire cache of books can be taken with you wherever you go.

4. *Personal preferences are accounted for.* Are the words you are currently reading too small? Too large? Too...**ANNOYING**? Paperback books cannot be modified according to personal preferences, but e-books can.

5. *Instant gratification.* Is it the middle of the night and all the bookstores are closed? Are you tired of waiting days—sometimes weeks—for online and offline bookstores to ship the novels you bought? Ellora's Cave Publishing sells instantaneous downloads 24 hours a day, 7 days a week, 365 days a year. Our e-book delivery system is 100% automated, meaning your order is filled as soon as you pay for it.

Those are a few of the top reasons why electronic novels are displacing paperbacks for many an avid reader. As always, Ellora's Cave and Cerridwen Press welcomes your questions and comments. We invite you to email us at service@ellorascave.com, service@cerridwenpress.com or write to us directly at: 1056 Home Ave. Akron OH 44310-3502.

Discover for yourself why readers can't get enough of the multiple award-winning publisher Ellora's Cave. Whether you prefer e-books or paperbacks, be sure to visit EC on the web at www.ellorascave.com for an erotic reading experience that will leave you breathless.

www.ellorascave.com